white lies

KRISTIN MAYER

White Lies
The Twisted Fate Series
Copyright © 2016 by K. Mayer Enterprises, Inc.
Book cover by JM Walker with Just write. Creations
(https://www.facebook.com/justwrite.creations/)
Interior design by JT Formatting
(https://www.facebook.com/JTFormatting/)
Editing by Nichole Strauss with Perfectly Publishable
(https://www.facebook.com/perfectlypublishable/)
Editing by Jen Matera at Write Diva (http://writedivas.com/)

All rights reserved. Without limiting the rights under copyright reserved above, no part of this publication may be reproduced, stored in or introduced into a retrieval system, or transmitted, in any form, or by any means (electronic, mechanical, photocopying, recording, or otherwise) without the prior written permission of the above copyright owner of this book.

This is a work of fiction. Names, characters, places, brands, media, and incidents are either the product of the author's imagination or are used fictitiously. The author acknowledges the trademarked status and trademark owners of various products referenced in this work of fiction, which have been used without permission. The publication/use of these trademarks is not authorized, associated with, or sponsored by the trademark owners.

White Lies / Kristin Mayer – 1st ed.
Library of Congress Cataloging-in-Publication Data
ISBN-13: 978-1-942910-13-8

VISIT MY WEBSITE AT
http://www.authorkristinmayer.com

To Timothy,
I miss you every single day. I thank God he brought you into our lives,
but wish I could have had you here on earth for a little longer. We miss
you, but talk about you often. Until we see each other again, know I
will always love you.
Love,
Kristin

Chapter One

The morning light kissed my skin as I stirred. The scent of his outdoorsy cologne brought a smile to my face as the memories of last night flashed through my mind.

Alex showed up after our fight—he came for me.

Me.

Through his kisses, I knew I still mattered. It was as if something awakened his need for me again... something that had been forgotten since we'd married.

I loved him.

He loved me.

We would figure everything out.

Last night was perfect; I treasured each memory. Each touch. Each murmured *I love you.* Through the night, he'd held me close. It felt like old times when we'd first met. My eyes fluttered open, and I turned over, ready to greet the love of my life.

The bed was empty.

Alex was gone.

Heart racing, I abruptly sat up. Had I imagined everything last night? Maybe he needed the bathroom. Impossible for last night to be a dream. No way. The connection I'd felt was too real, like our bodies connecting on a molecular level. From the moment I saw him, I was consumed. Nothing else mattered except Alex and me. I believed he felt the same way; I knew he came to talk, but our bodies demanded something else. From the instant our hands touched, the moment had enveloped us, all thoughts dissipating except for the need to have each other.

I stood still as I strained to listen for a sign of my husband in the room.

Nothing.

A defeated sigh left my lips. Why had he left? Last night had been incredible... the way it had been between us when we first fell in love, before Alex had been deployed. Alex had been in the military since he was eighteen until he was medically discharged seven months ago at twenty-seven.

I touched my lips, still swollen from our kisses. Last night, right before I touched him, Alex had begun to say something before he smashed his lips to mine. Had he changed his mind from what he was going to say?

I wasn't sure.

The soreness between my legs confirmed my memories were real and not the dreams I normally had—wishing for what was lost between us. Last night Alex hadn't been aloof or distant; he'd loved and wanted me. Me. I'd been enough.

The eerie silence served as a reminder that he'd left without a word.

"I'm such a fool." The words echoed off the walls, mocking me.

This was probably payback for me leaving after our fight yesterday. Alex was cruel at times—playing emotional games, and I was done. Yesterday, I had finally reached that point and left the estate in the Hamptons to check into a hotel room in New York City.

On the way into the city, I'd made plans to meet with my lawyer midmorning to talk about a legal separation.

Our fight was the same it had been since shortly after getting married six months ago—Alex wanted me to talk to Nonno, my grandfather, about giving me control of my trust fund. I refused. Being my dad's father, Nonno knew what Dad would have wanted. The trust set up by Dad gave Nonno the discretion to manage the funds and not hand over control until I turned thirty. At that time, the money automatically transferred to me.

That was still six years away.

The large inheritance totaled in the millions. Dad had made his money through good investments and his art. His side of the family had always been fairly wealthy, but he had taken it to a whole new level. His paintings were featured all over the world, including the Louvre in Paris. Money would never be an issue for me. I had plenty to live off. More than plenty. Nonno made sure, and I was thankful for the life I was blessed with.

I knew from when the trust was initially established that Dad simply wanted me to be ready to carry the burden of what large sums of money brought. It took a toll on people. I had seen it in high school with some of my friends. Sometimes it changed them... for the worst. The last thing I wanted was to be affected the same way. I never wanted to lose my morals.

Thank goodness Dad and I had discussed doing a prenup. Dad had it drawn up shortly after Alex and I met. We'd talked about it after he left. At first, I was hesitant about the whole prenup thing. When you married someone, it was supposed to be the merging of two lives into one. A prenup seemed to have the possibility to create a gulf between two people. In the end, Dad left the decision to me. I'd gone with my gut and asked Alex to sign it, which he did without any argument.

When he believed I was ready, Nonno would hand over my trust. I trusted him. My dad trusted him. I had faith Nonno had my best interests at heart and would know the right time.

My blood boiled remembering my fight with Alex yesterday. I was furious, thinking he only married me for the money. The thought had crossed my mind a couple of months after we married that he'd manipulated me in the beginning of our relationship.

But… something held me back from believing it entirely as I knew deep down our love started out pure before something changed. Honestly, I wasn't sure what to think at times.

None of it made sense.

Last night, I thought we were done for sure until, after crying in my hotel room for half an hour, Alex showed up. Came after me. Apologized for not protecting me. All he wanted was to focus on us at the moment. Nothing else mattered. He told me we would talk through it all today.

Confusion filled me.

Today was here… and he was gone.

Cradling my head in my hands, I moved the gold down blanket, revealing a piece of paper. I heaved a sigh of relief at the familiar script.

Sorry,
I had to leave before you woke.
There are a few things I need
to take care of for us.
I'll see you tonight.
I love you, Willow.
I never stopped.

Tracing my fingers over his words, I grinned. I felt bad for doubting him. It was easier to believe the bad over the good these days after all the events from the last six months. But maybe... just maybe, this time was different.

Things could have been different if it hadn't been for his last mission overseas. When he came back, I sensed something was off, but he hid it well. It wasn't until after we married that I realized how much he'd changed. War had that effect on people, which was understandable. We'd married so fast when he came back.

Too fast.

As I came to find out, Alex blamed himself for the death of someone in his unit. He told me his thoughts had been consumed with returning home... to me, versus keeping his men safe. Essentially, as per him, it was *my* fault. *If only I'd known prior to marrying him.* By nature, I refused to quit. That was why I stayed with him longer than any sane person would have.

Though I knew things would be tough, I hoped the love we shared would be enough to get us through. At first it was… then it wasn't.

I glanced down at the note again. The words were like a beacon. A new hope blossomed in my chest. I chased away the negative thoughts that reared their ugly heads with the memories from our fight. I loved my husband. Finding what we had was worth one more shot. Clutching the note to my chest, I giggled. There was no stopping the sound as I thought about our whispered words when he made love to me.

I love you, Willow. I never stopped.

I love you, too. I never stopped. I never lost hope. I knew we would find our way back to each other.

As I thought back to last night, I held onto the belief we had broken through.

A hand trailed up my back as Alex held me. Goose bumps formed in the wake of his touch as I lay on his chest in the darkened hotel room. My fingers traced the military tattoo on his chest I couldn't see but knew was there. The two knives intercepting each other with the inscription I will not accept defeat *were over his heart.*

"I miss this. Being together tonight feels like when we first started dating. I'm sorry I called you Gabe earlier. I know how you hate that. Old habits."

My husband's full name was Gabriel Alexander Thompson. All of his friends called him Gabriel when we first met while I was in college. He was on leave from the military. It had been a chance meeting in a random town as I crossed a street. Fate happened, bringing two people who were meant for each other together. Though I'd tried to take things slow, something between us clicked, and I fell madly in love with him before I realized it. Honestly, it was insane how fast we fell in love. Maybe too fast. But I don't believe I could have stopped it if I tried.

On our first date, I called him Gabe, and it stuck. At least until he asked me to call him Alex shortly after returning from his last military mission. All of his friends who died overseas called him Gabriel, and it was hard for him to hear a shortened version. I got needing to distance yourself completely from painful reminders. I hadn't been to Italy since Dad died for that very reason.

The muscles in Alex's body tightened and then released while he dragged his right hand through his dark hair. Even in the dark, I felt his emerald eyes watching me. His voice was strained when he finally spoke. "Sweetheart, we're going to find our way back to each other. We'll get back to the place when we were Gabe and Willow, not Alex and Willow. I'm working through it. I promise you, I'll never upset you again like I did this afternoon when I found you."

I kissed his chest and then sighed. "I'm not going to Nonno to try and get him to release my trust. It's not what Dad would have wanted. We have plenty to live on. I don't want to fight, but that point I'm not budging on."

Fingers paused on my back before continuing. I braced myself for the anger to return. "It's your decision. I'll respect that." A small victory—a step in the right direction.

After kissing him again, I laid my ear against his chest, listening to his steady heartbeat. "We might want to think about couple's therapy. When you came back after leaving the military, something has been missing. It might help us get a new start. I want to make this work."

"That's what I want too—a fresh start. For us."

I smiled at his words. "Thank you for coming back to me."

"I promised I always would."

The memory was beautiful. Magical. Through the night, Alex woke me up twice to make love to me. Love. It was the key to everything. For now, I would focus on the memories of last night in order to hold on to hope to save my marriage until I saw him again. I read his words again. *I love you, Willow. I never stopped.*

Inspiration struck.

I needed to get home.

Quickly, I grabbed my bags and checked out of the five-star hotel in New York City. I'd barely given notice to my plush surroundings in my suite last night with all the tears... then bliss.

The valet brought my Land Rover to me. The city felt alive. Dad and I used to come to the city all the time to people watch as we sipped hot tea in the park. It was amazing what you could learn about human interaction, which he believed helped translate emotions onto the canvas. I agreed.

On autopilot, I tipped the man with the tall black hat. I was in a fog as images of what I wanted to paint invaded my brain. The strokes of deep blues and greens would form the sky. Trees intertwined themselves like lovers. A light shone in the distance. The picture was crystal clear.

My fingers itched for my paintbrush to let the feelings and images within escape onto the canvas. It had been forever since the urge to paint struck me. I'd followed my father's, Alfonso Lorenzo Russo, footsteps and become an artist myself.

Since the Russo name was "famous" in the art realm, I painted under the name Willow Loren, my first and middle names. In the last year, the name Willow Loren had gained traction. It would have been easier—career wise—to paint under the Russo name, but I wanted to earn my way and not ride on the strokes of my father's paintbrush.

More pieces of the scene flowed through my mind as I catalogued the image mentally unfolding and where it would fit on the canvas.

After driving for almost two hours, the large estate my father left, which was also my childhood home in the Hamptons, came into view. The gates opened with a push of the button on my SUV sun visor.

Home.

Warmth settled over my body.

This place always brought me peace and perspective. It came to be the only home I knew except for the apartment I had through college up until Dad died.

The Tuscan-style house came into view with the expansive lawn, and I pictured my dad on the front porch waiting for me to come home like he always did. It was bittersweet thinking about it. Waves from the ocean crashed in the background.

This was paradise.

The gardener trimmed the bushes around the statues in the middle of the circular drive. Dad insisted we have as much Italian culture here to commemorate our artist roots.

I waved to Chris as he wiped his graying brow from the early heat of the sun. Years of physical labor kept him fit. He'd been in charge of our lawns since before I was born twenty-four years ago. His granddaughter came here often to swim in the ocean with her mother. Though not related, we were family.

I continued around the back of the house to the garages. Anxious to paint, I parked outside, not taking the time to raise the garage doors. The waves calmed as I jogged to the studio that stood off to the left behind the house. The stones crunched beneath my feet along the path that led to the studio door. It had been my father's studio before he passed away unexpectedly from a brain aneurism a month after I married Alex.

That was only five months ago. His death still felt raw. Too raw. I would have given anything to have him here to guide me.

My world fell apart when Dad died. Though things were rough between Alex and me since he left the military, I was more determined than ever to make our marriage work.

One of the last conversations Dad and I had was about Alex. His guiding words were to see it through the storm. Through the trials we then saw our triumphs. Over the last five months, those words were what kept me on course. When I drove into the city yesterday, ready to file for separation, the sting of failure was deep.

Through it all, I felt like a ship lost at sea, tossing and turning without a compass. Dad had always been my true north, providing guidance. Had our storm passed?

Last night had been my only reprieve since Alex had come back. I needed the connection more than I had imagined. There was no going back to the abyss I had let myself wander into.

What had clicked to make things better?

Was it another trick?

Would the same Alex I had last night be the one to come home today?

It was terrible to doubt your husband, but the scars were still fresh.

I was thankful I still had Nonno through all of this. Nonno was the only family I had left besides my best friend, Carson, and his parents, Bennett and Marie. Even though not related by blood to Carson's family, they took me in as if I were one of their own.

Mom died in a car accident three months before my eleventh birthday, shattering my world for the first time. Dad and I adapted, but the piece of my mother remained missing. Nonno was there for both of us, helping put our world back together again.

"Willow, do you have a second?"

With my hand on the wrought-iron door handle to the studio, I turned to the familiar voice of Chris, our gardener. He looked distraught. "Hey, Chris. Absolutely. I was about to start painting, so you caught me at a good time."

When I painted, I locked the entire world away. It was only me, the canvas, and the emotions flowing through the brush. I lived for the rush.

His hazel eyes warmed; he knew it had been a while since I'd been in the studio. In some ways, Chris was like an uncle to me. Through the years, he and my dad had become close. Since my father's death, he watched over me as if I were one of his children. I treasured the relationship.

"Did Alex tell you about firing Mildred?"

I gasped. "No! Why?"

There had to be a misunderstanding. Mildred had been the family housekeeper since I was in diapers. In many ways, she helped raise me.

Nervously, he shuffled his feet. "I don't want to cause problems, Willow. She's pretty upset. After you left yesterday, Mildred was in the study cleaning and found some papers behind a bookcase. Alex walked in, lost his temper, and fired her.

He said some terrible things. I came in from outside, and when I walked in the room, he stormed off in a rage."

A heavy stone landed on my heart. This was the crux of our arguments. He wanted everyone I considered family gone. The reasoning was he wanted to start out fresh—sell the house, fire all the staff, distance myself from my best friend, and us be in control of my multi-million dollar trust fund.

This was my home.

What I'd hoped to be *our* home.

Our children's home.

Frustration brewed within me. Had Alex played me last night? I blew out some air in a gust. "Yesterday was a rough day for Alex and me. Mildred isn't fired."

Chris nodded. I knew he was holding back what he wanted to say. For a while now, I suspected he didn't like Alex, but he supported me. Honestly, after how Alex acted, I doubted anyone was a fan.

I let go of the handle and exhaled, knowing painting would have to wait. Family first. "Is Mildred here?"

"She arrived just before you, after spending the night with her sister. I imagine Mildred is gathering her things from the guest house. Alex said she had until today to leave."

I gave Chris a quick hug. "Thanks. I know this has been a tough few months with Alex's condition. I promise it's going to get better."

"I worry about you, Willow." The tone in his voice told me there were doubts to my words, which was fair. I had said something similar to him and Mildred about two months ago.

The truth was I worried about myself, too. How long was I going to be able to keep piecing everything back together? Dad always said marriage should be a lifelong commitment. But were there extenuating circumstances?

At times, I hoped the answer was yes.

Alex and I still had a lot to work out even after last night. I was still processing the fact he didn't want kids. A month ago he informed me he'd changed his mind and kids were no longer an option for us.

"I appreciate you always looking out for me, Chris." I took a few steps. "I need to go convince Mildred to stay. I'll be back. I hope she will."

Chris nodded. "Of course she'll stay for you."

I hoped so. The thought of her leaving left another empty hole in my chest.

Baby steps.

One day at a time.

That was the advice my therapist gave me for dealing with someone who had PTSD. I held out hope Alex and I were able to figure it out because this was our last chance.

T he sun shone bright on this spring day in the Hamptons as I took off to the guest house on the left side of the painting studio. Landscaping hid the studio and guest house from the front.

Mildred's familiar black car was parked next to her garage. Thank goodness she hadn't left. As I got closer, I saw the door was left open. Sniffling sounds resonated through the air.

Pausing, I knocked. "Mildred?"

The air grew quiet, and then I heard Mildred answer. "Come in, Willow." A duffel bag was near the door. "My brother is going to come help me get the heavy stuff. My sister just left with a load."

Without thinking, I walked up to Mildred and threw my arms around her. "You're not fired. I just found out from Chris what Alex did, or I would have come home last night. I stayed in the city. Mildred, you have a place here for as long as you like. Please don't leave me."

Strong arms came around my back as the middle-aged woman brought me to her. "I'm so sorry, Willow. I had no idea I was messing with Mr. Alex's things. He lost his temper. I try. I really do. I love it here."

Putting a little distance between us so I could see Mildred's face, I felt the tears burning at the back of my eyes. At times, Alex had been a monster since he came back. "I love you here, too. Please stay. I will work everything else out. You're family, Mildred. You will always have a place here."

Later, when things simmered down, I would get the full story from Mildred. Right now, she was too emotional, and I knew she wasn't ready to talk about it.

The normal fiery redhead, who kept the house in tiptop shape, wept some more. "I love you, too, Willow. So much. You're like a daughter to me."

"Will you stay? Please."

She nodded with watery eyes. "I could never leave you, Willow. My heart broke thinking I had to leave."

I shook my head fiercely. "Never. You will never have to leave here. If anything ever happens, come talk to me first, okay?"

I had to remain strong when all I wanted to do was cry after the beautiful night Alex and I shared.

More sniffles came from Mildred. "Okay. I'm going to freshen up and then head to the main house. I'll have my sister bring back my stuff. How does lasagna sound tonight?"

The mention of lasagna made my mouth water. Being from a heavily influenced Italian ancestry, pasta was the way to my heart. "Mildred, please take the night off."

She squeezed me and then stood back to wipe away the remnants of her tear. "Nonsense. Cooking helps relieve stress. I'll make gelato for dessert."

Gelato was my favorite form of ice cream. In fact, it was my go-to comfort food because of Mom. Mildred knew she had won. There was no way I could say no to gelato. "Will you make mint chocolate chip?"

"You bet. Let me straighten a few things out and I'll be up at the main house."

Crisis averted.

My nerves were frayed, and I was feeling like the hope had been diminished and last night had been a fluke.

Regardless of how Alex had been at the hotel, we needed to have a serious talk. Some things would need to change if our relationship was going to move forward. "I'm going to be in the painting studio. If Alex comes home, call the studio phone and I'll be right up."

"I will. I'm sorry about this mess."

"It's not your fault. Things are going to change, I promise." My words were spoken as a vow.

Mildred gave me a small smile as the light in her eyes grew. "I'm so glad you're painting again. Off you go."

Mildred walked me to the door and we hugged again. With little shooing motions, she ushered me out. "I'll have dinner waiting. Take your time painting."

"I will. Thank you, Mildred. Thank you for staying on while it's been difficult. I promise things are going to change."

With a deep breath, she responded, "We'll get through this."

An unspoken statement came out in her words. *Life has been hard.* And she was right. How had I got myself into such a mess?

I meandered back across the lawn. My heart was torn. Last night, it felt like Alex was the man I fell in love with in college. The man I thought I'd married. But after hearing about the altercation with Mildred, I wasn't sure.

For good measure, I took out my phone and called Alex.

Ring.

Ring.

Ring.

"This is Alex. You know what to do." Beep.

He never picked up his phone. Internally, I wanted to scream. But I took a deep breath and hung up. Instead I would text him. When Alex got home, he would see how serious I was.

Me: Please call me. We need to talk about Mildred. She's staying and that is not negotiable. Hopefully, you were serious about things changing last night. I can't go back to the way they were. I won't.

I stared at the phone, willing a response to come. My message stared back at me almost in a mocking manner.

Were people able to be saved after they let a demon take root in them for so long? I hoped the answer was yes, that our story was just beginning after having a rocky start.

Hopefully, things would settle and rational Alex would walk through the door when he got home. Normally, I hardly ever called Alex because he kept his phone turned off and rarely had it with him being an undercover cop. However, he said he'd be home tonight in his note, which meant he wasn't undercover.

I let out another sigh. I hated Alex being an undercover cop because I knew the situation was less than ideal for someone diagnosed with PSTD. A few times, I asked him how he passed the medical assessments to become an undercover cop.

The doctor we'd visited together signed the release. No doubt the doctor was a quack. I hadn't trusted him from the second I entered his office. But Alex refused to get a second opinion. A shudder ran through me at the memory of some of the fights we had when I questioned him. The subject was closed. Period.

At times, I had to pick my battles, and the doctor's diagnosis was an already lost battle.

I had a number to call in emergencies while Alex was working, but wondering about his location wasn't justifiable. Thank goodness a need to use the number never arose.

My phone dinged, and for a moment I thought it might be Alex. The caller ID confirmed it as Carson. Still, a smile formed at the familiar name. We'd been each other's best friend since we were in preschool—a brother I never had. On the playground, I used to make him be my pretend husband when all the girls wanted to play marriage. He hated every second of being the groom.

Carson: Worried about you with how upset you were last night. How did it go with the lawyer?

Me: I didn't go yet. Alex showed up and we talked. He's coming home tonight and I'm going to see if it's salvageable.

Carson: I'm here for you. Let me know if you need anything even if it's simply to talk. I come home in a few days. Let's get together. Mom and Dad want to see you, too.

Me: I'd love that. Let me know when you're available.

Carson: I will. I'll check in later after my meetings.

Me: Knock 'em dead.

Carson: I'll try.

I tucked my phone away. Currently, Carson was overseas tending to his hotels. One of their hotels in Italy currently had issues. He'd been there a lot over the last two months. The Whitmore Hotels were a five-star hotel chain unlike any other in their extravagance. I was proud of my best friend and all he'd accomplished.

Entering the studio, I stopped and looked at the half dozen unfinished works taunting me to finish them. But nothing came. I had no idea what was missing in them. Another couple dozen blank canvases stared at me from against the wall.

For hours I stared at them, willing inspiration to strike. It hadn't in a long time. Nothing was going to be solved until Alex arrived home. Until then, painting would pass the time.

Quickly, I whipped my blonde hair into a messy bun. Then grabbed one of my white, paint-splattered, button-up work shirts that swallowed my small frame.

The images from earlier began to flow as I looked at the blank slate before me. Taking my paintbrush, I hovered over the pallet, figuring out which colors to pick. My hand shook as it had the last time I tried to paint. I tried to push the negative aside. My mind lost focus while the painting block returned, and my spirits plummeted as I worked to recapture the inspiration.

A picture of Alex and me caught my attention. It was from college before he left. We were happy. In love—like last night. His arms were wrapped around my shoulders while my lavender-grey eyes stared at the camera.

When the shutter on the camera clicked to capture the moment, I remembered thinking I'd found my happily ever after.

Love. We'd been in love then. I knew it.

I remembered the note from this morning and pulled it out of my jeans pocket, tracing the words. There was still hope. I looked again at the picture, wondering how we allowed ourselves to get so lost.

Grabbing my palette, I mixed my mediums as I kept glancing at the note, which now lay on the nearby stool. As I brought my paint brush up to the canvas, my hands shook again. I closed my eyes and felt the wood of the handle. I thought of the picture and the emotions I'd felt as my friend took several pictures.

The magic sparked through my fingertips as I let love encapsulate me.

Love.

That was the answer.

My eyes opened as a smile formed. The images from earlier came back, begging to be let out. I dabbed my brush in a blue-green mixture on my palette to make the mediums for the sky. This color was exactly as I'd imagined it. As I continued with my strokes, I felt at peace with my steady hand. My soul had found what it was looking for.

Finally.

Hours flew by as I got lost in the painting before me. It was like entering a trance. My father painted the same way. It wasn't until we stepped back that we were truly able to see what we'd created. Mom said it was our gift of being able to paint with our hearts versus our eyes.

I took a step back to see my creation and grabbed a Twizzler. When I was done painting, I always snacked on them while contemplating my art. Dad had always had peanuts. As I looked at my creation, I knew I'd gotten the habit from him.

Before me, a man walked through the forest toward a light at the end of the road. The hues became warmer as the light drew near. Darkness beckoned him from the other side. Though his hand reached toward the light, he was still only halfway through his journey.

I sat back on the stool, thinking about the precipice of the man's decisions. Whichever way he chose would affect him for the rest of his life. Dread came over me, feeling as though this was where my relationship was.

What if the man chose the darkness?

Where did that leave the light?

Was the light enough?

There was hope, though, where the light shone bright.

Knock.

Knock.

Knock.

I jumped at the sound. My heart slowed as I realized someone was at the studio door. "Coming!" I called.

I quickly stored my brushes and traipsed toward the door, unable to shed my deep thoughts of the meaning behind my painting.

The door swung open. Chris stood there with two officers—all with solemn looks. A ball formed in my stomach, reminding me of the time the officers came to the door to tell us Mom was in an accident. That was the last time they had beckoned our door. I still remembered standing behind Dad as they told us the news.

I'd never forget the sound of agony ripping from my dad's chest when he found out Mom was dead.

Hoping my voice was steady, I swallowed hard before asking, "What's going on?"

Chris was the one who spoke. "Why don't we go to the main house?"

This only raised my suspicions. When Mom died, they'd asked us to sit in the living room. Dad had refused and asked for the officers to get to the point. It was the worst type of torture knowing you were probably about to receive life-changing news.

I wanted to go back to ten minutes ago when I wasn't facing this.

Whatever had happened, I wanted to know now. "Is Nonno okay?" My voice cracked on the last word.

The officers looked at each other. I clarified, "Antonio Lorenzo Russo."

"Ma'am, we are not here regarding a Mr. Russo. We'd like to sit and talk if possible, even if it's inside your studio." The slimmer officer had a pleading look on his face. Chris's eyes filled with pity toward me.

My voice was stern. "No, tell me what is going on."

The two officers looked at each other silently communicating. The heavier-set man on the left nodded. "Ms. Russo, I'm sorry to have to tell you this—"

"Get to the point. Please." My patience was drawing thin as my mind went through a million different scenarios.

He coughed. "Your husband was killed this afternoon."

Everything went black.

Chapter Four

The crackling fire was unable to warm the chilled state of my body.

I felt nothing.

I was numb.

Alex was dead.

Burned.

Murdered.

The cops stated he'd been found at the edge of what they considered to be mob territory. They identified him by partial dental records after they found his driver's license discarded in the grass not too far away. Apparently, that was all that survived. I closed my eyes in anguish.

They'd mentioned the name Fabiano. I'd never heard it before.

Alex had been dumped on the side of the road, like a piece of trash, in the tall grass at the park. They were investigating, and wanted to know if I knew anything. It was terrible relaying everything back to them.

The last time I saw him.

What was his state of mind?

Any strange happenings?

Any enemies?

Per Alex's instructions, I told the officers I knew nothing. Repeatedly, it had been drilled into my head to trust no one. *No one.* Not many people had clearance to his cases. Plus, he never shared anything about the case he was on. It was a taboo subject. I'd been against the job from the beginning.

In the last two months, he'd been home sporadically.

Remember, Willow, tell them I am an independent consultant. Someone may be watching you. It might be a trap.

A sense of dread filled me thinking of Alex's words.

What if the mob came for me? What if they connected Alex to me?

Earlier, I'd asked Mildred to pull the curtains as an unnerving feeling came over me that someone was out there.

I closed my eyes in anguish, fighting the nausea.

The officers left shortly thereafter. They were unable to get much from me as sobs racked my body. Their parting words were *they'd be in touch.*

My mind swirled with unanswered questions. Different scenarios. What ifs. But nothing came into clear focus except the fact that Alex was dead.

"Sweetheart, drink this. It's hot tea. It will help." Mildred's voice brought my attention from the flames.

Absentmindedly, I took the cup and continued staring at the fire while letting the warmth of the mug seep into my cold hands. Only Chris and Mildred were here. Nonno was on his way but had been in the city at the time he got the call. After him, I'd called Carson. I was still a complete wreck and wanted him here, but insisted he stay to finish his business. I knew Carson would be here as soon as he could.

This had to be a dream.

Alex was dead.

My husband was dead.

Dead.

Death had such a finality to it. There was nothing that could be done to fix it. Death had the final word. I hated it.

There were no redos once someone was gone.

Whispers at the door between Chris and Mildred caught my attention.

There was a pause before Mildred continued, "I'm going to stay in the main house tonight in case Willow needs anything."

"I'll stay in the guest house. Call me and I'll be right up. I'll wait up here until Antonio arrives."

"Thank you, Chris."

I said nothing. The endless stream of tears flowed down my face without a sound. Alex and I had lost our second chance. Rage boiled within from all the loss. Everyone I love died. The only family left in my life was Nonno and Carson.

Only one way best described how I felt—alone.

Abandoned.

Empty.

All I wanted was the family I'd always imagined as a child. A family full of love, laughter, and happiness. My father, mother, and husband. They were all gone.

It was hard for me to care about much at the moment. Right now, being numb was all I had. I wasn't ready to give it up. When I did, the reality of what happened would be infinitely worse.

Per the police, Alex had been shot and burned. A finger was missing from his remains—potentially a trophy. The thought made me nauseous. It had to be connected to whatever assignment he had been involved with. The thought of him being burned ate away at me, churning the acid within my stomach.

Had he suffered? Was it quick? Did he know how much I loved him?

The thoughts chewed away at my soul.

More time elapsed.

I was neither here nor there.

I was stuck.

"Willow."

I turned, with my lip quivering, to the aging man with white hair in the doorway. He was my rock in so many ways. At the sight of me, he came to me and engulfed me in a hug.

"Nonno, he's gone."

"I know, baby girl. I'm here."

Unable to hold it in, a cry escaped, which opened the flood gates. Nonno held me until exhaustion crept into my bones. No words were needed. He knew nothing could be said to lessen the pain. "Let's get you in bed. You need your rest, Willow."

"I don't want to go to my bed. I want to sleep in here tonight." There were too many memories in my bedroom—mainly the bad ones of all our fights. We hadn't slept in the same bedroom since a week before Dad died. Before moving into the Hampton estate, I had a two bedroom apartment where we lived together.

Nonno's strong hands stroked my back in a comforting manner. "Let's get you settled here on the couch. I'll be over there in the chair if you need anything."

The comfort of him brought immeasurable peace to my broken heart, but I still worried about him being in his seventies.

I grabbed his hand. "Nonno, please sleep in a bed. I'll be okay."

"Shh, don't worry about me. If I need to go to bed, I will. Promise."

Mildred brought in blankets and a pillow. Begrudgingly, I lay on the brown leather couch while watching the flames dance. Murmurs were heard in the hallway. I didn't have the energy to care what they said.

The fire crackled.

If only I could go back in time.

If only I had Alex back.

If only…

Stretching, I reached for Alex, remembering our magical night in the hotel room.

He wasn't there.

Was I on the couch? I must have fallen asleep before bed when Alex hadn't returned from work. He never called when on duty. It was safer if I stayed in the dark regarding his assignments.

Cracking my eyes open, I saw Nonno in the corner chair with his eyes closed and head cocked back. A light snore resonated from him while his chest rose evenly. Worry lines were present on his face.

Why was Nonno here?

Memories rushed to the forefront in a blur.

Alex.

He was gone.

Dead.

Burned.

Reality washed over me as I sat up.

Without permission, my tears fell of their own accord. Nonno stirred and watched me for a minute as the anguish crept back into my bones. All I wanted was to go back to sleep and be in the moment before my world fell apart—the moment where I thought Alex was still alive and we had made love throughout the night.

"Can I get you anything, Willow?"

A sob escaped. "I want Alex back."

"I know, baby girl. I know."

Mildred appeared in a red sweat outfit, looking exhausted. I'd slept fitfully most of the night except for the last few hours when a deep sleep taken over me. Nonno had held me each time I woke up crying, which meant he needed rest.

A cup of coffee appeared before me, and I sat up. "Here you go, Willow. I can make you something if you're hungry."

"No, thank you, Mildred."

An uncomfortable silence fell over the room. Glancing up, Nonno exchanged a look with Mildred before she left the room.

Nonno rose from the red and gold upholstered chair. Even in his early seventies, he got around well. He swam every day in his indoor pool to stay in shape. Per his doctors, he was healthy. As my mind drifted, I thought about all Nonno had endured in his life. In his fifties, he lost my nonna to cancer, then my mom, who was like a daughter, and finally his son. It was unnatural to outlive your kids, Nonno had said at my dad's funeral.

How did he cope?

Sitting next to me, Nonno brought warmth and comfort with him. I leaned against him while taking a sip of caffeine. "What do I do next, Nonno?"

Without saying it, he knew I was asking how he dealt with all the loss. Losing my mother, father, and now husband was more than I could bear. He squeezed me gently. "You live it day by day. You'll see you're stronger than you think you are."

Day by day.

"I'd gone into the city to file for separation. Alex came to me. He wanted to make things right between us." I looked to Nonno. "I don't understand why life is so cruel. Why even let me believe we had a second chance? Why?"

He patted my leg. "I don't know. I often thought the same thing. We thought your nonna was cancer free, but the doctors were wrong. Before we realized the seriousness of her illness, it was too late. She passed within a week. Life is hard, and it's accountable to no one."

How true those words were.

I thought about the last night with Alex. Maybe if I focused on the positive, the negative would fade away. A thought belatedly occurred—Alex hadn't used protection. The doctors had taken me off birth control because of the side effects I was having. Alex knew and hadn't cared. Probably because we weren't sleeping together until the night before last. *What if?* No, I refused to think about it right then. It was too much to process.

My mood shifted. A month ago, he informed me his decision on kids had changed since being in the Middle East. He no longer wanted them. I was hurt he'd kept a game changer like that a secret until after we married. I touched my stomach, hoping we'd made a child our last night together—a piece of him to have. Wait... I was crazy. It had to be all the stress. How in the world would I ever raise a child on my own?

Push the thought aside, Willow.

Nonno's voice brought me out of my wishful thinking. "What about the funeral arrangements?"

I shook my head. "Alex wanted to be cremated. No funeral. No memorial. With him being an undercover cop, he said it could bring unwanted attention to me. I think he'd been on some sort of assignment this last month. His hours at home had been erratic. We never talked about it. Regardless, nothing can be done until the investigation is over."

If only I had been able to talk him out of being an undercover cop.

"I'll be with you through this every step of the way, Willow."

A sniffle escaped me. "Thanks, Nonno. I love you."

"I love you, too, baby girl."

Chapter Five

Three days ago, I'd come to my studio to escape, to paint, and I hadn't left. I needed the solace. Everyone watched me closely—asking me every five minutes if I needed anything. It became suffocating after a day. It was hard to believe it had been four days since Alex had died.

Out of the blue, different scenes fought their way to the surface, begging to be painted. At least it allowed the loss and pain to disappear for a bit—or maybe it was the missed opportunities we had as husband and wife that hurt more acutely. Life was precious.

We only had one shot to make the most of it.

Our shot was gone.

At meal times, Nonno came into the studio to eat with me. He'd stay until he was satisfied with the amount of food I consumed. As soon as the door closed, I returned to painting. At night, I slept on the couch for a few hours, took a shower in the studio bathroom, and then resumed painting.

I finished one painting after another. I was hardly able to keep up with the images as my brush furiously stroked the canvas.

The studio was a mess, and paint splotches covered my clothes.

Making the last brush stroke, I stood back and grabbed a Twizzler from the table. Canvases, dry and wet, littered every surface of the studio. I'd been busy over the last few days. I walked around eyeing each one. The beginning paintings were full of bright colors and love, showcasing the brightness of the light. Later paintings grew darker and more detached with always a symbolic light somewhere in the picture. Toward the end, the light faded and then became brighter. All the paintings led to the one I'd been working on the day I found out Alex had died.

The series was our story. Alex's and my journey. Our journey.

I kept staring at the figures in each painting. The weariness grew on the figures as the burdens of life weighed them down. At times, the vines nearly encapsulated one or the other.

The paintings were raw emotions exposed to the nerve—they were real life.

A sense of completion filled me. The process helped catalogue and decipher what happened.

Over the last few days, I questioned why I'd stayed with him when there seemed to be more bad times than good. At least I knew I gave it everything and had no regrets. Or at least regrets I had control over. It was hard giving up on the person you believed was your soulmate. Through sickness and in health, through the good times and the bad... those were the vows I took. They meant something to me.

Taking a deep breath, I flipped off the lights and left the studio. The wind picked up and whipped my messy bun around. I was probably a disaster with my paint-splattered face and clothes. The loss was still brutal, but I would survive.

The waves crashed against the shore as I made it to the back of the property.

Today, the sea was angry, which mirrored what brewed inside me despite all my revelations. Under the sadness, an irritation lurked as to all the unanswered questions. Why had Alex insisted he do such a dangerous job? Why had he come full circle all of a sudden? Why? Why? Why? There was so much unfinished between us.

"Willow."

I turned to the familiar voice of Carson, and relief swept through me having him here. I flung my arms around him, and he engulfed me in a hug. "I'm so sorry, sweetheart. So, so sorry." My nose was buried in his chest. "I would have been here sooner, but delay after delay kept me away. I'm so sorry."

"All that matters is you're here now."

With a gentle hand, he rubbed my back. "I wouldn't be anywhere else, Willow. You know that. I tried calling to check on you. I've been in touch with Nonno when you didn't answer."

Nonno was like a grandfather to Carson, too.

Pulling back, I sniffled. "I've been in such a fog. I just… I don't know. I turned off my phone and went into the studio to paint. It's such a mess, Carson." I shrugged, not sure what else to say.

Without warning, Carson pulled me back into his embrace. "Shh… it's okay."

The waves crashed against the shore while thunder rolled in the distance. I wasn't sure how much time passed before rain droplets hit my back. I still clung to Carson as the rain pelted a little more, causing a shiver to emanate through me. "Let's get you inside. The last thing you need is to get sick."

Staring into his eyes, I saw his concerned powder-blue ones staring back at me as his shoulder-length blond hair whipped in the wind. He was here for me. Throughout my entire life, Carson was always there when I needed him. I had more people in my life than I allowed myself to remember these last few days. The emptiness was all-consuming. "Sounds good."

Protectively, Carson walked me to the main house. Nonno and Mildred sat at the walnut breakfast table, sipping coffee. "There's my girl."

I hugged him tightly. "Thank you for staying. I know I've been distant." At meal times, I hardly spoke, focusing on the painting I was working on at the time. Dad would be gone for days sometimes. Mom would force him to eat like Nonno had me.

"Of course. Did you work through what you needed to?" Nonno knew I used painting to cope and express myself like Dad. The hurt was long from gone, but I felt as though I was beginning to function once again.

Mildred handed me a sweatshirt, which I slipped over my head.

"I think so. Did the officers call?"

Carson took a sip of coffee from the mug Mildred gave him, weary from all the travel. Nonno nodded. "They did about ten minutes ago. I was about to bring dinner and tell you. The investigation is still ongoing. No leads. They're releasing Alex's body to the crematory tomorrow. They have all the evidence they need to collect."

"Which officer called?"

"Officer Ashton. He was one of the detectives who noti-fied you."

Why hadn't Alex's supervisor called? Honestly, I knew nothing about how all this worked. Was it too dangerous to come to my house in case someone was watching? I would have thought at least his superior would have contacted me somehow. I'd met his superior once in the precinct when I needed the accident report from when someone rear-ended me.

A headache bloomed in the back of my head as I sat in the chair and took the offered coffee from Mildred. "I'll go to the station tomorrow and see what's going on."

Carson ran a hand through his hair and looked at me with caring eyes. "I'll go with you if you need me to."

I never knew what I did to deserve Carson as a best friend. Alex and he had gotten along great prior to him being deployed. After we were married, Carson was one of the major things we fought about. Alex wanted him out of my life, say-ing Carson wanted me. The notion was insane. I refused to give an inch on Alex's request regarding Carson. There was nothing sexual between us. Never had been. Never would be.

A sigh left my lips, and I took a sip of my coffee while a bowl of stew was set before me. The steam rose as the meaty aroma filled the room. Nonno raised his eyebrows at me as he had the last couple of nights when it was dinnertime. Begrudg-ingly, I ate. Carson joined us, sitting across from me. I lis-tened, not adding much to the conversation, as Nonno asked Carson about his latest trip to Italy. A vineyard came up. Some wine. Honestly, I zoned out, thinking about what I was going to say to Commander Taylor tomorrow.

"Do you remember the restaurant we found in Little Italy the summer we went with Dad to a business meeting, Wil-low?"

The question brought me back into the conversation. Carson smiled at me. *The delicious ravioli we found.* "They had the ham stuffed cheese ravioli we devoured. Your dad had some delivered for us every week from then on out because we wouldn't stop hassling him to take us back."

I remembered Carson and me eating until we lay on the floor, stuffed and moaning in pain from too much ravioli. Carson's dad, Bennett, had thought we were insane, filling ourselves like we did.

I giggled.

Carson's grin grew wider. "You're remembering how we ate until we nearly popped."

"I do. We were ridiculous about that ravioli."

Winking, Carson took another bite. I was glad he was here.

Chapter Six

S itting in the driver seat, I looked at the 24th Precinct, where Alex's boss, Commander Taylor, presided. I thought about Alex breaking the news to me about his new job as an undercover cop. A week after we got married, Alex had taken it without consulting me. I was furious but had let it slide because of his PTSD.

I sighed as my phone rang and sent it to voicemail. It was Carson. This morning, I'd left before he woke, needing some time to get my thoughts together. I'd asked him to stay the night in his old bedroom my parents had kept for him growing up. Having him and Nonno there helped. Tension in my neck grew as anticipation bloomed. I wasn't ready to speak to any-one until I got this over with.

I quickly typed out a text so he wouldn't worry.

Me: I'm okay. At the precinct. I'll be home shortly.

Carson: Thanks for texting me. Wanted to make sure you were okay. I'm going to head to my place to get some things if you still want me to stay at your house.

Me: Thanks, Carson. I'd like for you to stay a little longer if you can. It means a lot that you're here.

Carson: Wouldn't be anywhere else. I'll be back to your place as soon as possible.

I knew he meant it. There was no telling what was put on hold business wise for Carson to leave early.

I got out of my car and headed up the concrete steps to the state-of-the-art police station. Hopefully, Commander Taylor remembered our brief encounter and would give me something a little more than the "investigation was still open" like the other officers had done over the phone.

The reflective glass doors greeted me. I was dressed in jeans and a yellow summer blazer with my hair pulled back in a ponytail. Any happiness was devoid from my body language. Sadness rolled off me in droves. But I knew I had to keep pushing forward to make it through. When you stood still, you risked the chance of being washed away.

Plastering on a pleasant expression, I opened the door and mentally prepped myself. It was morning, and the place was deserted as I approached the front desk. Only the smell of stale coffee lingered in the air.

A female officer sat behind the desk in her blue uniform. "May I help you?"

"Yes, I'd like to speak with Commander Taylor regarding the murder of Alex Thompson. My name is Willow Russo." I never changed my name after we got married. Alex actually encouraged me not to. Only a few of my closest friends knew I was married, because Alex hadn't wanted me to broadcast it. It bothered me, but with the PTSD, I hadn't questioned it much. There were quirks that were better left alone.

She nodded after taking a few notes. "He's in a meeting. Do you want to wait?"

"Yes, please."

Keys clicked on her computer. "Perfect. I'll let him know you're here."

Making my way first to the coffee machine, I poured a cup and mixed in some creamer as I tried not to watch two officers chat with each other on the other side of the room. The coffee smelled old, but something was better than nothing at this point. The chattering stopped momentarily as they glanced my way, which caught my attention.

I met their gazes, and the officers looked away and continued their conversation. I felt paranoid and did another quick take of the place, finding it void of anyone else.

Idly, I wondered if they knew Alex and recognized me. Probably not since he was undercover and I'd only been here once. He kept no photos of us in his wallet. In fact there weren't any photos of us except on our wedding day in Vegas. If only I had done things differently, in retrospect, after all that had transpired through the last year.

It seemed like a lifetime ago that we got married. On a whim, shortly after he left the military, Alex surprised me with a trip to Vegas. It was an incredibly romantic weekend. Though I'd sensed a change, I loved him and agreed to marry him.

Something in the pit of my stomach had warned me, but I'd ignored it, thinking love conquered all.

Always go with my gut. I should have known.

My mind drifted to better times.

We were at the airport. I'd been an emotional wreck on the inside all morning but forced myself to be calm on the outside. The love of my life was leaving to head back to base. Within forty-eight hours, Alex would deploy. There was a chance I wouldn't hear from him again until he arrived at the base overseas. He explained that at times I might go weeks without hearing from him. Weeks. And when I did hear from him, it would probably only be through e-mail.

How was I going to survive going that long not knowing if he was okay?

"Sweetheart, don't worry. I know what I'm doing."

I laid my head against his chest. "I know you do. I'm trying not to be upset."

Fingers came up underneath my chin, and I looked into those gorgeous green eyes I'd become addicted to over the last few weeks. "Willow, I will come back for you. I'll make you my wife. We'll have a little girl and a little boy. That will be my perfect world."

A tear streaked down my face. "I want that, too."

He pulled out a picture from his bag. It was of me smiling up at him. This morning, when we were getting ready, I'd put on lipstick and put a big kiss in the corner of it. "I'll keep this close to me all the time. Even if you don't hear from me, I'll be thinking of you. I love you, Willow."

"I love you, too. I'll be waiting for you. I'll wait forever."

"You won't have to."

Thirty minutes passed while I was lost in similar memories before the officer from the front desk approached me. She grinned, which hopefully meant good news for me. "Ms. Russo, Commander Taylor is on his way up to meet with you."

"Oh, thank you. Perfect."

Sweat coated my palms as nerves settled over me. I wasn't sure what I should or shouldn't say. I noticed a gentleman reading a paper in the far corner and glancing my way every few minutes. Where had he come from? It was as if he materialized out of thin air. I kept looking at him, unable to look away, willing him to glance my way again. He stayed intent on reading the paper.

The officer cleared her throat, breaking my focus. I threw away my almost-full cup of coffee. It had only set my nerves more on edge.

As I grabbed my purse, the man caught my attention again. His gaze lingered longer than necessary. I was the only one in the area for him to be staring at. He was older, wearing a golfer's hat. Large glasses covered his face.

Again, his stare met mine and held for a few seconds before he looked away. Chills ran down my back. I wasn't sure why or what they meant. Was I being paranoid as Alex's warnings bounced around in my head?

One night, about two months after getting married and right before he left on an undercover assignment, Alex had said, "Willow, if they find out I'm an undercover cop, they could come for you. Be careful. Don't tell anyone we're married."

I'd packed my bags and stayed with Nonno for a week. I barely slept a wink until I got my fear under control. Then I decided he was probably being an asshole. But on the off chance, I'd remained cautious. What if there was some truth to what he said?

After leaving the military, Alex entered a self-destruct mode, which was common with PTSD. Nothing I said convinced him to stop. What if he had told someone about me?

"Ms. Russo?"

I turned to see the man I remembered meeting in the lobby. "Commander Taylor, thank you for seeing me. I hoped—"

"Let's go to my office to talk." His shortness caught me off guard. Had I done something wrong? My husband just died, and I had zero answers. I thought coming down here face to face was better than calling. To me it seemed normal for the wife of a murdered officer to come to the police station. Phone calls had the possibility of being taped.

Nodding, I followed the broad-shouldered man with the crew cut. His strides were heavy and his posture was unfriendly, which only heightened my anxiety. His fists were clenched at his sides, adding hostility to the air.

At the end of the hall, I was ushered into an office. Quickly, I glanced around. At the back was a bookshelf filled with awards and golfing trophies. In front, was a huge desk that made the room feel smaller and intimidating—like the commander.

Without a word, Commander Taylor sat behind his desk. His brown eyes grew colder. "Why the fuck are you here? Have you come to carry on your late husband's vendetta?"

What. The. Hell?

Vendetta?

Carry on?

This was bad. My spine shot ramrod straight as adrenaline pumped through my veins.

Taking a few steps back, my fingers wrapped around the door knob as my heart escalated. I worked to swallow the lump that had formed in my throat. The air became thick. I took a deep breath. It was time to leave. "I-I-I came to talk about Alex's murder." I took a steadying breath before I continued. "I wanted to know if he was undercover when he died. And if you could tell me anything to help explain what happened. I don't know anything about a vendetta. This was a mistake coming here today."

This was not how I imagined coming here would be. I thought, at worst, he would give me the brush off.

Maybe having Carson with me would have been for the best. I'd flung the door open when I heard, "Wait, Ms. Russo. Please." Slowly, I turned to see some of the ice had left the man's eyes. "Will you close the door?"

The door clicked shut, but my hand remained on the knob. I wanted to be able to escape quickly if I needed to. My instincts told me to stay, while my head said to leave.

Silence permeated the room.

"Are you playing a game?" His menacing tone rankled me.

My mouth dropped open. Was he testing me? Before I left, I wanted to put this man in his place as all the suffocating emotions made their way to the surface.

I practically spit as I said, "How dare you ask me that! I came here for answers. This isn't a game. I just lost my husband!"

My shouting startled me quiet. I took a deep breath and focused on the cream-colored walls before I met the commander's eyes again. "I'm sorry. I'm not a yeller. I honestly don't know what you're talking about with vendettas and games. All I want is some answers. Alex was with me the night before. Then he was gone. I know being undercover is dangerous. But as his wife, I thought I would be given a little more than 'the case is still open' and when his remains will be sent to the crematory."

A tear tracked down my face as I continued. "I know it's against protocol to come in. Alex repeatedly warned me against it. I get it, but I need something more. Anything. I loved him."

The commander stood, and I backed against the door, twisting the knob. With his hands up, he sat back down. "Please have a seat. I'll stay where I'm at. I understand why I've made you nervous."

This was a complete change from his earlier demeanor. He was softer.

Tentatively, I took a few steps to one of the chairs in front of his desk, not trusting this sudden change.

"Ms. Russo, I don't know how to say this. I hope you're not lying about the games. But I don't think you are." He paused, and I stared at him, not knowing what to say. He continued, "Your husband, Gabriel Alexander Thompson, was not an undercover cop. He blackmailed me to give you the illusion that he was. I kept up the farce at all costs. I don't know what he was involved in, but it wasn't good. His record is nearly blank. Trust me; I tried to find something on the bastard."

The blood drained from my face as the words registered. "Wh-what are you saying?"

This wasn't happening. No way. I wanted to leave, pretend the commander was lying.

Alex was a lot of things, but I never thought of him as a liar.

He leaned forward. "I've been reading people for a while, and I can tell you had no idea."

My only response was to shake my head.

Alex wasn't an undercover cop.

He blackmailed someone.

He lied to me.

Wait, what if this man was for some reason lying? "Why was he blackmailing you?" Commander Taylor began to respond, but I interrupted him. "How do I know you're telling me the truth?"

Assessing me, the quietness settled over the room for a couple of minutes. "I made a mistake once at a club in Philadelphia. If it got out, it would ruin my personal life. Bastard set me up a little over six months ago."

That happened right before we were married. I swallowed hard, still holding on to the chance he was wrong or lying. I wasn't sure what to say when he offered, "I have a recording of a conversation I had with Alex. Do you want to hear it?"

My insides shook with fear as the lies engulfed me. This was beyond anything I'd thought possible. I was scared to reveal the truth of the white lies. Betrayal sliced through me bone deep. How was I so stupid not to see the depth of his deceit?

By the seriousness of his face, I knew the commander was about to prove he told the truth.

Alex had lied to me.

Tears pricked the back of my eyes as my vision blurred. My heart ached. Barely above a whisper, I answered, "Yes."

Chapter Seven

In a fog, I left the precinct and stopped for a second as the sun's rays hit my face. It helped bring warmth to my chilled state.

The conversation with Commander Taylor repeated in my head. The menace in Alex's voice had been unmistakable. I hadn't known that version of Alex, even during the bad times.

Commander Taylor had told the truth. I shivered as the memory replayed.

Alex's voice came over the phone recording. "Are you prepared to sell it when you meet her at the precinct?"

A long pause ensued before Commander Taylor responded, "Yes, I will hold up my end of the bargain. Where is the tape?"

"Safe. Your wife will never know about Cocktails if you make sure Willow believes what we discussed. Understand?"

"Yes."

The recording had abruptly stopped, potentially at a part that put Commander Taylor in a bad light.

Acid churned in my stomach.

Commander Taylor had obviously cheated on his wife. I made no comment regarding this as I left. All I said was I would be in touch with the crematory to get Alex's remains and wished him well. What else was I supposed to do? I wanted Alex out of my life.

What had Alex gotten involved in when he returned? What happened to him? He was more far gone than I ever imagined.

But worse was the feeling I'd been living with a total stranger. Someone who had calculated his way into my life—sold me an illusion. If only, I'd listened to myself all those months ago and not married him.

If only…

Numbly, I walked to my black Land Rover and sat in the seat. Staring at the precinct, I wondered if ignorance was bliss. Alex was dead, and I wasn't sure what having this knowledge accomplished besides making me realize how naïve I'd been.

None of this seemed real.

My phone rang, which drew a small scream from me. The number was unknown. "Hello."

A male voice with a thick accent greeted me. It wasn't someone I recognized. "Look under your seat." Dread filled me as my eyes quickly scanned my surroundings. I was at a police precinct. Two people strolled down the sidewalk hand in hand walking their dog. They weren't on their cell phone. Maybe I should run back. What would I say to the officers?

My voice wanted to waiver, but I steadied it as I asked, "Who is this?"

A deep breath came over the line with a prolonged pause. I checked to make sure we hadn't lost connection, but my phone still showed that the call was connected.

"Hello?" I asked.

"Willow, I'm looking for answers as well. Alex wronged me, too."

This was the worst day of my life. This morning I was so sure of who I married. Yes, we had our issues—a lot of issues—but I never imagined. In a matter of thirty minutes, my world turned upside down and inside out.

I cleared my throat. "I don't know anything. Please."

"Willow, I'm not going to hurt you. I swear it."

Truth rang out in his voice, but my nerves were on edge. My eyes darted around the parking lot. "Why are you calling me?"

"I want to right a wrong… and make sure you're okay."

Make sure I'm okay? This was a little creepy. The hair stood up on my arm*s*.

Another sigh. "We can discuss more later. Check under the seat when we hang up. It'll be up to you if you want to find the truth. Regardless, you'll be safe."

The last statement seemed like an oath, and my insides warmed. But there shouldn't be a warm gooey feeling from a stranger calling me and telling me I was going to be safe from whatever Alex was involved in.

What was wrong with me? Stress, it was stress.

I shook my head to clear the muddled thoughts. Until I saw the information, I wasn't sure what I wanted to do. I hated that there were other people hurt by my husband. Part of me felt responsible, though I knew that was stupid. I whispered to keep my voice from shaking, "For what it's worth, I'm sorry for whatever Alex did to you if we don't speak again."

"We'll be speaking again. I'm certain of it."

The line went dead.

So frustrating. All I was left with was more questions.

The parking lot was deserted except for the old man with the cane from earlier. His gaze met mine before he turned and walked down the sidewalk. For good measure, I locked my doors before I reached under the seat.

There was an envelope.

My heart sped faster.

He had been in my car.

I gasped for air.

Disabled my locks.

Gotten around my alarm.

Who was this man?

I wasn't safe.

With trembling hands, I took the manila envelope and placed it in my lap. Glancing around, I saw a few officers ambling to their cars. The old man turned and disappeared around the corner.

Whatever was inside would alter my course. I knew it. Something within told me so.

I paused.

If I tossed the envelope aside, would it all disappear? Sometimes ignorance was bliss. But not knowing the truth would eat me alive later, when my thoughts settled. I knew it.

I ripped it open and turned it over to scan the pictures.

My fingers trembled.

There were pictures of Alex outside a club smoking a cigarette. *He smoked?* He told me he hated cigarettes. We never went to bars because of that. He was allergic to the smoke.

I shook my head. More lies.

Squinting, I focused on one of the pictures again. A woman stood beside him with her hands on his arm in an intimate gesture. They were definitely familiar with each other.

A bigger man stood in front of him, giving me a profile view. Alex had a scowl on his face.

Disgust roiled through me.

Betrayal wedged its way into my mind.

Whispering to no one but myself, I said, "What did you do, Alex?"

Acid fought its way up my esophagus. I was going to be sick.

Calm down.

Maybe he was undercover? The hopeful question sounded absurd, even to me in my stressed out state.

I needed air.

I needed to be out of this confined space.

Not thinking, I scrambled to unlock the car door. Barely making it to the bushes, I heaved the contents of my stomach onto the ground. Dry heaves wracked my body, causing tears to spill down my face.

This wasn't happening.

It all had to be a dream.

But… the pictures were real.

Alex was not the man I fell in love with.

Abruptly, I stood. Someone could still be watching me. Or worse yet, try to abduct me. My mind was out of control with scenarios. *Carson.* I needed to get to Carson. I'd be able to trust him with this, get his thoughts. Without a second thought, I dashed to the car and drove away, furiously wiping away the tears trailing down my cheeks. *Focus, Willow. Focus.* My heartbeat raced as I watched the rearview mirror to see if anyone followed me.

Two blocks. Right turn.

Was someone following me? My heart thudded in my ear.

Three blocks. Left turn.

My fingers slipped on the steering wheel as I hastily turned. I glanced again in the mirror. Nothing.

One block. Left turn.

My tires squealed as I made the turn too quickly. A red car appeared. *Oh shit.* My breathing sped up. Were they after me?

Four blocks. Right turn.

The red car went the opposite way, and I stopped, knowing I was on the verge of losing it. This was bad. I needed to regain control before I got into an accident. My hands shook as I made them into fists and released them.

I'm okay, I'm okay, I'm okay.

The mantra helped soothe me.

I checked in the rearview mirror again, and there was no one. My shoulders drooped as the adrenaline left me.

The streets remained vacant. No one was watching me.

Honk!

I screamed and saw I was blocking a dump truck from crossing an intersection. Not taking the time to apologize, I sped off again. My thoughts went every which way. Betrayal and hurt spread through me like a disease.

Alex was gone, and I would never know why.

Why? Why? Why?

The park outside of the city was ahead as I turned right again. Memories from the past tickled their way into my consciousness—something good to think about, which I needed. Almost past the entrance, I made a hard turn causing my tires to squeal again.

A few people stared my way as I parked the car. Their opinion was the last thing on my list to care about. I thought back to the day Alex and I came here after he met Dad.

◆━━━━━◆━━━━━◆

We lay stretched out on a blanket underneath the big tree in the park with my head on Gabe's chest. My hand was placed over his heart where his tattoo was. The birds sang a melodic harmony while a warm breeze rustled the trees. It was perfection, lying here with the love of my life.

Kids played all around, and the possibilities of my future with Gabe had my mind wandering with visions. A little girl no more than two giggled as she tried to kick a ball and kept missing.

I glanced over at Gabe, who watched the scene unfold. Pressure from his hold increased. Our eyes met, and I saw the same feelings in his eyes I felt.

For now… our life would have to wait.

He was returning to the military from leave in less than a month. I dreaded when that time came. Taking a deep breath, I smelled the fresh cut grass.

He sighed, breaking into my thoughts. "I hate that I have to leave you. If I'd known you existed, I would have never enlisted."

The words brought a smile to my face. Gabe always expressed his emotions in the sweetest ways with how much he cared for me. I felt cherished and loved. A feeling of content-

ment fell over me, and I raised my head. *"I'll wait for you. Always. Just promise me one thing."*

"What's that, sweetheart?"

"Come back to me."

Fingers trailed down my cheek as our eyes locked, the familiar intensity growing between us. "I promise. I'll always come back to you."

Our lips touched, igniting the chemistry that always lingered beneath the surface. "Let's go back to the hotel. I want to make love to you, Willow."

"Please."

A couple sat beneath our tree. Two nights before Alex left, he brought me to this place again and carved our initials in the trunk. We were so in love. While he was away, I came here often to sit and read beneath the tree.

Pain settled in my chest as the revelations from this afternoon refused to be ignored.

It was amazing how much the effects of deployment could change a person. I'd read about it multiple times since Alex was diagnosed with PTSD. At one point, I wondered if the diagnosis was true since the doctor had rubbed me the wrong way. I had gone into full research mode. After extensive research, I came to the conclusion that Alex had all the symptoms—edginess, nightmares, jumpiness, and the need to be isolated. Even though we were in different rooms, his nightmares woke me up frequently. Once, I tried to help, but Alex refused, slamming the door in my face.

But… lying was something I'd never imagined.

Truth was a fundamental building block of any relationship. The one thing I held onto through the rough spots was the honesty we had between each us, even if we weren't in agreement.

The manila envelope on the passenger seat caught my eye again. It was like a train wreck. I wasn't able to look away as I picked up the stack.

This time, I flipped through the remaining three pictures. They were from different nights, as Alex had on different shirts… shirts I'd never seen. In each one, the same woman appeared. The last one was of them kissing in front of the Club. I looked closer at the picture. The club was called Cocktails.

Cocktails.

Fuck.

In the phone conversation between Commander Taylor and Alex, Cocktails was mentioned. I bet this place was in Philadelphia.

"I made a mistake once at a club in Philadelphia."

Those were the words Commander Taylor spoke in his office. Why was Alex involved with such a place?

I stared at the picture of them kissing. Alex held onto the woman's ass. The way they regarded each other spoke of intimacy. More betrayal. The ultimate betrayal. My mind wanted to play this all off, but I felt the truth.

Ugh. What an asshole.

There was nothing pure left of our relationship.

A piece of paper on the seat caught my attention. Picking it up, I read:

Did the other woman know about you?

Cocktails in Philadelphia tonight.

Don't tell anyone you were married to Alex. Watch and listen.

Don't come alone. You will be safe. I'll make sure of it.

My emotions were a ping pong ball, moving back and forth as the questions came to mind.

He cheated on me?

The bastard had cheated on me after everything I'd done.

I felt dirty inside.

Who was this man with the accent?

A glutton for punishment, I looked at the woman more carefully. Dark hair, bright eyes. We were exact opposites in our appearance. The short skirt and the way she held herself gave me the impression of a hooker. Maybe that was the cynicism in me talking. She was obviously in love with him, considering the adoring expression she wore. Alex gave nothing away as he looked at her.

Was that why he hadn't wanted me to change my name?

Don't come alone. You will be safe. I'll make sure of it.

Carson was going to think I'd lost my damn mind wanting to go to a club over three hours away.

Chapter Eight

The night was upon us as we drove in Carson's gunmetal-gray Maserati toward Philadelphia. I'd been silent most of the drive as smooth tunes filled the car and helped to keep my anxiety at bay. Honestly, I was holding on by a thread. Carson knew I needed the silence for now.

After filling him in on everything, Carson hesitated to go anywhere without first scoping it out. It was true. This might be a trap. Maybe that was why the note told me not to come alone. But I had to find out.

The cops weren't to be trusted now. The only person I could trust with this information was Carson.

For good measure, I suggested we tell Nonno and his parents where we were headed. We told them Carson was taking me out to this place, on the recommendation of a client, to get me out of the house. No one thought twice about it. In fact, they all agreed it was a great idea.

Melancholy clung to me like a dark cloak. I needed to focus on something else before the negative emotions drowned me.

I took a deep breath and grinned as the familiar scent of the cologne Carson had worn since college filled my nostrils—fresh with a hint of spice. In Paris, I'd bought him a bottle for his birthday. Shaking my head, I chortled.

"What are you laughing about?"

"Your cologne. The inside of your car smells like you sprayed it in here. I remember when you sent me chocolate at college for a month as a thank-you gift."

The movement of Carson's wagging eyebrows brought a snicker from me. "The girls really loved it. They still love it. Do you remember when my friends tried bribing you to tell them what cologne it was?"

The laughter felt therapeutic. "I think the best present was from your friend, Richard. The Gucci watch was nice."

"Bastard. He was determined to get it out of you."

"I held firm. No one was getting the secret from me. Plus, you were one-upping them each time they sent me a gift. That month I made out like a bandit."

He shook his head. "Cost me a damn fortune. Dad called, wanting to know why the hell I spent two grand on a spa treatment. When I told him, he threw in another for you. Thought it was brilliant."

"Good times."

"The best."

Another comfortable silence filled the air, but the weight of what we faced crept back into my mind. Not in the clubbing spirit at all, I'd kept my hair simple, threw on a basic black cocktail dress, donned a pair of high heels, and put on a little makeup. From what I'd seen on the internet, this place was not upscale.

Honestly, this was the last place I wanted to be. On the couch in my pajamas with a tub of ice cream watching some comedy sounded better.

We entered the city limits of Philadelphia. I needed to go over the plan again for my sanity. "Remember, I don't want anyone at the bar tonight to know I was married to Alex."

"Not a word. If we see the people in the picture, are we going to try to sit near them?"

This afternoon, when I'd told Carson about the pictures, he'd assumed Commander Taylor gave them to me. I hadn't corrected him. And I'd left out any mention of the note. I wasn't sure why, but I followed my instinct. For the time being, I wanted to keep that private after hearing the conviction in the man's voice.

Carson patted my knee. "Hey, we don't have to do this?"

Realizing I hadn't responded to his earlier question, I snapped out of my thoughts. "No, I want to do this. If they are there, let's sit as close as we can without being conspicuous. I'll let you lead the way."

"Sounds like a plan. We'll figure this out, Willow. I'm not sure what the fuck Alex did, but we'll find out. At least kids aren't involved."

"Thanks, Carson."

My thoughts drifted to our last time together when we hadn't used any protection. If the need to ever came, I would think about it then. Today, it was too much to process.

The hot pink sign of the bar came into view. It reminded me of an eighties movie gone bad. There was nothing special about the bar from the outside. An ordinary place. The lack of a line wasn't a surprise, considering the day of the week.

After parking the car in the paid parking garage, we moseyed across the street. I grabbed Carson's hand for reassurance. I wanted to think I was a strong person, but inside I felt anything but. My nerves were rattled as all the facts continued to sink in.

I was at a bar.

A bar where my husband had been with another woman.

And a man I'd never met had left me pictures of them after breaking into my car.

Yeah, I was definitely treating myself to a pint of ice cream later.

The large bouncer greeted us at the door. The dark sunglasses obscured his eyes as he took us in. "There's a cover charge. Five per person."

Carson fished out the bills before I had a chance. We each received a stamp on our right hands. It was the outline of a martini glass.

A musky beer smell emanated from beyond the doors. This wasn't an average bar. It was a dive.

What the hell had brought Alex to this place besides that woman? Would she be here? An uneasy feeling ran through my body, and I focused on my inner strength. With my shoulders squared and head held high, I walked into the place, looking confident and feeling anything but.

Some cheesy song played low through scratchy speakers as women danced provocatively on stages throughout the place. Basically, it was a low-class strip club. Men sat at each table, their eyes glued to the nearly nude dancers. We made our way up to the bar when a familiar brunette turned my way for a minute, her eyes watery.

I froze for a second, feeling the sting of the pictures again. She was real. Of course she was real, but it was harder than I'd imagined.

I knew Carson saw her, too. He'd studied the pictures for a while with me this afternoon, looking for other clues. Besides the bar's name, there wasn't anything else.

Carson kept me moving, and I focused back on the bar while visualizing the picture where their lips were interlocked and Alex's hands were on her ass.

I added "Get tested for STDs" to my checklist.

The man with the short crew cut whom Alex had been scowling at in the photos had his hand on the woman's shoulder. No recognition flickered in the woman's face when we made brief eye contact. Nothing on the man's face, either.

Thank goodness. Alex kept me a secret, which was a relief. *Asshole. I shouldn't even have to be here. I should be able to mourn my husband like a normal person, not be on the verge of hating him.*

Carson led me to the bar and ordered us each a bottle of beer. I wasn't going to drink it, but the beer was probably the safest option from the looks of the place. The bar seats looked worn with a few tears, but we sat anyway.

Another thing to add to the checklist: sterilize our clothes. Or better yet, throw them away.

Sniffles came from Alex's other woman a seat away. With the music low enough, we were able to hear, "I can't believe he's gone. He promised."

"I know, sugar."

More sniffles. "I had to come to our place. We loved it here. He loved when I danced for him on stage. I know I'm a mess, but I needed to be somewhere familiar to us where we shared a lot of good times."

Who all played a part in his double life? Danced for him? Disgusting. It was hard not to look her way, but the last thing I wanted was for her to stop talking. Who told her about Alex dying? My fists clenched in my lap as I thought about the police keeping the lie for Alex.

Carson kept quiet beside me, listening to the conversation while pretending to check his phone.

The gruff man soothed her. "Sugar, Alex loved you. You know this. You can take as much time off as you need. I'll keep a dancing spot open for you."

She worked here? As a stripper? I felt a stab of pain in my heart and busied myself with the label on the beer in front of me. He sounded sure of Alex's love. I wasn't sure if Alex loved me. For the last six months I wondered if he hated me. Getting rip-roaring drunk and not having a care in the world sounded like the answer.

Immature, I know.

Carson raised an eyebrow, silently asking if I was okay.

I responded, "Feels nice to unwind after a long day." My voice shook a little as I blinked rapidly, willing myself not to cry.

Tipping his beer, Carson responded, "It does."

I dug my fingernails into my left hand, which was still in my lap, to focus on the pain. The female bartender walked up to Carson. "Can I get you and your girl anything else?"

I wanted to roll my eyes at the subtlety. "She's just a colleague. A friend told us about this place, and we thought we'd give it a try. He failed to mention it was a strip club."

She laughed and gave him a wink. It appeared she fancied Carson. I tilted my head to the side, trying to tune out their conversation and listen to the *other* woman's.

I quickly glanced their way. The man stroked the woman's arms, and she leaned into him. "Alex said we were going to be taken care of. He was working on a deal worth millions. He hoped to be able to pay you back. That's why he was gone so much. How am I going to take care of our son? My husband is gone!"

It all happened so fast—I lost my balance and fell on the dirty floor, drawing attention from those around me. Carson was beside me in an instant.

"Are you okay?" Carson asked with worry.

I looked up into his eyes as he hoisted me up and held me still. "Yes. I s-s-slipped."

The large man consoling Alex's other woman came to my side. "Darlin', are you okay?"

Staring at the man, I couldn't look away. This guy knew Alex in a way I hadn't. I wanted to ask a million questions, but I wasn't prepared to get tangled in this life Alex had separate from me. It seemed… dangerous. And not two feet away sat a woman who thought she was married to my husband.

"Ma'am?"

Carson looked me over and my senses came back to me. "Oh, yes. I'm fine. Just a bit too much to drink. I'm going to the restroom."

He nodded and returned to the *other* woman. I whispered to Carson, "I'll be back."

"Do you need me to come with you?"

"No, I need a minute." *Or a lifetime to recover from all of this.*

He was married.

He had a child.

He was working on a deal worth millions.

64

As I made a beeline for the restrooms in the back, a sleazy man winked at me. Gross.

Another item to add to my checklist: sterilize me.

I kept walking and tried to get my thoughts straight. But the woman's words kept repeating in my head.

Husband. Son. Millions.

Realization dawned, and I paused outside the utility closet in the musky hallway. I whispered to myself, "*I* am the other woman."

The door to the closet cracked open. Someone was in there, so I resumed my path to the restroom. As I passed, one hand yanked me inside while another came over my mouth to muffle my scream. I thrashed about as I was held against the wall.

This wasn't happening.

I thrashed more.

Carson. I needed to get to Carson.

The grip intensified as I used everything I had to get free. I was immobilized. The pitch-black room made it impossible to see. *They were here for me.*

My movements were restricted as panic surged through me. I wasn't strong enough, but I refused to give up as I clawed and kicked my way to no avail.

"Shh… I'm the man from the phone." I stilled. The voice with the Irish accent filled my ears. His strong frame held me, eliciting goose bumps from within. "I hoped you would come this way so we could talk." He paused. "I'm going to take my hand off and step back to give you space. If you want my help, don't scream."

I nodded, and instantly his hand left my mouth and the pressure of his body vanished. Even with my eyes adjusted, I was unable to make out anything.

My heavy breathing was the loudest noise in the room, followed by the sound of people walking by the door. He asked, "Did I hurt you?"

"You scared the shit out of me. You're a complete stranger who broke into my car and now yanked me into a closet. Who are you?" It felt good to release some of the pent-up emotions.

"Someone trying to right a wrong."

I snapped, "You keep saying that. What wrong are you trying to right? I'm tired of the games."

A few feet away I heard a sigh—like on the phone today. He sounded frustrated. "I can't share that yet. I need to know I can trust you."

"You're asking me to trust you blindly after everything that has happened to Alex?"

The voice was a little closer. "Yes, I know. It has to be this way for now, Willow. I wish I was able to tell you everything, but it will put you in more danger."

More danger? I massaged my temples as I listened to him. He stayed still and wasn't moving closer to me. I wanted to argue with him, but I didn't have the energy. Should I leave? Against my better judgement, I was going with my instincts, which were to stay and hear him out.

But... I needed a little more information. "Have we met before?"

"I've met Alex before. Did Candy or Harley recognize you?"

The acid feeling returned to my veins. The woman now had a name... Candy. "No. Did you know Alex had a child?"

"Yes, Alex is a bastard." The venom in his voice pierced the air. At least we felt the same about Alex.

How many other people knew? My fingers dug deeper into my temples. "I hope I'm not pregnant."

"What?"

Fuck, why did I choose this moment to have word vomit? The stress was getting to me. This information was too personal to share at this point, let alone admit out loud. "Nothing. It was nothing."

"Are you pregnant with Alex's child?"

The silence felt suffocating. "I don't want to talk about this." More silence, but I could hear his breaths. I wanted to move past this to see what else he had to offer. "I don't know if I am or not yet. We had a slip-up right before he died."

Another tired sigh. Oddly, he brought me comfort with his presence, which was insane, considering the circumstances. Something stirred between us. I was drawn to him… undeniably, as I felt myself wanting to gravitate toward him. With some effort, I forced myself to remain on my side of the room. Only so much crazy could be tolerated in one day. The automatic response toward this stranger jarred me.

"Did you tell anyone about me?"

I guess my reveal was too personal for him, too, since he changed the subject, for which I was thankful. "No. I went to Carson's after I opened the envelope. I left the part about you out of it."

No response. I felt the need to explain who Carson was all of a sudden. What if he thought Carson was someone I saw on the side since Alex had not been faithful to me? The last thing I wanted was for him to think I took my vows lightly. "Carson is my best friend. We're like siblings."

"Why?"

The man was driving me nuts with his nonanswers and rapid-fire questions. "Why are Carson and I like siblings or why didn't I tell him about you?"

"About me."

In the dark, I shrugged even though he wasn't able to see me. "I don't know." Every fiber in my being wanted to shut this man out of my life, but my heart told me I needed this man to figure out what was going on. If I wanted to know… if I wanted my life back… I needed him. Even with Alex's betrayal fresh on my psyche, part of me trusted this man, and I had no idea why. The thought both sobered and scared me at the same time. I found it hard to keep my guard up around him. An unstoppable draw kept me entranced. Fear shot through me at the strength of emotion I had around this stranger.

Panic ensued.

"I need to get back. Will I hear from you again?"

Again, a one-word answer that infuriated me. He offered nearly zero insight. "Yes."

Though I was the one ending this conversation, I wanted to prolong it. To give me something to hold on to. Maybe I needed to add "Get checked out by a psychologist" to my list. I was becoming certifiably insane. "Will I ever know who you are?"

"Yes."

The frustration created by this situation left me in a foul mood. "Can you give me anything? Something to go on?"

"You'll be safe. I promise."

The words stirred something within me, which filled me with guilt. I needed to get out of there and clear my head. "I have to go."

Without warning, I left the room and made a beeline for Carson. I looked at the other woman, and she appeared to be calmer. She hugged Harley. "Thanks for listening to me, Harley."

Seeing I was ready to go, Carson dropped some bills on the counter and led me out of the bar. Everything from the last few minutes in the closet was on replay in my head. The mysterious man seemed genuine. And he was certain we would meet some day. Why was that so important to me?

I wasn't ready to answer that. But I knew I wanted to talk to him again, and the truth of that reality scared me. *Shouldn't I be more focused on what happened with Alex?* Tonight, life as I knew it had altered.

Alex lied to me.

He had a wife.

All he wanted was my inheritance.

There was a possibility I was pregnant.

An even greater possibility I might not be safe.

What else was there to uncover? However, instead of worrying about the Alex situation, I was focused on the strange man I'd just met. The man who broke into my car and pulled me into the closet to talk to me.

What was wrong with me?

My defenses were helpless around this man. All common sense left me. And worst yet... I wanted more. Mentally, I scolded myself, knowing I needed to break this habit immediately in order to keep my wits about me. This was unlike me. Completely.

Once in the car, Carson said, "Shit, that was fucked up."

"That's putting it mildly."

Carson's knuckles were white from holding the steering wheel so tight as he drove. "I know once Alex got back, we had our issues about how he treated you. But he was a bastard."

Laying my head against the window, I watched the rain hit it. The tears tracked faster. "He was a bastard. A bastard who lied and cheated on me." A sob broke free. "But I was the other woman. He was married, Carson. I feel so disgusting inside."

He pulled the car over to the side of the road as I let the tears spill free. I sat further back into the soft black leather seats and let the anguish rip through me. The truth was hard. But I would be stronger than it.

"You did nothing wrong, Willow."

When his hand touched mine, I let it all go, yelling, "I hate him, Carson! I hate him with every fiber of my being!" Then I sagged. "I know it's wrong to hate someone… but I do! He stole so much from me that I'll never be able to get back."

I was barely able to see through the curtain of tears. Carson leaned over and hugged me. "He can't break you, Willow. You're stronger than that. I know it."

An unladylike sniffle came from me. "It gets worse."

Concern laced his face. "What else is there?"

I paused, hating to say it out loud. It only made the reality of all the lies worse. "I think Alex's business deal to get millions was to take mine. I think he was looking for holes in the trust."

"Oh fuck."

Chapter Nine

Two weeks had passed since Alex died. Nothing new surfaced on Alex, and I hadn't heard anything from the mysterious man. The entire situation was an enigma.

I wanted to hear from him, but I hoped Alex's double life stayed away at the same time.

Inside I was still a mess, but with painting, I began to heal. The loss of Mom and Dad helped prepare me for this, in a way. The hate fueled me, too. Three days ago, while I cried in my studio, I was glad Alex was dead and out of my life. I knew I wasn't taking the high road with those thoughts, but I truly despised him with all my heart.

Sometimes, I thought about the good times we had in order to rationalize why I had been so imperceptive. Love truly made you blind.

I'd debated with Carson about whether or not to go to the cops or tell our families about what we'd found out. For now, we were doing neither. Instead, we contacted an investigator named Trent. Apparently he'd done some work for Carson.

After I talked to Trent, I would determine if I wanted to use him or not.

With Commander Taylor being dirty, I wasn't sure who I could trust. It seemed smarter not to disclose everything until we knew more.

The waves crashed against the shore as I sat in a chair and looked out at the ocean. My bare feet sifted through the soft white sand. Seagulls dipped into the ocean for a snack. I loved it out here—always had, ever since I was a child.

I glanced back to the house and saw no one. Carson was going to join me when he finished his conference call. For now, I asked him to temporarily live with me. Since I decided not to go to the cops, I felt safer having him here, and he agreed. Before Carson left, the security system on the house needed upgrading. I also needed to look at the possibility of having someone added to the staff. That was on my list to talk to Trent about. Carson had done extensive background checks prior to using him. In fact, he helped him set up the initial structure for his company.

Once we decided on what to do with security, more would have to be explained to Nonno, Chris, and Mildred. I knew it was going to require telling them a version of white lies. The thought made me nauseous since honesty was so important to me. But hopefully when that time came, I had a better option.

I focused back on the soothing motion of the waves as they crested and crashed onto the shore and waited for Eva to emerge from my studio. She was an art gallery manager, in the studio looking at my latest paintings to see if she wanted them for a show. After I finished the last one the day before yesterday, I called her to see if she was interested.

Now that the emotions lay on the canvas, I wanted them out of my house. These paintings were a little darker than my norm and I was nervous what her response would be.

I closed my eyes and listened to the ocean as my thoughts drifted. Part of me wondered what Commander Taylor had to gain by sharing the conversation with me. There had to be more to that. When we met in his office, he'd only revealed part of the puzzle. Why that piece, I wasn't sure. He was still in it somehow. After all, Candy knew Alex was dead. Since his office handled the case, they'd had to orchestrate telling two wives their husband had died. How could each of us get remains?

Maybe Commander Taylor was involved in the scheme to get my trust fund. It was easier to go with the words of the mysterious man and trust no one… with the exception of Carson.

Five days ago, Nonno picked up the remains from the crematory. When I received them, I idly wondered who got the real remains… me or Candy.

For now, Alex's *supposed* ashes were in a closet to keep me from dumping them down the garbage disposal where they belonged. Part of me felt guilty I wasn't mourning Alex, but then I remembered all he'd done and anger diminished the guilt. My eyes were now opened to his true self.

All I wanted was to piece my life back together and move on.

The thought that he had a son kept occupying my thoughts. What kind of father had he been? What did the kid look like? How old was he? I pushed away the thought of meeting him. It wasn't worth the potential consequences, but the fights Alex and I had had about children made the revelation hit home.

Going to the precinct two weeks ago left me with more questions than I ever thought possible. If only I hadn't gone to the precinct that day… *if only.*

The biggest hurdle I had left was getting my period—less than two weeks away. I relaxed back and my thoughts wandered back to a time when I was truly ignorantly happy for the last time with him.

He moved within me, and I arched my back, relishing the friction. My nipples tingled as they brushed against his chest while he thrust in and out of me.

I was close. So close.

Gabe kissed along my collar bone before sucking the sensitive flesh of my neck. I reveled in the moment since he was leaving tomorrow to return to base.

On a plea to reach my orgasm, I whispered, "Gabe, please."

A light sheen covered our bodies. "I'm with you, sweetheart."

Our orgasms rolled through us as we called out each other's name. Gabe collapsed on me and quickly rolled me on top of him, keeping us connected. "I love you, Willow."

"I love you, too."

Fingers trailed up my back. "One day, I'm going to make you the mother of my children."

I wanted to be with Gabe forever and have his children.

"Hey, angel."

Leaving the bittersweet thoughts, I smiled at the term of endearment Carson had used since we were younger. One time in the tree house, the light shone behind me, and he swore I looked like an angel. Plus, I'd helped bail him out of more than one situation throughout our childhood, earning me the name.

Opening my eyes, I responded. "Hey, you. Is your conference all done? I thought it would be longer. Eva is still looking at my paintings."

Wearing athletic shorts with a T-shirt, Carson squatted, bringing him eye level with me. Those blue eyes were gorgeous—they always had been. "It is. I have an idea."

I quirked a brow. "That sounds dangerous. You've gotten us into a lot of trouble throughout the years with your ideas."

A hand went to his chest in mock surprise. "When?"

"The time we played hooky from school and got caught drag racing your father's car along the shoreline."

His eyes lit up as a hand raked down the stubble on his face. "You may have a point. Are you in the mood to be daring?"

"I could be, depending…"

He gave me a mischievous wink. "Good. I need you to pack a bag."

"A bag?"

"I need your help."

Standing, I watched Carson. He was serious. "Help?"

He chuckled. "Are you going to answer everything I say with a question?"

"Hey, Willow. Am I interrupting?"

I turned to see the brunette art gallery manager approaching. Her attire was not appropriate for the shore at all as her heels sank into the sand. Carson stood beside me as the familiar artistic nerves took over while I waited for her verdict. Ultimately, I never had to sell a painting and I would be financially secure. But I loved it and wanted to be successful on my own.

"Of course not, Eva."

Since I let them observe my art by themselves, I was never able to ask what gallery managers thought about my work after they looked at it. I was fine with criticism, but asking felt like it forced people to give disingenuous compliments if they didn't like it.

Bringing her fingers to her mouth, she kissed them before moving them away in an exploding motion. "Willow. My word. I must have all of them for a show. You can't say no. I have to have them."

Eva was my favorite art gallery manager because of her energy and passion for art. The gallery on Madison Avenue in Manhattan drew huge crowds any time she hosted an event and generally sold out within hours. "Wow! Are you serious?"

I was stunned. Eva rarely took entire collections. She was very selective.

She waved her hand. "Of course I'm serious. They're fabulous! I'm going to showcase them as soon as possible."

Nearly hugging Eva, I remembered myself before exclaiming, "Yes, yes you can have them! This is amazing!"

She gave a quick clap. Needless to say, she was… eccentric. "Oh, you've made my day! I'm going to get to work on this immediately. We'll go through any you want to keep and all the specifics later this week, if that works."

In all the excitement, she leaned in to kiss both my cheeks, like in Europe.

"That sounds great. I don't want to keep any."

Squeals erupted from her, and I took a step back at the unexpected screech. Eva was oblivious to the scene she was causing. "This is your best work yet, Willow. They are so raw and emotional. Oh, I love them. Okay, I need to get back to the gallery. Can I send someone to get all the paintings tomorrow?"

"Yes. Thank you, Eva!" I remembered Carson asked for my help and told me to pack a bag. He knew he'd be able to get me to say yes. "I may be out of town. Mildred and Chris can let them into my studio."

Carson beamed, knowing I basically agreed to go.

"Perfect. Let me know. I have their numbers from the last show, in case you do decide to leave town. I've got to go plan this fab event." Eva waved as she walked to her car, completely ignoring Carson.

I hadn't spoken to Eva since I got married. I wasn't even sure if she knew I'd been married. Alex stayed out of the public eye with me. And with all his issues, I'd only told a few close friends about us. It shamed me that I allowed him to control so much of my life.

My own show… it was unbelievable. Astounding. Surreal. Normally, I'd share the showcase with several artists. This was the perfect timing for something positive to happen, giving me a glimpse that hope existed. I was truly achieving my dreams regarding my career.

A hand patted my shoulder. "I'm so proud of you, Willow. Your dad would be proud, too."

A lumped formed in my throat. "That means a lot, Carson."

I often wondered what Dad would think of my life now with all the mistakes I'd made. Mom, too. At least they were together now. Their deaths were sudden, and I was missing so many words of wisdom. Nonno had many for me, but it wasn't the same.

Carson walked toward the house and called over his shoulder. "We're leaving in one hour."

"Where?"

No answer. Half the time, I thought he aggravated me on purpose.

Four hours later, we pulled up the drive of a gorgeous two-story house located on a private beach in Newport, Rhode Island. I wasn't a fan of flying, especially in small private planes like the one Carson owned. Heights made me nervous. Carson knew this, of course, and drove instead.

The front porch lights were on, and the sun was setting behind the house, creating a cascade of orange and red. "Who owns this place?"

"Potentially me."

I spun around. "Carson, this is gorgeous."

We walked around as I took it all in. The place was amazing—definitely Carson's taste. There were cobblestone paths surrounded by plants. I meandered about as Carson stayed near the car. It was as if I'd entered another place—truly mystical.

Birds chirped in the distance, bringing a smile to my face as I touched a red petal from a rose bush. I plucked it and smelled it, appreciating the beauty.

I emerged back onto the driveway and found Carson leaning against his car, waiting for me.

Looking up, I saw a glass deck that disappeared around the back of the house on the second story. The view must be amazing from up there, creating an artist's paradise. If Carson bought it, no doubt I would be over here to draw.

"How did you find this place?"

The house was modern with metal trimmings and windows. It was impressively large. I lived on the beach, but this was a dream vacation home. I stepped up onto the front porch to keep looking.

Carson joined me. "I've been looking for a place to relax and unwind away from the Hamptons. This came on the market, and they're holding it for me."

I quirked a brow. "Holding it for you?"

"Yes, for a price. They're giving me a few days to make an offer without entertaining any other bids. It's why they staged it for us to spend a couple of days here. After we leave someone will come to clean."

Carson had expanded the family business internationally. Whitmore Hotels was a chain of five-star hotels that put all others to shame. With Carson being an only child, he was inheriting a multi-billion dollar business. The plan was in five years his father would step down as CEO. Until then, Carson learned every aspect he could. "Workaholic" was an understatement when it came to him.

Turning, I gave him an incredulous look. "Well, hopefully they'll put whatever money you put down toward the purchase price. This is amazing. It'll be good for you to unwind. You work too much."

The slate entrance led to the massive metal doors. He entered a code, the door clicked open, and we walked inside. Someone had been here to stage the lighting. The interior decorating was phenomenal. It was modern, edgy, and comfortable. As I walked toward the glass windows, I wished I'd brought my paints.

"I brought you a sketch pad in case you get inspired while you're here. I know I sprung it on you last minute."

I gave him a quick hug. "You're the best. I think a change of scenery was just what I needed."

Thunder rumbled, interrupting the slice of heaven before me. A storm brewed in the distance, dimming the bright colors of the sunset. I loved when the sea was choppy. It was beautiful watching the waves thrash about, creating sprays of color when they crashed into each other. Right now it mirrored me, internally.

"Let me get our stuff. The fridge is stocked. I figured it would be nice to stay in, relax, and roast marshmallows in the fireplace like we did as kids."

Our parents let us have sleepovers as children. I missed those times. "That sounds heavenly. It's been a while since we've done that."

"I know. I think we're overdue."

Chapter Ten

"**O**h my gosh! These are so good!" I popped another perfectly browned marshmallow into my mouth. The rain beat against the house, which—given the amount of glass—echoed throughout, creating a cozy feel. I loved rain storms.

The air conditioner worked to keep up with the heat from the fire. Pillows and blankets were sprawled beneath us as I put another marshmallow onto my roasting stick. It was late… nearly midnight. We couldn't stop laughing as we reminisced about our childhood.

Carson's marshmallow burst into flames, and I snickered. He never had the patience to hold it at a proper distance to get the perfect golden color. Moving his stick rapidly, he tried to extinguish the flame, but that released his marshmallow right into the fire. "Damn it. Such a fucking pain. Why the hell can't I get this right? I run a fucking empire of hotels and can't roast a damn marshmallow."

Whistling, I twirled mine in slow motion, not saying a word. A minute later, perfection was achieved again. I brought the stick toward my mouth when Carson snatched it. "Carson! That's mine."

He shoved the marshmallow in his mouth and smiled around it in victory. Smacking his lips together, he nodded his head. "That was good."

I put down my roasting stick and picked up a nearby throw pillow. "You stole my marshmallow. You must pay!"

"You've had like six of them. I've only gotten two." Carson backed away a few inches, bringing him closer to another pillow.

I giggled. "Then stop trying to incinerate them."

As he turned his attention to reach for his pillow, I launched mine at him, landing a direct hit to his head. "Hey, you're firing at an unarmed man."

The bag of marshmallows was closer, and he abandoned his reach for the pillow. He grabbed the handful of the sugary goodness, instead. "Carson, you're going to make a mess!"

He shrugged. "Are you scared, Willow?"

"Never!" Another laugh escaped before the marshmallow hit me smack in the face. That meant war. My skewer still had some gooey stuff on it. I picked it up and swiped it across his cheek.

Carson's eyes grew big, and he snatched my foot and began to tickle it. I was going to pee my pants. He knew my weaknesses. "Are you ready to call *uncle*?"

I thrashed, trying to fight him off. "No!"

The tickling persisted. I would not give up. I refused. I reached for a pillow and hit him on the side of the head, causing him to release me. We laughed as we scrambled to our feet, preparing for what the next one would do.

"Do you want to call a truce?" His blue eyes danced with fun. This was exactly what I needed. "What's it going to be, Russo?"

CRASH!

We jolted and swung our attention to the back porch, where the noise came from. In a flash, Carson headed to the door. The rain pelted harder. It was like a monsoon. The weather was unseasonal.

"Be careful out there. Do you want an umbrella?"

He flicked on the back porch light. "Nah, I'm good. Let me check. I'll be right back."

He opened the door, and the sound of the storm intensified. Carson stepped outside into the rain. The door remained open as the rain made its way in. Quickly, I grabbed one of the kitchen towels to clean up the mess.

Lightning struck, illuminating the angry night sky.

The storm was getting worse. I waited and watched for Carson to come back. When I was on the verge of going after him, he came back inside and shook out his long hair. It sent rain droplets flying everywhere. He was soaked. "The storm knocked over the umbrella. It's getting bad out there."

Another flash of lightning streaked across the sky. "Do we need to secure anything?"

"No, everything else looks good."

Carson headed to the guest bathroom and reemerged with a towel to dry off with. A yawn escaped me as I took in our mess. "I'll clean up the rest of this in the morning. I think this girl is headed to bed."

"Night, sleepyhead. I'm going to work a little bit in the study. The Italy hotel should be getting in any moment."

Placing a few of the pillows on the couch, I asked, "Are they getting any better?"

"I don't think so. We've had several reported thefts. So we're adding some security per Trent's recommendations. I'm hopeful it gives us some answers."

The fact that Carson allowed Trent so close to his hotels spoke volumes. The problem in Italy sounded terrible. Managing people was not my forte. I preferred it to be me, the canvas, and the paint. It was a perfect combination. "Ugh. Better you than me. Enjoy working while I get my beauty sleep."

"Night, Willow. Trent is headed back from Italy in a couple of days. He said he would make his schedule clear whenever you wanted to meet."

"Sounds good. Night, Carson." I walked up to him, and he gave me a brotherly hug. "Thank you for the wonderful evening. It was what I needed after the hellish couple of weeks."

"Anytime, angel. I'll see you in the morning. Get some sleep."

"I will."

Heading to a bedroom upstairs on the opposite end of the house from Carson's, I got under the covers. I was so exhausted, I barely remembered my head hitting the pillow.

I felt a light pressure on my cheek. *Wait... someone touched me.* A startled scream was cut off as a hand covered my mouth. I froze, terrified. On the verge of thrashing, the familiar accented voice said, "Shh... it's me."

The low, hoarse whisper sent a warmth through me. He was here again. Abruptly, I sat up and scooted away. "What the hell are you doing? You can't come in here unannounced like this and scare me like that."

I felt him shift further away. "I'm sorry about that. I forgot to give you something last time we talked to keep that from happening. I don't want you to be frightened of me."

My heart slowed as I drew my knees up. "I don't have any idea who you are. I'd be crazy if this didn't make me a little nervous."

He chuckled. It was deep in tone. "Very true."

The room was pitch black. The curtains were drawn and nothing was detectable. Again my body felt drawn to him and I had no idea why. The realization scared me. I wanted to reach toward him, but I ignored the urge. To feel such familiarity with someone I knew nothing about scared the hell out of me.

"How did you know I was here?"

"I have my ways."

I blew out a frustrated breath. This was getting me nowhere. My logical side said to scream bloody murder and get him out of my life. But... there was something else... something big holding me back. "Willow, I swear I'm not here to hurt you. If you want me to leave, I will."

His weight left the bed, and I blurted, "No, don't go!"

My hands went to my mouth. I sounded desperate, which was unlike me. I wasn't in complete control of my thoughts around this guy.

"I'll stay. But if you get uncomfortable, tell me and I'll leave."

Where was his accent from? It had to be Irish. I racked my brain, but I wasn't able to think of anyone I knew with an accent this strong.

I blindly reached for the light, but his grip stopped me. Tingles erupted all over my skin where we touched, and I sucked in a breath of air. He didn't release me, and his grip was fuzzing my thoughts. I needed to regain control. "Why can't I know who you are?"

"For now, it's safer this way, Willow. I promised someone I would always protect you."

Promised someone? Who? The possibilities raced through my head.

"Was it my dad?"

"Yes."

He'd known my dad. "How'd you know Dad? Do I know you?"

His hand touched mine, bringing an odd comfort. "I promise you, I'll reveal everything when I can. I'm trying not to lie to you, Willow. I know after what Alex did to you, along with things to come, you need honesty."

I blew out a frustrated breath. "Why are you here if you're not ready to give answers, only more riddles?"

A pregnant pause permeated the air, and his thumb brushed against my lower lip. "I needed to tell you something. It wasn't safe to call you."

Closing my eyes, I focused on his touch—strong yet gentle, rough yet soft. In the blink of an eye, the warmth was gone. Instantly, I missed his touch. What the hell? *I missed his touch?* The pressure of my teeth against my lower lipped helped eradicate the feeling, giving me something else to focus on. Without thinking, I reached forward, and his hand stopped me again. A quick intake of air settled between us.

Was I affecting him?

"What did you need to tell me?"

"Commander Taylor is having you followed. Your phone is tapped."

I leaned against the headboard, feeling all of the air leave me. "Why?"

"He knows you visited Cocktails. The paperwork to get the tap cleared showed it was to monitor for any clues about Alex's death. It was tapped within twenty-four hours of your visit."

Who knew me at Cocktails? I replayed the events from that night. No one had seemed the least bit interested in me or even showed the least bit of recognition. I'd never been there before. The only connection was Alex, and I highly doubted he'd told his other wife about me. That would have gone over like a house on fire. Was Commander Taylor having me followed?

I went through the possibilities as dread filled me. On a whisper, I asked, "How did he know?"

"Harley called him. He knew about Alex's plan."

My spine went rigid. When I'd seen Harley at Cocktails, he'd given no indication. None. "H-h-he knew?"

"Yes." My heart was racing, and I realized the man had his thumb on my wrist where my pulse pumped through my veins. "I'm going to keep you safe. I swear it. I get you're scared, but this is why I have to work in the dark like this without you knowing."

His honesty took me back. It was confusing, finding comfort in his words. What was I getting myself into? I wasn't sure.

All I knew was Alex had royally fucked up my life. Each day, it grew easier to hate him and not feel guilty. I swallowed hard, preparing myself. My voice quavered. "What did he say?"

A thumb stroked my bottom lip, and I realized it was quivering. It was as if this man had the ability to see in the dark. I found myself calming as he continued his soft, reassuring touch. "Harley asked Commander Taylor what he told you when you visited the precinct. Commander Taylor lied and left out the majority of it, saying he let you keep believing the lie. Harley demanded you be watched. Today the patrols let up since you've done nothing for almost a week. It was the first time I've been able to get to you."

Harley, Commander Taylor, and God only knew who else were in on Alex's games. "Did Alex come after me because of my money? Is that why he was so insistent Nonno hand it over?"

I knew the answer, but I wanted it confirmed. The thumb disappeared again, but his hand remained on my wrist. "Alex had a lot of debt."

"What kind of debt?"

"He owed a few different loan sharks several hundred thousand dollars. So far, I know of at least two million dollars he was on the line for."

Over two million dollars. That was an insane amount of money. "Does Candy know about the money?"

"From what I can tell, she knows a little but not the full extent. She's stripping again at Cocktails."

Wow, that was fast. I knew what I was asking was trivial, but so many questions still remained unanswered. "How long had they been married?"

"Five years."

Five years! Five years! Five damn years! I felt sick and grabbed my stomach. Alex had already been married long before I entered his life. I was for sure the *other* woman. The man's hand followed. "Did you find out if you're pregnant or not?"

I shook my head but then remembered we were in the dark. "No. I won't know for a couple more weeks." I paused as my mind wandered. Harley knew about me. No doubt there had been a plan. "Are they going to come after me?"

"I don't know. There are a few more things I need to find out first."

"Like?"

"Like what their plan was to get the money and who was in on it."

These people were dangerous. "How will you find out?"

"I have my ways, but I can't share yet. I need you to be careful by staying at your place as much as possible. I'm going to give you a burner phone so we can keep in touch. I meant to give it to you at the bar the other night."

Things were spinning out of control. No, wait. Things *were* out of control. This was crazy. I was trusting this man way too fast. I scooted back, needing some distance between us to clear my head. He followed.

His forehead came to mine, and I stayed completely still. "I get that I'm asking for a lot of trust after you've been to hell and back. Maybe this will help. Your dad told me something only you and he would know." He cleared his throat while I worked on staying unaffected by the minty smell of his breath brushing across my face.

"Wait? My dad told you what?"

"He told me about when you went to Italy, how you would go to the spot in the woods behind your house where he proposed to your mom. You both would lay flowers in the spot and share your memories. Even your Nonno didn't know this."

A tear slid down my face. That was something only Dad and I knew about. It was our secret—something we'd done to treasure Mom's memory. No one knew but us. "Why did he tell you that?"

"I don't know. Honestly, I have no clue, Willow."

I was a little hurt Dad would share something so personal with someone and not tell me. But I knew Dad loved me and wouldn't have done it without a reason. Maybe he died before he was able to tell me.

I stared into the darkness; my voice was stern and left no room for misunderstanding. "Don't ever lie to me. If you can't answer, just say so. But don't lie. I'm going on faith that Dad told you that story for a reason. I'm going to try and trust you. Don't prove me wrong."

A sigh escaped him. He was closer than I anticipated. On instinct, I turned toward him, causing my lips to brush his. The connection sizzled, and neither one of us moved. Every fiber of my being was aware… acutely.

This was crazy.

I was crazy.

Suddenly parched, I licked my lips, touching his. Without warning, his lips crashed to mine.

Warm.

Commanding.

Desperate.

I moaned into his mouth. My hands moved to touch him, and he pulled away, leaving a void my body craved. *What is wrong with me?*

Only our ragged breaths filled the room. As I opened up to him, he pulled back. I wanted to taste him.

"I need to go, Willow. The phone is on the dresser. Don't tell anyone about it. Does Carson know about me?"

"No. What do I call you?"

I felt him move closer before his lips were on my forehead. "Tack."

"Tack."

And just like that, he was gone.

Chapter Eleven

I tossed and turned all night, thinking about the men who might possibly be after me, Tack, a potential pregnancy, and Alex.

My life was officially a monumental fuckup.

Again I lifted my fingers to my lips. He was familiarly comforting, and I wasn't able to place from where.

His voice.

His touch.

The way he made me feel.

Tack consumed most of my thoughts. And I loved his accent. How long had he lived in the states?

His kiss.

Since that first night in the closet at the bar, my body came alive thinking about Tack, but I refused to admit it. My dreams focused on what his kisses would be like.

Now I knew his lips were strong and commanding and set me on fire.

It had been since the night before Alex died I felt alive like that. Truly alive… not manipulated alive. Alex had ruined so much with his lying, cheating, bastard ways. But nonetheless, it hurt to be betrayed as I'd been.

He knew a secret I'd had with my dad. I still wasn't sure how I felt about that, but I was going to give Tack a chance to prove he deserved my trust. I hoped to hell he wasn't playing me. It was probably stupid for me to give him as much trust as I had.

I waited for the warning bells to go off in my head, but they were oddly silent. It was truly an enigma.

I glanced over at the phone on the dresser. Now I had a direct line to Tack. Excitement raced through me. I closed my eyes for a second. *Calm down, Willow.* I stared at it, wondering if I should grab it. It was hard not doing the logical thing.

The phone vibrated, and I made my choice. Throwing back the covers, I ambled over and looked at the text message I'd received.

Tack: Good morning. Please let me know when you plan to leave there.
Me: Good morning. I will.

His response was almost immediate.

Tack: I haven't been able to stop thinking about last night.

How was I supposed to respond to that? Did Tack regret thinking about me? Did he wish we'd gone further? I tapped the dresser as I thought about it. Hell, I hated lying. Honesty was best.

Me: Same here.
Tack: You feel it, don't you?
Me: Yes.
Tack: You have no idea how happy that makes me.

Say what? That threw me for a loop. Things were progressing at the speed of a freight train, and I needed to slow things down for my sanity.

Me: This is all going too fast, Tack. Just because I've decided to semi-trust you doesn't mean anything else is going to happen.
Tack: I know.

He knew? What the hell kind of response was that? I ran my hand over my face and mumbled, "Men. They say women are complicated, but men… they're just… ugh."

The faint smell of bacon had me ravenous. Carson was up cooking. I deposited the phone in my purse, abandoning Tack's cryptic texts. I needed food. Coffee was also in order after the confusing text exchange this morning. I was stepping from one minefield into another.

Since I wasn't ready to tell Carson about Tack, I wasn't able to get his manly advice. Through the years, I'd helped him plan romantic evenings with girlfriends and he'd deciphered what guys said. It was a win-win situation having a guy as a best friend. However, Carson and I disagreed on which was the more complicated gender.

At the cream marbled counter top, Carson stood in his low-slung pajama bottoms and loose fitting T-shirt. Over the years, he had most definitely filled out. His hair was a mess and tucked behind his ears. Seeing me, he grinned.

"Good morning. How'd you sleep?"

I poured a cup of coffee. Not telling him about Tack felt dishonest, but I wasn't ready to complicate things. Carson raised an eyebrow, and I remembered he asked me a question. "Oh, sorry. I tossed and turned all night. Good morning."

I wasn't a morning person.

He pulled the remaining bacon from the pan and the last pancakes from the griddle. "Why?"

I took a sip of coffee before answering. "I was thinking about all that's happened."

"Understandably so. You've had a shit couple of weeks, Willow."

I decided I was ready to share one of the thoughts occupying my mind. "I might be pregnant."

His shocked expression confirmed what I was feeling on the inside. He knew Alex and I hadn't shared a bedroom in a long time. Shock then morphed to concern. "I thought Alex didn't want kids?" My eyes cast downward. "Shit, I'm sorry, Willow. I just… this just caught me off guard. How are you holding up?"

I let out a deep sigh. "It's all coming at me fast. I'm not sure."

There was more to that statement than Carson knew.

"You know I'll support you whatever you decide to do."

"Decide?"

"Keeping the baby or not."

I set my cup down. Irritation spread through me. I flexed my fingers a few times. I took all the pent-up anger I'd been holding inside and unleashed it on Carson. "You're right. Alex didn't want kids. Or at least kids with me. I went off birth control a while ago because of the side effects I was experiencing. Hell… Alex and I hadn't slept together since we got married—

at least not until the night before he died. I don't know why I wasn't thinking, but we didn't use protection." I stood taller. "There won't be an abortion. If I'm pregnant, which is a slim chance, this baby will be part me, too."

His arms wrapped around me in a friendly hug. I shook I was so mad. "I know you're angry. I know you're hurting. I think you misunderstood what I meant. It's your choice. But whatever you choose, I will support you."

My muscles were strung tight, and I worked on relaxing them. "I know. I'm sorry."

In my bedroom at home, I flopped down on my bed. The bedding had been stripped and replaced with a pale yellow duvet and matching curtains. It went with the light blue room for now until I found something better I liked. While I was gone, I'd ordered a new mattress, too. It felt comfortable.

The thought of sleeping on the mattress I'd shared with Alex disgusted me, even though he'd been in here only a handful of times to sleep.

Carson went to the Whitmore Hotel headquarters after dropping me off. I needed some distance. He knew it after I erupted at him in the kitchen at the beach house. They say you hurt the ones you love the most. I owed Carson an apology when I saw him again.

Distance normally helped put things into perspective.

I sighed. Once I had the courage to take the pregnancy test, I would have a better idea what my next steps were. It was stupid, but I needed time to mentally prepare for the answer... either way. If I missed my period by two days, I would take the test.

One day at a time.

Ring.

My phone rung inside my purse. I rummaged through it to find my phone.

Ring.

Finding it, I gazed at the blank screen.

Ring.

Oh, the burner phone. I dug deeper and gripped it after pressing Talk. "Hello?"

"Is everything okay?" He sounded worried.

It was Tack. "Yes. Why?" I remembered he asked me to tell him when I was leaving. "I'm sorry I forgot to tell you I left. Something happened and I forgot."

"What happened?" Was it wrong that the genuine concern I heard made me relax a bit more?

I took a deep breath and let it out, needing to share it with someone. "I overreacted when Carson brought up—in a roundabout way—that it was my choice to keep the baby or not. If I was pregnant. He tried to tell me he would support me, regardless."

Silence was all that met me on the other end of the line. "Tack?"

"What did you decide?"

I analyzed his words quickly. No judgement or indication as to how he felt about the subject. I was glad I hadn't made a mistake in telling him. "If I'm pregnant, then it's a miracle I was meant to have."

No response.

"Tack?"

He coughed. "Sorry. I thought you were going to say something else. Life is a precious thing, Willow. If you are, you'll make a great mom."

Being a mom was something I knew nothing about. Time would tell if I was. Softly, I said, "Thanks, Tack." I needed a subject change. "Have you found anything else out?"

"Not yet, but I will. Do you mind telling me a little more about Alex's and your relationship? Maybe that will help fill in some gaps or give me a lead I haven't thought of yet. So far, it's been hard to get information on a rather hated man."

Walking around the room in aimless circles, I thought about how to begin. Scenes from our life together passed by. "I met Alex at the end of college. It was love at first sight for me when he crossed the street in a small town I was visiting with friends. Something changed within me when our eyes connected. We were inseparable during his leave from the military. I loved him with my entire being."

A lump formed in my throat, and I worked to swallow past it. "He left for deployment in the Middle East. We stayed in contact through an occasional e-mail, which wasn't often due to his deployment. But I didn't care. I would have waited forever for him. One day I found him on my doorstep—emotionally darker, broodier, but he was home. That's all that mattered."

I took a deep breath. "I found out later he'd left the military. An incident occurred where his comrades died because of a poor choice Alex made. He said his head had been focused on me and not the mission. I felt guilty."

A faint swearing came over the line. "What a motherfucker."

No doubt Alex was indeed a motherfucker. "Anyway, we married quickly after he returned. He signed a prenup without question, which is odd considering he wanted my inheritance. Shortly after, we got the PTSD diagnosis from some quack of a doctor. He refused to see anyone else. We fought a lot about the trust my dad had set up. Nonno has the authority to hold it until I'm thirty or release it when he thinks I'm ready. If Nonno passes before I'm thirty, then it automatically goes on lockdown until I'm thirty. Alex was furious Nonno wouldn't turn it over. Now I know why he pushed me so hard on the issue."

It hurt being used. More than I ever imagined. Alex was calculating. He probably never left for overseas. Hell, he probably never actually joined the military. That thought sobered me, and I had to ask. "Tack?"

"Yes, Willow?"

"Was Alex in the military? I need to know. Please tell me—even if you don't think you can, for whatever reason."

Without hesitation, he responded, "No, he wasn't."

My lip quivered.

"Willow, if I could make the bastard pay, I would." His words rang true as they were spoken with such conviction. "I know this hurts, but you are strong enough to beat this. Alex isn't going to win. We're going to figure this out. I promise you will be rid of Alex and able to live your life. Just give me a little time to figure it out."

Tack was understanding and sincere. "I don't know what I did to deserve your help, but thank you, Tack."

"You're welcome. Thank you for giving me a chance to prove myself. Call me if you ever need to talk. I won't ever be without my phone."

Goose bumps covered my flesh. "Tack?"

"Yes?"

"Be careful."

"I will, sweetheart."

As the phone call disconnected, I touched my lips, remembering his bruising kiss.

Chapter Twelve

"Willow, are you in here?"

Sitting up on the bed, I answered, "Yes, Mildred. Come on in."

Since hanging up with Tack, I'd lain back and thought about everything we said. Why was he so concerned for me? What made him want to keep me safe? Questions, questions, and more questions. And he knew me. Where? Why was he familiar, yet I was not able to place him?

"Willow?"

Without me realizing it, Mildred had walked in and set something on the table near the fireplace. She looked at me, waiting for a response.

"What did you say? Sorry."

"Were you thinking about someone? By the grin on your face, it looks like it was a good memory."

Chewing my lip, I looked down. Tack was on my mind. I had no idea who the man was, but he had gotten under my skin. "Do you think it's too early to move on?"

Mildred scoffed. "Willow, dear, after what Alex did to you?" I looked up, shocked and filled with shame. She continued, "You did nothing wrong, darling. Through it all, you stayed faithful to your vows. He was a truly nasty man for what he did to all of us. There aren't many who would have stayed with him after all the terrible things he said to you. Chris and I pretended not to hear the fights, but we did."

And she only knew a portion of the story.

"He was a piece of work. Why do I keep remembering the good times? Shouldn't I be able to just be over it all?" If only she knew everything…

A soft sigh filled the pause. "Sometimes remembering the good helps validate what we did." The bed dipped beside me. I liked her thought process about validating—it made sense. "It's okay to move on, Willow. Who's this man you're thinking about?"

I shrugged. "I was curious."

She patted my leg. "Don't rush. Follow your heart."

That was tough as I worked through it. I played with the hem of my T-shirt. "What if my heart tells me wrong… again?"

"Did it the first time? Was there no doubt?"

Her words penetrated through my thoughts. There had been some—no, actually there had been a lot of doubt when Alex asked me to marry him. It was the guilt that persuaded me. Alex had played the guilt card perfectly, manipulating me with his accident along the way. Prick. His fake accident since Tack confirmed the military was all a lie.

My silence was answer enough.

She stood. "I thought so. Willow…" She paused while I looked up. "I'm not saying go marry the first guy who makes you feel something. But don't beat yourself up for Alex's lies and deceit. Don't be afraid to put yourself out there."

With Gabe, initially there had been no doubt about my feelings. I would have risked everything for him.

But was I ready to put myself on the line like that again? I wasn't sure. All I needed was to remind myself of Alex's betrayal.

"Thank you, Mildred." I stood to give her a hug and she brought me to her. "I appreciate you always being there for me since Mom couldn't be."

These were the conversations I imagined Mom and I having while eating a pint of ice cream. After all, she believed ice cream was the be-all and end-all. Her words brought happiness to me. *Willow, if every argument had ice cream, the world would be a better place.*

Mom may have had a point.

Mildred patted my back. "I wouldn't dream of being anywhere else." We stayed in our embrace a little longer before she let go. "Dinner will be ready in about fifteen minutes. I made homemade ravioli with the primavera sauce."

I raised an eyebrow. "That's Carson's favorite. He may tackle you from happiness."

She giggled. "I hope so."

"Mildred!"

She moved her hand in a dismissing motion. "Please, I have eyes. I can appreciate and hope for a little hugging."

A full smile stretched across my face. Carson was definitely easy on the eyes. Most girls flocked to him. Whenever he dated someone, apprehension initially filled their eyes about our relationship and what I meant to Carson. Because of our closeness, most girls worried we were undeniably in love with each other. However, after hanging with us a few times, those worries eased as they experienced our platonic relationship.

Once, in high school, we tried kissing. Terrible was an understatement considering how brotherly and awkward it felt. *Ugh.* I shivered unpleasantly at the thought.

Before leaving the room, she pointed to a small manila folder on the table. "Since Carson was using the office, I cleaned out Alex's old paperwork I found the day he fired me. I found those on the floor behind a bookshelf. When he fired me, he threw them on top of a stack of books. I noticed today they were still there."

She shook her head, distancing herself from what I assumed was the memory, before looking at me again. "Thought you might want to go through it."

That was not my idea of a good time—going through Alex's stuff—but probably a good idea. "Thanks." The door nearly shut when I called, "Mildred."

"Yes?"

"What happened that day in the house when Alex tried to fire you?" Tears formed in her eyes. "You don't have to tell me."

Picking at an imaginary piece of lint on her apron, Mildred said, "I was in the office cleaning, when I saw this folder on the floor behind the bookshelf. As I placed it on his desk, Alex walked in, his foul mood evident. Asked me what I was doing. I said cleaning. Called me a few names and said to pack my bags and leave. I think he wanted to start something with the first person he saw."

"Thank you, Mildred, for staying with me and putting up with all you did."

"We're family, Willow. That's what family does. You'll find your way again. I know it."

The door shut without a sound as she left me alone with my thoughts.

I hoped so.

Why had I fought for my relationship with Alex for so long? Now that I was free from the toxicity, I knew I'd made the wrong choice staying with Alex. I'd helped in a few battered women's shelters. It was always similar stories. The woman loved him, believed her companion had changed, was unable to leave… until it was almost too late.

The same held true for the relationship I'd been in. I also wondered how someone wasn't able to see what was going on. Now, I knew. Sometimes the trees grew so thick around you that you weren't able to see where you came from or where the path led.

Seeing the papers, I was not in the mood to deal with them today, even though I knew I should be. Later.

My real phone rang. It was Marissa. We'd been friends for a long time but drifted apart over the last year since Alex had come back into my life. She was one of my few friends who knew about my marriage.

Come to think of it, I isolated myself from almost everyone since marrying Alex. He hated crowds, he hated my friends, he hated going out. How had I let this happen? It had been slow, but he'd nearly managed to do it. I used to be extremely active, socially. Now, I painted and had spent an enormous amount of energy keeping my life together.

Was that his plan all along?

It wasn't until I distanced myself from the situation I saw all he'd truly done.

The phone rang again. "Hello."

"Oh, Willow, it's so good to hear your voice. Is this a good time?"

I missed my old life as I heard Marissa's voice. "It is. How have you been? I've missed talking to you."

"I've missed you, too. Willow, I'm so sorry about Alex. I called Carson to check on you and he told me. I know how much you loved him."

Marissa had always been a good friend to me. At one point, Alex was truly nasty to her and she stopped calling. We fought, but he won in the end since he removed her from my life. "I did. It was rough, though. Enough about me, how have you been?"

Definitely time for a subject change.

Excitement greeted me on the other end. "I'm getting married in six months." A pause. "Oh, shit. Willow, I'm so sorry. That was unthoughtful of me with what's going on. I didn't call to tell you that. I honestly called to check on you."

Marissa was always putting everyone else's feelings first. She was the last of my friends to distance themselves. "Don't worry about it at all. I'm glad to be getting good news for a change. When did he ask?"

"Two months ago."

Since marrying Alex, I'd missed so much. Regret washed over me. But I was finding myself again. Repairing the damage. I pushed forward. "I'm sorry for everything." My voice sounded thick with emotion.

"Willow, don't you dare think twice about it. You had to do what you had to in order to make your marriage work. The girls and I are still here for you."

"I love you guys."

"We love you, too!" A knock on the door from her side broke her focus. "Give me ten." A few words were exchanged, and then Marissa's voice came back on the line. "Since I let the cat out of the bag, I do have a question for you."

I stilled myself for what was to come, hoping Marissa hadn't seen Alex tromping around town with anyone. With trepidation, I asked, "What's that?"

"Will you be a bridesmaid? I know it's short notice, but I've been holding a spot for you."

Wow, she was serious. Even though I'd been out of their lives since marrying Alex, Marissa had kept me in her thoughts. Hope flowed through me. I hadn't lost everything. Alex hadn't been successful with everything he did. "I would be honored. What do you need from me?"

"Nothing, the dress shop had your measurements on file, so you have a dress being made. We'll have to get fitted." She sighed. "I hate talking about the wedding. I feel like I should be there for you. Can I do anything?"

"Trust me. I need the distraction. I want to be there for you guys."

A pause stretched on noticeably long. "We're having a weekend getaway in two days at Martha's Vineyard. It's a huge group of us going."

"Just girls?"

"No, the whole gang."

That sounded heavenly—seeing everyone again. Maybe that would jolt me into moving forward faster. "Do you mind if I bring Carson?"

She squealed. Actually squealed. "I love Carson. Yes, bring him. It'll be like old times."

Through our school years, we all hung out together. Generally, Carson and I went together unless we were seeing someone. "It will be. I can't wait."

Marissa went on to say, "Okay, I'll send over the details of where we're staying. I'll put you down for two bedrooms in one of the houses."

"Sounds perfect!"

A weekend with my friends was enough to lift my spirits. Though hard times had fallen, my true friends were still there for me.

Ignoring the pile of paperwork, I made my way down to the kitchen. The smell of oregano and cheese greeted me. I was ravenous. Carson was there serving two plates in business slacks and a dress shirt. His sleeves were rolled up to his elbows, and I could tell he was stressed from the way he held his shoulders. "Hey there, I was about to come find you. Mildred made my favorite."

"She told me. She hopes you tackle her. I'd watch your step."

The serving spoon stopped halfway between the ravioli and the plate. His eyes widened. "You're fucking with me."

I shook my head and tittered, "I swear. Scouts honor." I pressed on. "Want me to see if she wants to come to your place and play house?"

The giggles came unbidden from me. They escalated at the look of horror on Carson's face. "Willow, she's like a mom to me. You're scaring me. That's just... no." He shook his head.

A snort broke free. "Your face."

Carson placed the spoon back into the warming tray and shivered. "It's good to see you happy again." He walked closer. "Are we good?"

"We are. I'm sorry I snapped at you. It's just... I shouldn't have done that."

Strong arms came around me. "I understand. You're strong to be handling all this. Just know I'm here."

"Thank you. Now let's go upstairs on the back deck and eat our ravioli while you tell me about what happened in the hotel empire world today."

Chapter Thirteen

❝**W**ake up, sleepyhead."

Groggily my eyes opened. The plane was quiet. We weren't moving. "Did we land?"

"Yeah, about five minutes ago. I had to finish a phone call with my European managers."

The drive to Martha's Vineyard was around five hours with an hour long ferry ride on top of it. With work piling up, Carson suggested we fly so he could get some work done. As soon as we boarded, I went to the bedroom at the back of the plane and fell fast asleep.

The interior was masculine and trendy, exuding power. Sleeping was the easiest way to get rid of the nerves of flying. Popping my neck, I sat up. "Is everything okay over there?"

He dragged a hand down his face. "It will be. I checked on you a few times and you were out. How are the nerves?"

"Good." I stretched and felt a cool breeze on my stomach where my shirt rose. Quickly, I pulled it down. "It's a lot easier when you fall asleep before takeoff. I like the new plane with the bed."

When Carson took the hotels international, the company invested in this plane to expedite his travels. "I'll let Dad know you approve of the purchase so we won't have to return it."

I swatted him on the stomach. "You're crazy. I like this one better than your other one. I didn't wake up once." My voice turned serious. "Carson, if you need to travel for work, you know I'll understand, right?"

"I know. I will be soon. I'm able to still manage things if you want me to stay with you a little while longer."

I was relieved. It helped having him around. "Yeah, I'd like that. At least through the week, if that works."

Hopefully by then we'd have a few more answers.

He looked at his phone and responded to a message. "Are we ready to head to the house?"

"Yes." I had left out a teeny tiny detail of who might be staying in our house with us. It was hard maintaining a straight face.

Skeptically, he raised a brow. "What are you hiding from me? I know that look, Willow."

I tried to contain my happiness, but there was no holding it in. "We're sharing a house with Brie, Rosie, and Kurt."

Carson's eyes snapped to mine. "Oh, hell. Rosie? Are you fucking with me?"

I snickered. "No, I promise. I think Marissa is trying to give her one last shot with you."

"Fuck. Fuck. Fuck. I'll never get any work done with her antics. You're going to have to be my wingman."

Tapping my finger to my chin, I said, "Come up with a good bribe and I'll think about it."

A megawatt grin spread across his face. "I know just the thing."

"What?"

He shook his head. "Not ready to divulge yet."

Oh geez, here we go again. Thank goodness my phone chirped with a text message, distracting me. I hated when he baited me.

Marissa: Have you guys landed?

"It's, Marissa."

He deadpanned. "Ask her to change the house."

"Nope. It'll be fun to watch you suffer some or get my bribe."

Singsonging, he responded, "Payback's a bitch."

"Yes. Yes, it is. I think I'm paying you back for the time you put food coloring in my toothpaste in college."

Now, it was Carson's time to laugh. *Ass.*

The pilot came on the intercom asking for Carson. I took the time to respond to Marissa.

Me: Yes. We're about to get in the car and head that way.
Marissa: Yay! I'm jumping around like crazy. Hurry your ass along.
Me: We will. Can't wait to see everyone.

Faintly, I heard Carson talking to the captain. I took out my burner phone from Tack, figuring I had a minute or two.

Me: We're in Martha's Vineyard about to head to the house.
Tack: Be careful.

Me: You, too.

Tack and I hadn't talked since the other day when I came home from the beach house. We'd texted, but that was it. I wasn't sure what I thought about the whole "Tack" thing. On the one hand, I looked forward to talking to him again. On the other, I'd become comfortable with him faster than I'd anticipated. If Tack wanted to hurt me, he had the opportunity. I hoped trusting my feelings turned out to be the correct choice.

I gathered my things and met Carson in the main area of the plane. Today he was casual in his shorts, Sperry's, and Polo shirt. "Are you ready? The luggage has been loaded in the car."

"Yes."

After thanking the captain, we got off the plane. A nice shiny red sports car waited for us. As soon as we left the tarmac, his phone rang.

"Whitmore... yes... that's unacceptable, Beatrice... you know my expectations..."

Carson always answered his phone with his last name. It sounded more... intimidating, with his raspy booming voice. Tuning out all the business talk, I watched out the window as we passed through the area. I loved how green it was. From the airport, we were about an hour away from the tip of the island where we were staying. The hum of the engine had me nodding off again.

———◆————◆————◆———

Tapping on the window caused Carson to curse and me to jolt awake. Rosie was peering in my window. "Willow! Oh my gosh! Willow! It's you!" Then screeching. "Carson! You came! My day is made!"

I was not prepared for her as I woke up, blinking my eyes a few times. A white two-story house with burgundy shutters sat to the left of the driveway.

More banging. "Hurry and get out! I need to see you!"

This. Was. Too. Much.

Carson muttered, "This was your idea."

It had been a bad idea. I should have asked for another house.

The window still hadn't been rolled down, and my eardrums were about to rupture. I chanced a sideways glance over at Carson, and he was tense as he muttered, "Fucking, Rosie."

Jumping like a jack rabbit, she rounded the hood.

"Oh, shit! Willow, you better save my ass."

A giggle escaped. I saw my opportunity and got out of the car. Before shutting the door, I winked. "I think you've got this, macho man. You reduce scary businesspeople to puddles of nothing in a boardroom. You can handle her."

I heard him calling after me through the window. Marissa engulfed me in a hug. "I missed you, Willow. I'm so excited you're here. Everyone is. It's good to see you."

A part of my broken heart mended as I pulled back to look at my friend. "It's good to be seen. Congratulations!" I looked over to Clay. "You've got yourself a fantastic girl."

My friend's brown eyes sparkled with love as Clay swept aside some of her dark hair and kissed her cheek. Her skin glowed.

"I know. I'm damn lucky to have her."

Carson joined us and glared at me while I gave him an oh-so-sweet smile. Rosie was staring up at him all googly-eyed on his other side. It was no surprise she remained single with her obnoxious compulsive tendencies. She was adorable with her five-foot petite frame. Her blue eyes were expressive as she looked at Carson with longing.

Everyone exchanged pleasantries. I felt alive. Marissa and Clay had rented out five houses next to each other. Her family owned the global Cream Factory ice cream chain. Yesterday, I'd offered to pay for our house. So had Carson. Of course, she'd declined.

Entering the house, we found more friends who greeted us. With Carson's hectic schedule lately, he'd been around as much as I'd been over the last six months. This trip was good for both of us.

The house was cute, with two bedrooms upstairs and three bedrooms downstairs. Rosie was upstairs, which meant Carson would be downstairs. Taking my bag, I headed for the stairs and gave Carson a cheesy grin. He knew what I was doing.

Rosie called from above, "Carson, where are you sleeping?"

Everyone giggled as Carson made a run for me. In one fell swoop, he scooped me up and grabbed my suitcase. I was in hysterics as he all but shoved me into the room next to his, fearing Rosie would relocate. Kurt and Brie were in the other room down here.

Rosie was still calling Carson's name. Carson stood in my doorway, panic filling his eyes. I was a terrible friend, but I loved torturing him sometimes. And like Carson wouldn't do the exact same thing if given the chance.

I playfully whispered, "I'm going to offer to switch rooms."

"Oh, Carson. Where are you?" Rosie's voice sounded so… scary.

This was more therapeutic than I ever imagined, giving me a reprieve from my new reality. It had been a great idea to get away. My focus now was to create as many positive moments as possible to replace the bad and distance myself from the loss.

He shuddered. "I'll give you an all-expense-paid trip to Italy if you'll be my wingman."

Not hesitating, I stuck my hand out and he took it. "Deal. I think this is your best bribe yet. Even better than the spa day."

I beamed, and Carson gave me the evil eyes as Rosie appeared. "There you are. There's a room next to mine if you want to stay there."

Carson mouthed the word *Italy* knowing Rosie wouldn't listen to a word he said.

"Oh, that's sweet, Rosie. Carson and I already picked rooms down here. He's helping me with some estate stuff. It'll be easier if we're closer."

Disappointment filled her face when Kurt called from the front. "Rosie, we're headed to the store. Do you still want to come?"

"Yes!" Sashaying up to Carson, she fluttered her eyebrows. "I'll be back before you know it. Leave your bedroom unlocked if you want me to come in." She turned without a word. No doubt... Rosie was a weird chick.

Carson breathed a sigh of relief. "Thanks, wingman. She is off her rocker. I hope to hell these doors have deadbolts."

"Anytime. I think I'd like to sketch a sunset of the Duomo from a rooftop."

He chuckled. "Sure thing. This trip is going to cost me a small country."

"Well… there's always sleeping in the room next to Rosie's."

He shut the door on another muttered curse. I couldn't stop giggling as I unpacked alone. Even without the bribe I would have helped him, but it was fun to playfully blackmail my friend. And now I was going to Italy for free.

Reading in the chair near the bedroom window, my door burst open and quickly closed behind Carson. He was slightly out of breath. Clicking the lock, he leaned against the door and closed his eyes. "I'm going to hire a bodyguard before this weekend is over."

"What's going on?"

"Rosie."

I whispered, "Did you forget to lock your door?" To keep from laughing, I mashed my lips together. He was obviously in distress. A knock sounded and Carson's eyes grew wide.

"Willow?"

The sweet feisty redheaded Rosie sounded so innocent. "Yes?"

Carson tiptoed to me.

"Have you seen Carson? I saw him come into the house, but then lost him. I wanted to show him something I bought him at the store."

I got glaring eyes from the man staring at me. "Don't you dare say a word, Willow. Italy. Wingman. She's grabbing my ass." Laughter bubbled to the surface.

Another knock. Then the doorknob turned—Rosie knew no bounds. "What was that, Willow? Did you say you saw where he was?"

"No, I've been in here unpacking."

"Thanks, I'll keep looking." A defeated-sounding Rosie left the door.

Carson flopped on the bed, sending a few of the nautical throw pillows onto the floor. "Holy hell. That girl is tenacious."

I sat next to him. "She's keeping you on your toes. It's good for you."

A groan emitted as his arm flew over his eyes. "I'm sleeping in here tonight on the couch. I bet she has a lock pick to get past the lock."

"She may have a key. It would save all that lock picking time," I concluded matter-of-factly with a straight face.

Carson shivered. "This is terrible."

"But so entertaining. At least you have me as your wingman."

As he went to grab my feet to tickle them, I warned, "I'll scream your name and say I found you."

"You wouldn't." His hands paused, knowing my threat was real.

"Oh, I so would, Carson. You know it. And then I'll take myself to Italy."

I got the Whitmore glare he used to intimidate people. It had no effect on me. "Traitor."

Rosie was being a little more ambitious than she normally was. "Maybe we should invent you a girlfriend. She always backs off when you're dating someone."

He raked a hand over his eyes. They twinkled when he looked at me. "I think you may have just earned your Wingman title."

"Glad I could help."

Chapter Fourteen

Carson slept on my bed. I'd snuck out to say hello to everyone, avoiding answering Rosie directly when she asked where Carson was. Somehow she fit into our group, even with her neurotic obsessed tendencies. It was expected as she took turns choosing which guy to obsess over.

Rosie and I ate pizza in the kitchen. Most everyone else was in the backyard drinking. Our house had somehow become the central party location. Part of me wanted to tell her where he was, but I couldn't. I snickered at the thought.

She sighed. "So, what color lingerie does Carson like?"

I started choking and grabbed my drink. "Umm… I have no idea. We've never discussed it. Honestly, I don't want to know. He's like a brother to me."

She twirled a finger in her hair, revealing a clover-shaped birthmark. "I brought this teal blue nightie with feathers on it. It's perfect. Don't you think? It'll drive Carson wild for sure."

Sometimes, I thought Rosie had a few screws loose, but I wondered if it might be an act. I wasn't sure. "Umm... Carson may not..."

Daggers filled her eyes as she took a huge gulp of her martini. "How would you know if he's like a brother?"

"Good grief. No." *Think, Willow. Think.* "He's got a lot of work. I know he's behind."

She took a drink. "I'll be able to help ease that stress." She teetered, sloshing her drink. "I need a refill. Be right back."

I sighed. Rosie was drunk. She hid it well until she tried to walk. Time to abort this conversation. Quickly, I cleaned up my dinner and went to my room. I closed and locked the door. Carson slept peacefully with his eyelashes fanned across his face. Always on the go, he never got much sleep. Rosie had started tapping on his window while he unpacked. He'd been camped out in my room ever since. When I told him about the blue nightie with the feathers, he was going to barricade himself in my room. We were officially roomies for the weekend.

I settled on the couch near the bay windows where the blinds had been shut in case Rosie stooped lower than expected. Carson had insisted. Soon, if she kept drinking at the pace she had been, Carson would be the least of her concerns.

The folder Mildred had found caught my eye. It stuck out of my bag, where I'd packed it at the last minute in case I had some free time.

Alex hadn't kept much in the office. I hadn't noticed until I packed up his stuff, but he'd been like a guest in the house. I always thought he was a minimalist, but he was actually only passing through my life and using me.

Asshole.

I would've given him the two million to avoid the heartache he caused. It worried me that he'd ruined me for any future man.

Flipping open the file, I saw one sheet from a bank statement. It was missing all the other pages—almost like it was left on accident. I skimmed through it. Each week, money transferred from his account to Apple Blossom in the amount of one thousand dollars.

Above it were transactions from ten of my accounts for one hundred dollars. I opened up my bank account app on my phone and pulled up one of the accounts, finding the withdrawal last month. I dug into my settings.

Son. Of. A. Bitch.

An automatic withdrawal had been setup on this account to send the amount from me to Alex every other week. I pulled up another account.

Motherfucker.

Same thing happened on alternating weeks. I pulled up another. It was like the first account. Such a small amount would never be brought to my attention. I knew my accountant would think I was giving Alex money.

He stole from me? Why was I surprised?

I put the paper to the side, making a mental note to research the school, and shut off the automatic deposits.

The next paper listed numbers with letters beside them. Some sort of code… maybe coordinates… I wasn't sure.

Behind were printouts of a hotel in Manhattan with another set of numbers and letters. I recognized this hotel. It was posh like the Whitmore chain.

Cryptic.

I took a picture and sent it to Tack, furious at the depth Alex went to.

Me: Found this in Alex's stuff. He stole from me also.
Tack: Can you send me those details?

After taking more pictures, I sent what I had.

Me: Does that code make sense?
Tack: Not yet. Is it safe to call?
Me: No, Carson's asleep. He's hiding out from a crazy friend in my room. I'm on the couch going through the papers.

I wasn't sure why I felt the need to clarify why Carson was in the same room, but I did.

Tack: Call me tomorrow when you can. I'll make myself available.
Me: Did something bad happen?
Tack: No, I just need to hear your voice.

There it was again… raw emotional honesty. It was my turn to give him the same.

Me: I'm scared you're playing me like Alex did.
Tack: I wish we could talk so you could hear the honesty in my voice. I'm not playing you. Only time will prove I'm telling the truth.
Me: I like the sound of that. I'm going to go to sleep. Night, Tack.
Tack: Night, Willow. Call me if you need anything.
Me: I will.

I tucked the phone away into the zipper part of my purse and straightened the papers. A small envelope fell onto the floor. Odd. I turned over the stack and noticed a paperclip on the last page. No wonder I hadn't seen it. With shaky hands, I opened the envelope and took out a photograph of a little boy, no more than five or six years old, sitting on Alex's lap. Alex's eyes were bright as he lovingly held onto what had to be his son, who was the spitting image of him.

Hurt spiraled through me as his words replayed in my head.

"I don't want any fucking kids, Willow. Get it through your damned head. I don't care what I said before. I'm in this mess because I focused everything I had on YOU!"

My body flinched, hearing the words as if they'd been spoken out loud. Life had been terrible.

I brought the picture closer, scrutinizing every detail.

Alex loved his son. It was obvious.

He'd wanted kids… just not with me. If only I had the ability to turn back time. Make different decisions.

Regrets were poisonous to the soul. I hoped I was able to move past them and not be too damaged.

I flipped the picture over, noting a woman's elegant script across the back—probably Candy's.

I'd reached my breaking point, and now I was done. After putting everything away, I stood and walked toward the door.

It was the final blow.

I needed a drink.

A strong one.

Laughter subsided. I wasn't sure what made me laugh so hard, but it had been funny. The world swayed as I sat on a lawn chair.

My mind was fuzzy. Any negative thoughts weren't able to penetrate the thick haze I'd surrounded myself with.

Alcohol was my friend. My best friend. The most wonderful friend in the whole wide world.

"I wuv you, Willow."

I glanced over to Marissa. "I wuv you, too."

She leaned over, beer sloshing about. "Remember the time Carson and Clay hauled us out of the bar? It was so much fun dancing. We were drunk like we are now."

I believed I'd been drunker than Marissa. I snorted. We'd just turned twenty-one. Hard to believe it was three years ago.

"Party pooper shamooper." A giggle escaped at my new word. Marissa laughed, too. Alcohol was her best friend tonight, too. I think alcohol was a lot of people's friend tonight.

The alcohol no longer burned as I took a sip. "I going get anoder beer."

I stood and swayed. Clay looked at me. He was drunk, too. "You good, Willow? Need any help?"

"Nopers. I gotz this."

Putting one foot in front of the other, I took baby steps and started clapping. It was a good idea.

"Why the hell are you clapping, Willow?" Marissa called.

I made a shushing sound with my finger to my lips. "It's my tracking device. You need to know wherez I am."

"I wuv you, Willow."

"I wuv you, too, Marissa."

So much love. I loved everyone. The world was a better place with alcohol. Mom was wrong. Ice cream was not the solver of world problems. Alcohol was.

Almost to the cooler, I stopped and announced, "I needz to pee. I'm going to clapz my way to the poolz house instead of anoder beer."

Clap.

Walk.

Clap.

Walk.

Giggle.

This was funny. Marissa laughed, too.

Clap.

Walk.

Clap.

Walk.

Giggle.

I died laughing.

Stopping, I squinted back over to the campfire and yelled, "Can you guyz track me?"

"Got you loud and clear!" Marissa stood and then fell over into Clay's lap.

Now, that was funny. *I need to pee. Focus, Willow. Bathroom.* I was almost there. The door was close.

Clap.

Walk.

Clap.

Walk.

Giggle.

"I'm herez! Goingz to pee!"

"Okay, pee!"

The room was darker, and I felt my way to the bathroom. I couldn't find the light switch at first. After taking care of business, I left the bathroom. Wow, the dark outline of the room swayed. Maybe another beer was a bad idea. Yeah, it was.

I stumbled, and strong arms caught me. "I got you, Willow."

Happiness filled me. Everyone was my friend. I screeched. "It's you! Tack! My best friend phonez buddy. I love you! I love everyonez tonight."

"Shh…" The voice vibrated through me.

Oh la la. I hoped Tack was a hottie. In my dreams, he reached hot factor nine. It was going to be very disappointing if he wasn't. "You have a sexy whisper."

"How much have you had to drink?"

I put my fingers in front of my face and lost count a few times. "A bunches."

"Fuck, Willow. You shouldn't."

I held my finger to my lips. "No party poopersshamoopers allowed. Why are you whispering?"

He mumbled something, and I stumbled as I took a step toward the door. "You need to lie down, Willow."

"No, I wantz to drink anoder beer." Maybe beer was a good idea.

My feet left the floor, and I nuzzled into his chest. Oh, he was warm. Comfy. Lips touched my forehead.

"Sweetheart, I don't think that's a good idea. Stay strong for just a little longer. I nearly have it all figured out. What happened since we texted?"

"I sawz a pictures of hiz son. Alex blamed me for all those deaths." My head lolled to the side. No more bad thoughts. My vision was fuzzy. "Are you old?"

"Old?"

I snuggled into his chest again. "Yeah, I hope you're not old. That'd be yuuuck! Ewww to the you."

125

"Why?"

"Because I fantasize about you." I wasn't even ashamed as I sniffed him, making a big production. "And you smellz good. Fresh."

He chuckled.

"Are you cute?"

"Let's hope so."

A wave of nausea hit. "I need to lie down. I feel sick."

We moved a little. Or maybe the room was spinning. I wasn't sure. "There's a couch here. I'll stay with you until someone comes."

"Okay."

My eyes were already sliding shut. I felt a pressure on my wrist, and then I found the soft couch. Was he taking my pulse? Lips came to my ear. "I won't leave you."

"Stay."

Tack was here, and as my eyes closed, I knew I would be safe.

P ound.

     Pound.

     Pound.

"Make it stop. Please." I was in agony as I pleaded with someone, anyone, to make the pounding cease.

Pound.

Pound.

Pound.

I groaned. "I'm dying. Stop."

Squinting my eyes open, I saw Carson asleep on the couch that was pulled up alongside the bed.

Pound.

Pound.

Pound.

Another groan emitted.

Carson stirred. "How are you feeling? You had a rough night."

My eyes closed as I muttered, "I feel terrible. What happened?"

Pound.

Pound.

Pound.

The pounding was inside my head. *Shit*.

The vibrations from Carson's voice had me wincing. "I found you on the couch in the pool house when I woke up. You scared me shitless with how out of it you were. Everyone was wasted. No one knew where you had gone."

A hand touched my shoulder. "Take this aspirin and drink some orange juice. It'll help." I shot up and then grabbed my head in pain.

"Fuck!" My outburst caused the ache to worsen.

Orange juice and two white pills were put in front of me. "Here you go. What do you remember?"

I took the aspirin and prayed they helped sooner rather than later. The orange juice burned going down. I closed my eyes as flashes from last night came back. "I found pictures of Alex's son. After that, I went on a mind-numbing mission. Not my finest moment." Being upright hurt, so I lay back down. "I haven't been that drunk since my birthday our sophomore year in college. Never again. I don't feel good."

He patted my back. "Get some sleep. I'm going to work for a bit. You'll feel better after you rest. If Rosie mentions a Francesca, just go with it."

"I will. Sorry your wingman is out of commission. Is Francesca your made-up girlfriend?"

He shrugged. "I've been on a few dates with one." *Later, I'd ask him more about this Francesca chick.* The throbbing in my head kept me from diving too deep on any subject. We'd talk later. My eyes closed but opened again when I felt a gentle pat on my back. "I'll think of some sacrifice you'll have to make on the trip since you're slacking on your wingman duties."

I loudly groaned at the displeasing thought.

I heard him chuckling as the door closed. *Bastard.*

<hr>

Hours later, I woke up to a plate of crackers and more orange juice. I caught a glimpse of a note.

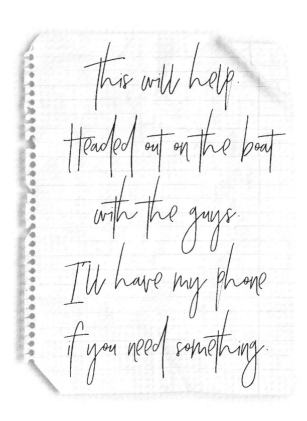

I was glad Carson took time to hang with the guys. It gave me some time to piece myself together after last night.

I headed to the bathroom to I clean up, which helped me feel more human. I was never ever drinking like that again. I hated that I let Alex's double life bring me down to a place where I turned to alcohol. Normally, I was more in control, but for some reason, seeing the picture of the boy sent me over the edge.

As I was combing out my hair, a knock stopped me. The door opened before I said a word. It was Rosie.

"Hey, Willow. How are you feeling?"

"Better. Almost human."

"Good. Do you have a second?" I nodded. "How serious are Carson and Francesca?"

No wonder Carson felt safe to leave his hideout. "I'm not sure. I haven't had time to talk about her much with everything that's been going on."

"That makes sense." My burner phone dinged from within my purse. "I'll let you get that. I'm going to go lay out by the pool and wait for the boys. Mitchell went with them, too."

Poor Mitchell. He was in for the Rosie ass-grabbing next. Hopefully he was dating someone. She bounced out of the room without a care in the world. Sometimes I needed a word stronger than odd for her. I was never able to figure it out, but we weren't close.

Grabbing my purse, I dug out my phone and sat on the couch Carson had moved next to the bed last night. I remembered being sick.

Ugh. Poor Carson.

Tack: How are you feeling?
Me: Better now that I've got some food and aspirin in me.

Tack: Do you remember last night?

I remembered he'd been there. Until now, I hadn't thought about it. *Oh my gosh.* I nuzzled him. I said I fantasized about him.

Another text came in from Carson.

Carson: How's it going?

Me: Better. I'm feeling human. Thanks for the crackers. The Francesca thing worked. Rosie has her eyes set on Mitchell now.

Carson: Poor bastard. Trent called. He rerouted his flight from Italy. He wanted to meet with us. Said he could meet in town if you want.

Me: Yeah, let's get it over with.

Carson: Okay, you want me to arrange or do you want to?

Me: I'll let you.

Carson: Sounds good.

Then Tack texted me again.

Tack: You there?

My eyes were tired of reading. I called Tack instead. My heart raced thinking about speaking to him again.

The phone connected. "Hello." That voice was too sexy for his own good.

"Hey." Oh geez, I was having word vomit thoughts now. *I mean, yes his voice is sexy, but I cannot have these thoughts.* It was the hangover. Hopefully, I kept them to myself.

"Are you going to answer my last question?"

It was time to give Tack a taste of his own medicine with one-word answers. "Yes."

A pregnant silence followed. And then a chuckle. "Yes, you remember or yes you're going to answer?"

"I can't believe I said those things."

Another laugh. "By the way, I'm not old."

Oh shit, I asked him if he was old. And told him I had fantasized about him. Fuck. I shook my head and then held it from the pain while I emitted a groan.

"You okay, Willow?"

"Everything hurts. And I'm humiliated. Around you, it's like my mouth has a mind of its own. It's terrible. Did you stay with me last night?"

"I did until Carson came for you. Then I disappeared out the back. You talk in your sleep."

Oh my gosh! I not only had to worry about my thoughts coming out when I was awake, but apparently when I slept, too. This was not good at all. My subconscious was doing a damn good job of forcing me to acknowledge a few things I was not ready to.

I leaned back. "What did I say? Please tell me it was about puppies or something unimportant."

"No, it wasn't about puppies." He paused. "You're scared. And hurt. And worried."

Well, that was obvious. Nothing too earth-shattering in those confessions. "I am. Was there anything else?"

"You miss what you had with Alex in the beginning."

Apparently, I shared a lot last night. Tack waited for me to respond. Not pushing, just being there in case I wanted to talk. I liked it. "I do. It's hard to explain. Have you ever been in love?"

"Yes. And then she broke my heart into a million pieces."

So he knew what I was feeling. "I know I shouldn't give Alex a second thought, but I was madly in love with him. The soul-shattering kind that leaves a void when it disappears. When he came back, all I tried to do was rekindle it. But it was all a lie. I imagine our meeting was planned. Somehow I was an easy target. And I don't know what I did. I'm terrified of making the same mistake. What did the girl do to break your heart?"

The conversation had taken a dramatic turn. "I've never told anyone this." He stopped speaking while he probably got his thoughts together. "She broke up with me, and I found her with another man."

So he knew what it was like to be cheated on, too. "Do you think your heart can ever heal?"

"I do, Willow. I think it takes time, but I hope to hell that's the case."

"Me, too." My words hung out there while we both reflected. Tack had depth, and I was drawn to him. Maybe it was two battered souls recognizing each other.

It was time to change the subject. "What are you doing right now?"

Seemed like Tack agreed, given the quick release of air I heard. "Sitting at a restaurant. Looking over the pictures you sent me."

"Have you found anything out?" If he had, I hoped it was good news versus another piece of the puzzle.

It was quiet for him to be at a restaurant. I looked at the clock, noting it wasn't exactly a meal time. "Not yet. I think there are some missing pieces." Of course. "Can I ask you something?"

"Sure."

"I know this is personal, but I was worried about you last night. Are you relieved the test came back negative?"

Lasts night's antics were definitely slowing down my thinking. I wasn't even going to try and follow. "Negative? Which test?"

"The pregnancy test."

Things clicked into place. "Oh *fuck*."

"What?"

What did I do? What the hell did I do? The throbbing was a jackhammer in my head. "I never took a test. Not yet. I'm not late yet. Tack, what have I done? I need to go."

"Willow!"

"I'll talk to you later."

I hung up and grabbed my computer to quickly boot it up. With all that had happened, I forgot about the possibility of being pregnant. A lump formed in my stomach as I thought about the damage I might have caused.

After forever, the browser came up and I typed *"what happens to the baby if I drank the first month of pregnancy"* into the search field. I never turned to alcohol to drown my sorrows. If I was pregnant and there was something wrong, I'd never forgive myself.

The search results came back. I found case after case where the same thing happened. Of course, it wasn't recommended, but nothing significant had been linked to the baby's health. I leaned back and breathed a sigh of relief. While I was thinking about it, I plugged a reminder into my phone to take the pregnancy test in a week, when I would be two days late.

The burner phone rang, startling me. "Hello."

"Are you okay?"

The headache was back in full force. "Yes. Sorry, I needed to look up the effects of what I did last night if I was pregnant. I'm still not ready to find out if I am. I know that may not be the most mature, but I have to take this in baby steps."

A week. I had a week to get mentally prepared.

"I think you have to do what is best for you. What are your plans today?"

Massaging my temples, I closed my eyes. "Meeting with a private investigator, who also happens to be a security advisor. Then probably coming back here. When will I see you again?"

Oh shit! Why the hell had I asked that last question? It was best not to backtrack. Otherwise, I was going to look like a bigger idiot than I already did. I shut my eyes tight, bracing for his response.

"Soon." I blew out some air, relieved when that was all he said. "What's going on in that head of yours, Willow?"

I was tired and exhausted from all the revealing. "I'm not sure. I probably need to get ready for my meeting with this security advisor."

"I'm glad you're getting extra security to make sure you're protected, just in case."

Just in case. That was what worried me. "There's something that's been bothering me that you may have the answer to."

"What's that?"

"How did Commander Taylor coordinate Candy and me finding out about Alex? He didn't come to my house. Officers did."

I heard a chime on the door, the first sign he was out and about. "Most of that precinct is dirty and on someone's payroll. The same officers who informed you told Candy also."

So, my instinct had been right about not sharing anything with the police. "I want all this to end, Tack."

"That's what I'm working day and night on."

I was bone tired. "Thank you, Tack. I'll see you soon."

"Soon, Willow."

I hung up the phone, forbidding myself to think about Tack for now.

Chapter Sixteen

"Poor Mitchell." Carson closed my car door as I watched Rosie hook her arms around our friend. He had been drinking last night with the rest of us, but staying in one of the other houses.

They walked rather fast to his house. Maybe he was still drunk? That was a terrible thought, but I imagined the teal nightie with feathers making its debut shortly with the way they looked at each other.

Shaking his head, he said, "Poor Mitchell's ass."

"He looks like he's about to get lucky. His ass may not mind."

We chuckled. "Better him than me." Carson shuddered with a *blech* face and then put the car in drive.

"How was the boat?"

We turned down a nice little street that looked like it was out of a magazine with the white picket fences and pristine yards. "Good. I got some waterskiing in. Caught up with the guys. It was nice. They're going on a trip together to the mountains later this summer. I think I'm going to go, too. We'll see."

People milled about as we drove through the center of town. "Hopefully you can. You know I think you work too much."

"I'll make time to go. Promise."

My phone chirped. The burner one was on silent. I knew I missed a text message on it, but nerves kept me from looking at it right away. We had shared a lot with each other as if we'd unknowingly taken things to another level between us. Now I wanted to share things with Tack.

"What's got your mind thinking so hard?" I looked over at Carson. "You had a smile one minute, and now your brows are all pinched together."

For a moment, I thought about telling Carson about Tack, but I wasn't prepared for the onslaught of questions. Hell, I wasn't sure I knew how to answer yet. The headache from drinking made its presence known again. Never again. "My head still hurts from the hangover." I wanted to change the subject before Carson realized there was more to the story. "How did you find this Trent guy?"

"Actually, your dad introduced us a little over a year ago, I think at an art show. You were overseas for a school trip. We got to talking, and I offered to look at his business plan. Turns out he was pretty damn good at security."

Dad had always tried to help people whenever possible. Especially ones where he saw potential. I loved the legacy he left. It helped feel more at ease with Trent, knowing Dad had given his approval. Giving someone power over your security was not an easy decision.

Carson's phone rang and mine vibrated with a text from Eva. I wasn't expecting to hear from her until early next week.

Eva: How does two weekends from now work for the show? I had an unexpected cancellation. I think there will be a lot of interest once I start circulating information, if the date works for you.

Excited butterflies danced in my stomach now that my first solo show was going to be only two weeks away.

"Eva wants to do my art show in two weeks. For solo shows, it normally takes six months to pull together."

Carson made a right. "That's amazing, Willow. I'll be there. Wouldn't miss it for the world."

Nonno would be so excited. He knew it had always been a dream of mine. Until we had a date, I had wanted to keep it low key just in case something fell through. The last thing I wanted was to give them something else to feel bad about for me.

Quickly, I typed out.

Me: That works perfect. Can't wait!

Eva: Wonderful! I'll e-mail you the details. I'll have a few press junkets prepared. I may need you early for an interview or two.

Me: Just let me know and I'll be there.

"All set. I'm nervous." I turned in my seat unable to contain the excitement. "Carson, it's just unbelievable. My own show." I squealed. "My own show!"

He beamed. "It's going to be fantastic! My parents will be there, too, once you give me the go ahead to tell them."

"After we meet with Trent, I'll call Nonno. Then, we can let them know."

"Perfect." Carson's phone dinged again. It had been over-active today. He read a message and sighed before putting his phone down. "I'm going to have to travel this next week to Florence. Do you want to cash in your trip to Italy now for being my wingman?"

I loved Italy. Our parents insisted Carson and I learn Italian when we were younger. We spent many family vacations over there as kids. Thinking about the memories filled me with a little trepidation since I hadn't been back since Dad died. Italy had been our special place.

It was time to go back. I knew the time had come to take this step. However, I wasn't ready to stay at our home there. Carson waited for me to answer, probably knowing my internal debate. "I think Italy sounds good. I'm not ready to stay at the estate there, though."

"We'll stay at the hotel. It'll be fun to have a friend there. You'll be able to meet Francesca."

I pointed my finger at him. "Okay, spill. How long have you been dating this girl?"

"On and off for a little over two months. It wasn't that serious in the beginning. On this last trip, it got more serious, I think."

Why hadn't Carson mentioned her to me? We told each other almost everything.

"You think?"

We turned into a parking lot and parked. He shut off the car and looked at me with wide eyes. "It scares the fuck out of me. It's the only reason I haven't said something sooner." He scrubbed a hand down his face. "I really like her."

My best friend was falling for a girl. I put my hand on his. "I can't wait to meet her."

He nodded his head, a little nervous. "Yeah, it makes it more real. I think I avoided bringing her up because I was in denial."

The words he spoke hit home about my situation. I understood. I hadn't asked if Carson was seeing someone. If I had, I knew he would have told me. "Carson, seriously, don't think twice about not telling me. I understand."

I wanted to add more, but stopped. This was not the time, nor was I ready, to discuss Tack.

Leaning over the console, I gave Carson a quick hug. "I'm so happy for you. Does she live in Florence?"

He sat back, obviously relieved to be talking about her. "No, on a vineyard outside of town. We met while I was there trying to talk her dad into letting me buy their wine for the hotels. Remember those bottles I brought back with me a couple of months ago?" I nodded. "That was the trip. Anyway, things progressed, and so far it's been great."

I wagged my eyebrows. "It was the cologne."

A vibrant chortle filled the car. "Best damn cologne. I think I owe you another spa day for bringing that back for me from Paris."

"You won't hear any complaints from me."

Laughing, we got out of the vehicle and made our way to a mostly-deserted restaurant. The quietness within the restaurant lot reminded me of being in a library. After speaking with the hostess, she led us in to a private dining area where a man who I assumed to be Trent waited. Standing, he greeted me. He was a lean, muscular man who looked ex-military with his crew cut.

He gave me a friendly nod and shook my hand. "It's nice to finally meet you, Ms. Russo."

I momentarily paused at his accent. It was exactly like Tack's. Odd. But, the voice seemed to be a tad different. "It's nice to meet you, too."

He cleared his throat. "Your father was an extraordinary man. I owe him more than I could ever articulate."

The way he spoke of Dad seemed to imply more than a passing relationship. Odd. Twice in a matter of a minute, Trent gave me pause. Carson watched Trent with a cocked head, too, no doubt having picked up on the same thing. I decided to go with something nonchalant while I tried to figure more out. "Dad was a wonderful man."

Trent gestured to the table, and we sat on the opposite side. "He talked about you often," Trent added.

Say what? A sense of familiarity came over me. It was hard to explain. It felt like constant déjà vu.

I cleared my throat. "I'm afraid you have me at a disadvantage. I don't recall Dad mentioning you."

Trent wasn't surprised at my statement, which brought me further unease. "I know." He let out a breath. "I'm a little nervous about meeting you. Your dad was like a second father. I knew him for a couple of years."

Couple of years? I mean, I knew I probably had no idea all the people Dad knew, but with the fondness Trent spoke about Dad, they'd been close. More than acquaintances. Carson watched him with calculating eyes as he said, "You never mentioned knowing Alfonso this well. I thought you guys met a year ago, right before we did?"

Trent shook his head. "This isn't going how I imagined it would. As Carson knows, I met Alfonso at an art event where I worked security. The timetable is a little off. We talked. What Carson doesn't know is he funded the startup of my company. I owe him a great deal."

I glanced at Carson, silently asking if he knew Dad had given Trent the money. He shook his head. This was all a surprise to Carson as well.

Dad was always kind and compassionate. He had a knack for seeing a person's true colors and helped in any way he could. It was one of the ways he made his money in addition to his art. That told me a lot about Trent—if Dad helped him that way. Carson took this in as much as I did.

"Why did Dad never mention you?"

Earlier, Trent had only confirmed I'd had no clue about him. "It just never happened. You were busy with school and I was busy starting up my company."

I was done with riddles, and I motioned for Carson to stand with me. Trent stood, too, about to speak. I raised my hand, stopping him. "I'm sorry, Trent, but this was a mistake."

He slid a letter to me from his back pocket. "This is from your dad. A letter to you."

"What?"

Never in my dreams did I imagine the conversation turning this way. I was stunned. The envelope had my name written in his perfect penmanship. I'd recognize it anywhere. I reached for the envelope. My eyes stung seeing his writing. A piece of my Dad resided in there.

I held the envelope close to me. Under no circumstances did I want to do this in front of Trent. "I'm going to read this in the car."

Trent remained calm, but an imploring look from his vibrant green eyes begged me to come back. "Of course. I'll be here if you want to give me a chance after reading the letter. I want to help you, Willow."

Without a word, I took the envelope and walked out the front. Carson silently followed. Not a word was spoken until we were in the car and the doors shut. "Willow, I had no idea."

"I know."

We stared at the envelope in dismay. Carson appeared to be just as shocked. I traced my finger over the envelope again. These were words Dad wrote. He had been prepared for my path to cross with Trent. The last thing I wanted was to feel betrayed by him... but a small part did. It was a peculiar feeling not knowing this aspect of Dad's life. For him to have been close to a man who obviously felt close to him and say nothing to me... left me feeling adrift.

We never kept secrets from each other. Ever.

Carson spoke. "Do you want me to step out of the car while you read the letter?"

Desperately, I grabbed his hand. "Please stay. I may want to leave immediately."

"Whatever you want, Willow." He patted my hand before I moved it back to my lap.

I slipped my fingers underneath the seal. The stationary was the same from his desk. It was the same stationary Mom gave him right before she died. He had never used a piece that I knew of… until now. The inside envelope had a silver embossed lining with my parents' initials intertwined in an intricate pattern. As a child, I spent a lot of time in Dad's office looking at it, especially when I missed Mom. Dad kept it in a special drawer behind his desk. When he died, it had been moved to the safe and put with my most-treasured items.

Only I had the combination.

This was his. Most definitely. Carefully, I opened the envelope and pulled out the folded matching paper. I swallowed hard at the tears simply seeing his words caused.

My Dearest Willow,

I know you've met Trent if you are reading this and probably feel a little betrayed. My heart hurts knowing I'm not there right now to explain everything. I hope you can forgive me.

Trent is a good man — a trustworthy man.

The reason why you don't know about Trent is because of an incident I needed his assistance with. Only a handful of people know. The fewer the better. I've asked Trent not to tell you unless it becomes imperative. I know you're going to be angry. Please trust I know this is the right decision. I would never knowingly hurt you.

Remember, Trent is only following my directions to keep you safe.

You are the most important person in my life. I will always love you, Willow. Never forget that. You made my life com-plete being my daughter. For that alone, I was the most blessed man in the world. I know your mother and I are smiling down on you, seeing what a beautiful wonderful person you've become.

I love you more than you'll ever know.

Dad

I had to put the paper on the dashboard as my tears poured out. Carson's arms wrapped around me. "Shh… I'm here. I'm here, Willow. It's okay."

More sobs. Those words were from my dad. I missed him so much. He knew me so well. If only he were here with me.

Finally, the tears subsided, and I straightened up. I handed the letter to Carson; I desperately wished things were different.

I knew Dad loved me. But after having the most horrendous five months of my life, it was something I needed.

"Wow, Willow. I don't know what to say."

With a watery smile, I turned back to Carson. "Me, either."

Gently, he folded the letter and put it back into the envelope. "What do you want to do?"

"Hear Trent out, I guess. Dad wanted me to."

I took a few more minutes to calm down before I announced I was ready to go back.

He gave me a slight nod. Trent looked relieved when he saw us, as if he hadn't expected me to return. I sat in the chair across from him. "Did you know what the note said?"

"I have no idea."

There were still so many questions. "When did Dad give it to you?"

"A little under nine months ago. He told me that if you ever needed help, this might help you trust me."

"Why did he think I would need help?"

Trent shifted in his seat. "Something happened." I began to speak, but Trent held up his hand. "I can't share it yet, Willow. Your Dad gave specific parameters on when I could tell you. I wish to hell I could, but I can't betray my word to him. If I don't have my word, I don't have much left."

Just like Dad predicted, anger rolled through me, but I kept it at bay. It was so frustrating. "Was Dad in trouble?"

"No, he was fine. The situation was handled."

I racked my brain for what could have happened eight months ago—I'd just finished the last semester of my master's degree.

This was the worse day to have a hangover. "Honestly, Trent, I don't know what to say."

He cleared his throat. "Let me tell you what I've found out. We can go from there. I'll help anyway I can, but I won't force anything on you."

It was easy to see why Dad liked him… if this was the real him. Not so long ago, I had been deceived by my husband.

"Carson only setup the initial meeting. Nothing else was discussed." Trent looked to Carson for confirmation, which he gave by nodding. Carson hadn't said anything. I wasn't sure what he thought right now. "I know Ms. Russo was married to Gabriel Alexander Thompson. From her father, I know she didn't take his name, he had PTSD, and acted erratically different from when he left for deployment. Since he died, I found he had a wife named Candy and a son named after him. And was involved with some shady people."

I sat there a little stunned. That was almost everything I had learned about him since Alex died.

Trent took my silence as the opportunity to continue. "Alex had quite the gambling addiction. He used his leverage to get his debt reduced. At one point, he owed the owner of Cocktails money. You know him as Harley."

I processed everything for a second. "Did you find anything else out?"

"Honestly, Ms. Russo—"

"Willow, please."

His eyes lit up. "Willow, when your dad died, I kept tabs on Alex because I know your dad was worried. I contemplated how to come to you with the information when he was killed. Then I wasn't sure what to do. I've been keeping tabs from a distance to make sure you were safe, but I knew I was already overstepping my bounds by doing that without your permission."

"Do you know about Commander Taylor?"

"I know he's a dirty cop. Most of his precinct is." Trent knew his stuff.

I sat on the precipice of a decision, knowing what Dad wanted me to do. For now, I wanted to see where this led. "What do you think you can do for me?"

"Design a protocol that keeps you safe until we figure out how deep the rabbit hole goes."

We drove back to the house on Martha's Vineyard. Everyone had gone into town to eat dinner. They'd texted earlier, saying they were going drinking again, and invited us. It was an easy decline with my head feeling as though a wrecking ball had made a few swings inside of it. Carson had been on the phone arranging the trip to Italy, leaving me with my thoughts.

Trent was an enigma. He seemed honest and to have loved Dad, but what incident had been kept from me? It drove me crazy. The fact was I had no idea when in the last two years the incident occurred. It was hard not to feel a little hurt at Dad for not trusting me with the information. Maybe he hadn't thought I was strong enough to handle it. How could it be worse than my current situation?

"What did you think about him, Willow?"

I looked around, realizing the car had stopped at the house. "I'm not sure. I guess we'll see what he recommends for security and go from there." Facing Carson, I asked, "Was there anything Dad or Trent said that would have led you to believe they were as close as he said?"

"No. Nothing. Trent never mentioned him. He came to the funeral."

There were so many people who had been there it was impossible for me to remember.

We got out of the car. The cool breeze from the ocean felt refreshing. "Let's see. I know Trent is clean. I've had him extensively investigated prior to using him for security at Whitmore Hotels."

I figured as much since Carson had helped him. A yawn escaped me. "I think I'm going to turn in. With Rosie having moved on to Mitchell, I think you're safe to sleep in your own room."

"Yeah, I'm going to call Francesca. See you in the morning, angel."

"See you."

After changing into my pajamas, I charged my phone and saw the notification on the burner from Tack. It was from earlier.

Tack: Thanks for this morning and listening to me.

Something gooey melted inside me, but I forced it away. I was too on edge with all the revelations of the afternoon. Tack remained an unknown, too, and the realization of how much I had let my guard down with him scared me.

Dad's note became my focus for now.

Me: You're welcome. Thanks for listening to me. I'm exhausted from last night. The bed is calling my name.

Almost instantly I got a question in response.

Tack: One question... how did the security guy work out?
Me: We'll see. Not sure.
Tack: Sleep tight, Willow.
Tack: Night, Tack.

I threw on my pajamas and quickly got into bed. Before I knew it, I was out—with all my problems from the day put aside.

Chapter Seventeen

The car pulled up to the Whitmore Hotel in Florence. It was magnificent with the old stone architecture and Italian sculptures recessed within the walls.

This was a new hotel Carson had acquired six months ago, and it was giving him troubles. My mouth dropped in awe. "Carson, this is beautiful. I can't believe I never looked this place up on the internet."

"Do you remember the Rinaldis?"

Memories of the older man brought happiness to my heart. When Dad brought us to Italy, we always stopped by the Rinaldis for tapas and pasta. Dad and Marco were able to shoot the shit for hours. Their parents had been best friends. "Yes, of course."

"Your dad insisted I stop by Marco's for tapas and pasta about a year ago." I chuckled and Carson beamed. "Best damn pasta I've ever had. Beats the ravioli we found in New York City with Dad." I nodded in agreement. Carson continued, "Turns out Marco was ready to simplify his life. He'd asked your dad if he knew of someone who would cherish his building as much as he did. It took a bit to work out the details and renovations."

Dad would have loved to come here and see this. "Did Marco's sons not want to carry on his legacy?"

It was rare a family let go of historical places such as this. The Rinaldis were extremely tight knit.

Carson held up a finger to an approaching bellman to hold him off while we finished our conversation. "No, his sons are executives at different companies. They had no interest."

"Dad would have been so proud of you, Carson. I'm proud of you."

The pride showed on Carson's face. He was so accomplished for someone so young. "Thanks, Willow. Means a lot. Let's get you situated. I have a meeting in thirty minutes with the management."

We got out of the car, and I whispered, "Do they know you speak Italian yet?" Over the last week I noticed Carson only spoke in English when dealing with this office. They weren't aware of Carson's linguistic abilities. He learned a lot when they broke out into their Italian rants.

"No."

A giggle escaped as I said, "When they find out, I bet they panic."

He shrugged. "If they did their fucking jobs, there wouldn't be a reason to talk behind my back."

Carson raised his hand for the bellman to come get our bags. This was Carson's hardcore business persona. He kept his cards close to his chest except with me. From business dinners I'd attended, Carson was a different person to the public. Guarded. Untouchable. It always shocked me to see the harder side of him.

The bellman unloaded our luggage, and it disappeared into the hotel as we made our way through the revolving door. Thick marble stone etched in fleur-de-lis framed the archways.

Soft classical music filled the atmosphere. The white marble floors had distressed gray marks through them. Everywhere you looked, another treasure waited to be discovered.

A giant crystal chandelier—wider than I was tall—hung massively over a ginormous flower arrangement.

Amazing.

I spun around slowly as Carson talked to someone. The corners of the lobby had Italian sculptures prominently displayed.

Beautiful.

We opted for the grand staircase made of marble. It was obvious that attention had been paid to the smallest of details, like the accented cord on the lamps with the Whitmore insignia. Carson spoke about how the elevators were too small. Apparently, it would have caused more headache than it was worth to have them expanded due to the infrastructure of the building. Currently, architects were seeing if a larger elevator could be added at the far end of the lobby.

I brushed my fingers along the finely-polished marble banister as we climbed the three stories. Chandeliers twinkled, and the scent of fragrant white lilies and violets permeated the air—both symbolic flowers of Italy.

Perfection. True perfection.

My heart burst with pride. Carson knew his hotel business. The staff made a fuss of providing Carson the best service possible. I'm sure they knew he was pissed. A theft problem, as well as a few management issues, had brought Carson here. People needed to know their stuff was safe when paying near eighteen hundred American dollars a night to stay there.

Security was now top-notch, thanks to Trent, and today the thief would be arrested. On the trip over, I found myself softening a little toward him after hearing all he had done for Carson. He'd been on a few of the conference calls where I'd heard him over the speaker. He never faltered in his professionalism or crossed the line when asking about my case. I respected that.

We rounded the grand staircase to the next floor. Leading us down the corridor, we came to a stop in front of a door. The bellman prattled details to Carson as they walked in. I was too enamored to pay attention.

"This is your room, Signorina Russo. Your things have already been placed in your bedroom. Signor Whitmore, you are in your normal room with your things as you have specified them to be. Is there anything else I can assist you with this evening?" The bellman clasped his hands in front. So far the service here was impeccable.

Carson looked around the room. "That is all, Tomas. Thank you. I'll be down in a few minutes."

I took in the room. It was decadent in cream, gold and black. When we were alone, I spun around and grinned at Carson. "This is gorgeous. I can't believe I didn't get over here sooner."

The view caught my eye as I traipsed toward the balcony. The *Duomo* was in the distance with an unobstructed view. I murmured, "Breathtaking."

"I promised you a view of the *Duomo* to sketch at sunset. Do you think this will work?"

Throwing my arms around Carson's waist, I gave him a quick hug. "It's perfect. I'm going to order room service and sketch to my heart's content."

For a moment, Carson's brows pinched. "I hate leaving you here while I see Francesca."

I was excited to see him with Francesca tomorrow. On our trip over here, he seemed softer when he spoke of her.

I waved him off. "I'll get to see you guys tomorrow for dinner. There are a few places around town I want to visit while I'm here. I think I'm going to schedule something with the Uffizi, too, so I can see Dad's Botticelli while I'm here." He began to argue, but I stopped him. "I'll be fine. I promise."

Right before Dad died, he had loaned the piece to the museum indefinitely and under the condition the family was able to have a private viewing whenever we wanted. I never understood why, and the will gave no indication. My mother had given him the painting she procured at an auction on their first wedding anniversary. He loved that painting. Going there was one of the things I dreaded doing but needed to do at the same time.

It was time to face that part of my life. And I was scared how I would feel seeing it for the first time without Dad.

Carson watched me skeptically. I reassured him. "I promise I'll be okay. I need to do this by myself."

"Okay, but remember, I'm a phone call away."

He stood there, looking like he wasn't leaving anytime soon. I waved my hands. "Shoo! Go arrest thieves and get managers in line."

Carson laughed and gave me a salute. "Will do." As he walked away, he added, "Call the front desk with anything you need. I'm the next room over. Anything you want from the spa is yours. I've let them know to give you carte blanche. I have to take care of my wingman."

"I love being your wingman. Sign me up anytime." I winked.

157

He grinned. His phone rang as he walked out, leaving me alone.

I looked out at the view again and sighed. It was perfect. I thought about the conversation I had with Tack yesterday as I packed.

I pulled out my suitcase to begin packing for Italy.

Tack had been on my mind since we'd returned from Martha's Vineyard. We talked a few times, but it had been sur-face level. I think our discussion the day of my hangover had affected both of us, baring ourselves to each other.

I threw in some more clothes.

Last night I promised to call him before I left for Italy. Rummaging through my purse, I found the burner phone.

I blew out a big gust of air as I looked at the phone. A small grin emerged as I typed out the message. Maybe I would see if he called me after I texted. I wasn't sure why I wanted him to call me, but I did.

Me: Headed to Italy tomorrow.

The phone rang almost instantly, and a wider grin spread across my face. "Hello."

"Hey, there. How was your day?"

I settled into the chair. "It was good. I'm nervous about going to Italy tomorrow."

In that moment, I knew I'd wanted to talk to Tack to help calm me. He had that effect.

"Do you think you'll go see the painting?"

Of course Tack knew about the Botticelli if he knew about Dad's and my special tradition of going to the place where he proposed to Mom. "I'm not sure. Probably. Maybe. I guess I'll see when I get there. I reached out to the curator."

"I'm always a phone call away if you need something, Willow. Always."

Again, I wanted, not for the first time, to feel Tack's presence again. Anything. A small touch on my lips or his forehead to mine. "Thank you, Tack."

"How are you feeling since your talk with the security guy? I think something happened that day that bothered you. Are you okay?"

I was stunned. "H-h-how did you know?"

"Sweetheart, I was able to tell in your voice, but didn't want to pry. You seem more settled tonight, and I wanted to make sure." That concerned Irish accent had me internally swooning. "Willow, you don't have to answer. I don't want to scare you."

I stood and began to pace. "Dad knew this security guy, Trent O'Malley. They were friends for almost two years, and he never said a word. There was a note in Dad's writing on stationery my mom had given him but he never used. In it, Dad asked me to trust Trent."

"That must be hard."

Tack understood where I came from, which helped. "It is." I got into bed. "Will you read me something, Tack?"

I heard shifting on the other side of the phone. "What would you like me to read to you?"

"Anything."

Tonight, the last thing I wanted was to be alone with my thoughts. Tonight I wanted to distance myself from it all.

"It was a time of old. A time of new. It was a time for all men to unite." Tack's voice chased away all of my demons as I settled into a deep sleep.

Last night had been intimate as I fell asleep to the sound of Tack reading to me. There had been no nightmares to chase away. I had peace while I slept.

The tolling of the bells brought my attention back to the *Duomo*. People milled about below. Tourists were easy to spot with their maps and confused looks. Some looked up at the *Duomo* with awe. I loved watching people fall in love with Italy.

From the first time my parents brought me here, I'd been a goner as I fell in love with the city. Early in the mornings while Mom slept, Dad would bring me to one of the artesian squares. We'd set up our canvases and paint the dawn until Mom called us home for breakfast.

Those were happy times. The best. I wished I had them back.

The beautiful city's sounds comforted me as they wafted in through the open balcony door while I set about unpacking. Halfway through my suitcase I remembered to let Tack know I'd arrived.

Rummaging through my bag, I was unable to find my phone. "Shit. Where is it?"

Then I remembered stuffing it in the side pocket.

Me: Made it. I have a beautiful view of the city.
Tack: I'm glad. I hoped you thought of me on the plane over there.

Me: Are you flirting with me?
Tack: Maybe. Is it working?
Me: Hmmm... send me chocolates and I'll say yes.
Tack: Done.
Me: Thank you for reading to me last night.
Tack: Anytime, sweetheart. It was my pleasure.

Tack was kind. I wondered what the woman he'd loved had done to break his heart. It had to have been terrible. My mind became occupied with possibilities while I finished putting my clothes in the armoire. Yawning, I decided to take a nap. My energy was zapped.

Chapter Eighteen

It was a perfect morning. Manicured within an inch of my life after using the spa services, I was fresh from a nap, sitting on the balcony and sketching in my notepad. My damp hair piled on top of my head allowed the fresh air to invigorate me. Being a wingman definitely paid off.

Knock.

Knock.

Knock.

"Ms. Russo. It's Tomas. I have a delivery for you."

I put my sketchbook aside as I called, "Coming!"

When I opened the door, the bellhop looked at ease. Things must have gone well today, which was good. "Good evening, Ms. Russo. This came for you."

I didn't expect anything.

A cream envelope was adhered to a black box with a ribbon. "Thank you, Tomas. Have a wonderful evening."

"You, too, Ms. Russo."

It had been a while since I received a gift. I figured it was from Carson, who was always doing small things like this for me.

The door closed. As I took the envelope out from underneath the silk ribbon, I noticed my name was written in an elegant script.

Slipping my index finger underneath the seal of the envelope, I pulled it apart.

I opened it and covered my mouth.

Willow,
I'm counting down
the minutes until
I see you again. I
hope you feel it, too.
Jack

My heart skipped a few beats with the romantic gesture. Tack. I was filled with anxiousness to be near him again. Over the past week, things had changed—or rather I allowed them to change. There had been something more since the moment we first met, but the timing was off. The timing was still a little off considering the uphill battle I faced. But it had become impossible to keep my emotions at bay. I wanted to feel again. Even if this went nowhere, I wanted to enjoy the journey.

Words from Dad echoed through my mind. *"To take a chance on love is worth everything."* By no means were we in love, but sometimes it was important to let your heart guide you, regardless of how fragile it felt. Hopefully, through this journey, my already-broken state wouldn't become shattered.

Inside the box sat elegant chocolates wrapped in tissue, like I'd asked for. In fact, they were dark chocolate truffles—my favorite. An excited giggle came out. I took a bite, and the chocolate melted in my mouth. It was succulent. I let out a small moan as the rich chocolate assaulted my taste buds.

Not able to wait a minute more, I ran to the burner phone and dialed his number.

Me: I got your gift. Thank you! Truffles are my favorite. Especially Italian truffles.

Tack: I'm glad you like them. Did you read the note?

I wasn't able to wipe the grin off my face as I gave a very Tack-like response.

Me: Yes.

I let out a little surprised scream when the phone rang.

Tentatively, I answered. "Hello?"

"Are you going to keep me waiting?"

Those butterflies returned in full force. "Maybe."

The deep vibrations from his chuckle brought more excitement. This was crazy how utterly schoolgirlish I felt.

"Can you give me a little more? It's been a while since I've put myself out there like this. I'm nervous."

That sobered me. Again, Tack was transparent in so many ways when it came to his emotions, it felt like I knew him on a deeper level. It both thrilled and daunted me at the same time. "I feel it, too, Tack. But it scares me. You say we've met, but I don't know who you are."

"I'm scared, too. You know me, Willow. What we've shared over the last few weeks is more than skin deep."

I listened to his words. "It is."

Knock.

Knock.

Knock.

"Willow. It's Carson."

I let out a deep breath, not ready for Carson to see me using a burner phone. "Carson is at the door. I need to go."

"Be safe. Call me if you need anything."

"I will. Thank you…" I wanted to say *for bringing me back to life, giving me faith in finding something more again, protecting me.* But I ended it simply, hoping he understood my meaning. "For everything."

"You, too, sweetheart."

Disconnecting the call, I said to Carson, "Coming. Give me just a sec."

There wasn't proper time to dissect our conversation and soothe my frayed nerves.

Opening the door revealed a freshly showered Carson in a gunmetal gray suit. "Aw, you look adorable for your date."

Tonight, Carson was seeing Francesca alone at my insistence. They needed it. And now, I was glad I would have time to myself, too.

He dragged a hand down his face, and I saw the panic in his eyes. "I'm nervous. Can you come take a look at something and tell me what you think before Francesca gets here?"

"Of course."

I grabbed my room key and followed Carson down the hall, enjoying this new side of him. Never before had he acted like this over a girl. I wanted to gibe him about it, but by the looks of him, it might push him over the edge. I mashed my lips together to keep from chuckling at the poor guy.

He walked faster. It took a slight jog for me to keep up with him. No doubt he was more than nervous. Turning the corner, I saw white rose petals on the floor forming a trail to the end of the corridor.

I picked up a petal and smelled it. Roses were my favorite. "This is so sweet. Where do they lead?"

No response. Carson took off again. Looney bird. *No. Lovesick looney bird.* I quickened my pace as we followed the trail and made a left at the end. The sign on the door read Rooftop Access.

What does he have planned? Is he proposing? I kept my questions to myself.

The door opened, and we walked up a small set of stairs. There were more flowers and lighted luminaries along the path.

It was brilliantly beautiful.

The sweet smell of roses and begonias filled the air. Twinkle lights hung from the pergola as the last rays of the sun cast oranges, reds and purples across the encroaching night sky. It was as if the stars were falling from heaven. I never wanted to leave.

In the middle of a table sat a covered dish and a bottle of Cristal.

Up here was most breathtaking view of the *Duomo*. Before we left, I was going to come up here and draw.

"Are you proposing?" I had to ask. By all means, I was happy for him—just surprised if he said yes, considering no one had met her yet.

Carson turned white as a ghost, and I suppressed my laugh. I had my answer. "No. Fuck no. I mean, not now. It's too soon. I just wanted to do something special for her."

I put my hand on his arm. "Calm down. She's going to love it. And if she doesn't, then she must be crazy." Carson still looked nervous. "Relax."

"Look at this one last thing. She'll be here in about twenty minutes. I figured we'd have dinner over there and then maybe…"

The doors opened to what was probably some sort of entertaining room but had been turned into a bedroom. For the second time tonight I gasped loudly, getting what the *maybe* implied. "Carson… wow."

I walked to the four-poster canopy bed in the middle of the room. Candles burned, giving it a faint aroma I wasn't able to place, and added to the ambience with the flowers. The sheer drapes of the canopy were soft as silk as I ran my fingers over the fabric.

"This is truly amazing. If she doesn't like it, tell me. I want to sleep up here. It's like a fairytale."

Finally, my best friend released some of the tension in his shoulders. "Good. You don't think it's presumptuous?"

I turned my hands up. "I mean, it says you plan on some festivities happening. But, I assume you guys have already… umm… had a few festivals." Carson laughed, and I was glad to see him loosening up. Placing my hand on his arm, I advised, "I would have dinner first and see how it progresses. But if it progresses, yeah, this is perfect."

"Good. I want her to have a perfect night. She's had a rough few weeks."

My heart melted.

A slight breeze blew from the windows up along the top of the wall.

"It is perfect."

He checked the time. "Okay. Fifteen minutes."

Giving him a kiss on the cheek, I wished him luck before I hurried back to my balcony. On the plane ride over, Carson had showed me a picture of Francesca. She was breathtaking.

It was a candid shot of her, which showed off her simplistic beauty and chocolate-brown eyes so full of life. Her kind smile reached all the way to her eyes.

I felt like a stalker watching the entrance, but I couldn't help it. A white car pulled up, and she got out. She laughed with the bellmen as she handed him her keys before disappearing into the building.

Francesca seemed kind and loving. I was beyond happy for Carson. He deserved to find love.

Chapter Nineteen

Not hearing from Carson all night probably meant the festivities had indeed occurred. That was about as in depth as I wanted to think about my friend. Any more than that became a no-go area for me. This evening we were eating at a restaurant on the Ponte Vecchio. There was a café there I loved. Dad and I had eaten there with Carson many times. Visiting would be bittersweet as I knew memories of Dad might become overwhelming, but I wanted to embrace those times and not shun them like I had.

Baby steps.

I checked the time. It was midmorning. Soon it would be time to head to the Uffizi around noon to see my father's painting, *La Primavera* by Botticelli. The museum had been more than accommodating. The painting would be relocated to a private viewing area.

As the time moved closer, a lump formed in my throat. Anticipation filled me at the thought of seeing it for the first time since Dad's death and knowing it was never coming home again. Dad knew I would never go against his wishes and remove the painting.

This would be tough. Taking a sip of my hot tea, I watched the birds fly around the Duomo, finding solace in the beauty. The caretaker of our villa here had reached out to me this morning after hearing I was in town. He wanted to know if I planned to come home. *Home.* The word had struck me hard in his message. It was too soon, the memories too raw. Maybe toward the end of summer I'd return and take that step.

If only I had one more trip here with Dad. If only a lot of things were different.

My phone chimed with a text from Carson.

Carson: Are you in your room? Can we swing by?

We? I set my tea down as I quickly typed out a reply. Maybe, I wasn't going to have to wait until this evening to meet Francesca.

Me: We? Sure. I have to leave in about an hour to head to the Uffizi.
Carson: Francesca is with me. I'm glad you're going. If you need me to come, I'll be there.
Me: I know. But, I need to do this on my own.

Oh, la la. I was going to meet Francesca.

Knock.

Knock.

Knock.

Geez, they must have been outside my door already. Quickly, I jogged from my balcony to the door. Carson beamed as Francesca stood beside him. There was a glow about her. Love. No doubt about it. Dad always said someone's soul shined brighter when they found their true match. It was truly a magnificent thing.

I greeted her in Italian. "You must be Francesca. Wonderful to meet you."

She stepped forward. "So nice to meet you, Willow. I've heard so much about you. Carson is truly blessed to have a friend like you. I'm sorry about your late husband."

Pity clouded her eyes. I knew Carson hadn't told her everything. It was my story to tell, and the fewer who knew the better at this point. "Thank you." Gesturing to the room, I said, "Come in. Please."

Carson put his hand on Francesca's waist, and she responded by leaning into him slightly. I loved the involuntary reactions love brought out of a person. "Francesca has to get back to the vineyard, and I have a meeting across town. We can't stay, but she wanted to meet you."

"I'm glad you stopped by. I can't wait for dinner tonight."

Leaning in, we did the European two-cheek-kiss thing as we said good-bye. Francesca responded, "Neither can I."

She gazed at Carson as they walked down the hall. She spoke English flawlessly. My friend's life was about to change forever as he fully gave his heart to someone. I loved being able to be part of this. Bennett and Marie were going to be thrilled when Carson told them.

Ten minutes after they left, I grabbed my purse and slung it over my head so it draped across my chest. The anxiousness of going to the museum had returned tenfold. I needed some fresh air to soothe my nerves.

The sun greeted me as I left the hotel. Scooters zoomed by. The streets were alive with people. I loved feeling the cobblestones underneath my feet as I wandered the city in aimless circles. On a whim, I got some gelato, knowing it would help. Like Mom said, ice cream could solve any problem. I always ordered the stracciatella. It was similar to chocolate chip ice cream… but better.

From time to time, it felt like someone was watching me, but I never noticed anyone out of place. It was probably my imagination.

As I finished the last spoonful in my cup, I arrived at the Uffizi. I remembered the first time I came to this museum with Dad. He spent hours telling me about the amazing works by Anna Maria Luisa the Medici family had preserved and later donated for the world to enjoy.

At one time, the Uffizi had been a palace belonging to the Medici family. The first time I saw the *Birth of Venus* by Botticelli, I'd been mesmerized by the masterpiece. It nearly encompassed an entire wall. The colors. The attention to detail. The symbolism. All of it captured my heart, forever sealing my fate as an artist.

Dad had been beyond thrilled we were able to share that love. Mom had always said we spoke our own language.

I took a deep breath as my foot landed on the first concrete step. I stared at the building, knowing it was time to see the painting. The wind blew, and I felt a sense of peace. *Dad.* It was as if his presence wanted me to know everything was going to be okay.

My lips tightened as I regained control of my emotions. I wasn't through the door yet, and I felt the tears building.

A middle-aged man, whom I recognized as the curator, met me in the lobby, and we conversed in Italian. "Signorina Russo, it's so wonderful to have you here. We have everything set up. Do you need anything?"

"I'm good, Signor Penzo. Thank you for being so accommodating on such short notice. I wasn't sure if I'd be ready to see the painting so soon after Dad's death."

He shook his head. "Your father was one of a kind. He loved this city. We are honored he chose to loan his artwork to the Uffizi indefinitely. It is truly a masterpiece meant for the world to see." That was what Dad had said in his will. He wanted to the world to benefit from the beauty of the painting. I understood, but it was hard letting something so close to my heart remain halfway around the world. Signor Penzo gestured to the right. "This way, Signorina."

The wood floors creaked beneath our feet as we left the main tourist area and headed to a secluded part of the gallery. As I passed the last entrance way, I looked to the left. Goosebumps covered my skin, and I paused.

"Signorina Russo, right this way. We have the Botticelli in a secluded area." I gave him a slight nod and followed. We came to a door, and the man stopped. "You won't be disturbed. Philipe will be standing at the door if you need anything. Take as long as you like."

"Thank you." I gave the man in the officer's uniform a smile and received a nod in return.

Signor Penzo left, and I stared at the doorknob. This was it. *I can do this.* With a fortifying breath, I opened the door.

At the end of the room, the painting hung in all its magnificence with the correct amount of light shining on it to display it perfectly.

The painting still took my breath away.

After closing the door, I walked closer. An unbidden tear slid down my cheek. Then another. I had missed this painting more than I imagined and regretted not coming sooner.

When I was within a few feet, I stopped and stared, letting the beauty encompass me.

I could gaze at it forever. The allegorical meanings unraveled inside my head from memorized teachings. My hand hovered over the picture of Venus under the archway as a sob left me. Dad said he believed Mom watched over us through this painting. He'd spent hours in front of this painting in the years following her death. On what would have been their twenty-fifth wedding anniversary, I found him sobbing on the floor in front of it. It was their private moment, and I'd left him there knowing the gap in our hearts would never be filled.

"Mom, Dad, I'm so sorry it took me five months to get here. I just wasn't ready. I miss you so much."

Tears overtook me, and I let the monumental moment take its course. This wasn't something to be rushed. Finally, after what seemed like forever, I stepped back to take in the beauty of the painting like I had so many times before.

I remembered all the discussions we'd had about the theories surrounding this painting.

Dad loved the fact that it evoked debates amongst the generations, which meant it was a true work of art, speaking to so many people differently as it did. Dad had believed there were no wrong or right answers when it came to how a piece of artwork moved someone.

As I sat in front of the painting, I found a white rose with red tips and a note on the chair.

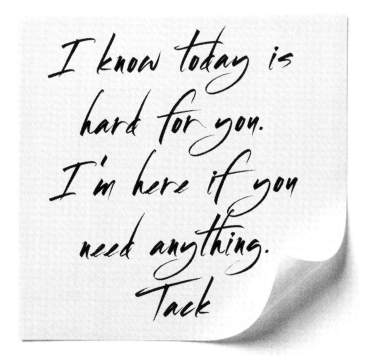

I had no idea he was in Italy, but again Tack had made my needs a priority. I knew, on some level, it should have freaked me out since I had no idea what he looked like, but it didn't. I think because I felt like I knew him on a deeper level, in a sense. I brought the rose to my nose. It smelled heavenly.

I sat down in the upholstered chair with my legs folded underneath me and gazed up at Venus, who was known as the Humanitas, or the goodwill, as she distinguished the material from the spiritual.

I wondered what Venus would have thought if she looked at me. My charcoal pencil found the paper as I absently let my fingers draw.

Time passed, and I flipped another page. The images flowed free. I was relaxed and comforted being here. I would never let fear keep me away again.

When I stopped, I noticed I had drawn a picture of Tack and me. I flipped the page, and another scene I'd envisioned revealed itself. More images of us followed.

Us in the closet at Cocktails. His face obscured by the dark.

His forehead pressed to mine in the bedroom in the beach house.

Me nuzzled against his chest in the pool house.

Before I was conscious of the decision to do so, I texted him.

Me: Thank you for the rose and note. It made today easier.

Tack: I'm glad it helped. Wish I was in there with you.

I wondered if Tack had been the one to deliver the note and rose. It had to have been after they set it up, but before I arrived for it to go unnoticed.

Me: Did you deliver the note yourself?
Tack: Yes.

He'd had been in the museum. I glanced around knowing, he wasn't in the immediate area, but wondering where he was.

Me: Are you still in the museum?
Tack: Yes, I needed to make sure you were safe.

A grin stretched across my face while warmth spread through me, further breaking down my walls with him. But then I wondered if he knew something I wasn't aware of yet.

Me: Is there something you're not telling me? Is someone after me?

Tack: I'm not taking any chances. It's only precautionary.

I truly believed he cared and wanted to make sure I was okay.

Me: Where in the museum are you?

Tack: Close. Don't cut your visit short because of me. We can't meet yet.

I grabbed my purse after storing my sketchpad. Leaving the area wasn't going to cut my time short. I was able to come and go as I pleased. I wanted to search the museum for Tack. My heart raced a little faster thinking the mystery could be solved.

Would I be able to recognize him? The accent alone was a giveaway. We'd spent countless hours talking, so I knew I would recognize his voice. If I had to ask everyone in the museum to speak, I would.

I left the room and saw Philipe at the door. "I'll be right back."

"Take your time, Signorina Russo."

Where was the most logical place for Tack to be? He wanted to make sure I was safe. The back of the museum wouldn't make sense. It had to be in one of the rooms with a view of the exit to this corridor.

Signor Penzo met me in the hall. "Is everything okay, Signorina Russo? Can I get you anything?"

"I'm good, thank you. I needed to stretch my legs but plan on going back in a bit, if that works." I knew it was fine, but I didn't want to come across as entitled.

"Oh, yes, yes. That is totally fine. Please let me know if I can help you in any way."

"I will. Thank you."

He continued on his way, and I made it to the end of the corridor. There were three rooms. One to the left, one to the right, and one straight ahead that led to the lobby. Tack was here, somewhere close, I knew it. I closed my eyes and decided to go right.

Excitement coursed through me. I knew Tack wouldn't expect me to leave like I did. My eyes darted around the room, searching all the tourists. Women, children, men. I searched the faces of all the men ranging in their twenties to thirties. One man caught my attention; he looked my way and waved.

I stared at him.

None of the normal tingles came. Was this him? My brows pulled together, and I froze, wondering how this was him. He walked toward me. My heart sped. This wasn't how I imagined it would be the first time. There seemed like there would be something… more.

An easy grin broke free, lighting up his hazel eyes.

Almost to me, he veered to the right. A woman leapt into his arms.

Inside I jumped for joy. Something inside told me he wasn't Tack. Internally, I sighed and shook my head. I was crazy. Certifiably insane.

I kept searching… looking in the faces of the men.

Nothing.

I changed rooms. Repeated the search.

Nothing.

I went to the last room. Repeated the search.

Nothing.

Where was he?

It was as if Tack was so close yet so far away. Feeling dejected, I walked back to the first room. Only a few of the people were new and no one who fit within the age range.

Ambling around, I kept looking. Had he left? Maybe. A bench along the back wall caught my eye as I felt my gaze pulled to the back of the room where an older man with a cane sat.

In Italian, I asked, "Do you mind if I sit?"

"No, please. My old legs aren't what they used to be. I needed a rest."

I sat and scanned the room again. Nothing.

"Are you here on holiday?"

"Yes, you?"

"I just came by myself to look at the beauty within the place."

Glancing toward the paintings, I saw a Rembrandt I knew well. "It almost seems like it would be a sin to have all this beauty in one place."

"It is. Did you find what you were looking for?" I glanced back to the old man and pinched my brows together. He gestured with his cane. "I walked in and took a seat while you walked the room."

A laugh broke free, and I quickly covered my mouth when I garnered unwanted looks. Museums were normally a place of reverence, an unspoken awe. I sat up straighter. "I guess I made a spectacle of myself. I was searching for someone but didn't find him."

I glanced to the man and he looked at me with confusion. "Well, hopefully he shows. Otherwise he needs a good talking to about leaving a beautiful woman waiting."

The man was kind, easing the sting of not being able to find Tack. I stood. "Thank you. I must be going. Enjoy your visit."

"I will. Enjoy your time in Italy."

Bidding him farewell, I headed back to my room. Philipe let me in. The door closed, and I walked to my chair.

My burner phone vibrated.

Tack: Did you find what you were looking for?
Me: You know I didn't.

I was frustrated, but it was my own damn fault. Tack had gone through a lot of trouble to keep his identity a secret. He wasn't going to just be waiting at the Uffizi with a flashing light on his chest. What was I thinking?

Tack: Willow, please just be patient a little longer. I know you're frustrated.
Me: I will try. I don't understand and I want to.
Tack: I know you do. Just give me a little more time.
Me: Please don't hurt me.
Tack: I feel it, too, Willow, and I'm just as scared.

Blowing out a pent-up breath, I tucked away the phone and focused back on the picture.

I worked on centering myself, thinking about the good times.

My lips turned up as I thought Dad and Mom dancing in front of the Botticelli. Every anniversary, Dad played an Italian opera favorite of mine, "'O' Sole Mio" by Luciano Pava-rotti. I pulled up my phone and played it. It was the same song he'd played when he proposed. I wished I had Mom's ring. After he died, I searched the safe for it, but had no idea where it was. I wondered where he put it and hoped one day I'd find it.

Tears gathered in my eyes as I remembered sitting on the couch and watching them dance while I stared up at the painting.

The opera was the most beautiful love song about the love of his life being more beautiful than the sun. It's about how, without having the love of his life with him, he becomes sad and only wants to be near her. They were the definition of love, or as they said in Italian, *amore*.

And I wanted to find the real thing.

Chapter Twenty

Carson, Francesca, and I were under a tree at the Boboli Gardens. Unexpectedly, dinner had been canceled when Carson's meeting ran late last night. He'd been at a local vineyard about an hour away. Actually, it was a competitor of Francesca's father, Bernardo. At this point, Bernardo still wanted to keep the wine local and not sell anywhere but at his winery. Business-wise, the concept wasn't the best, but it was probably the way his father and grandfather had done it.

"Are you sure you don't want any wine, Willow? It's some of Father's best."

"I've had a headache all day. I'd love to take some home to my Nonno. Carson told me how magnificent it was."

"Yes. Yes, of course. That would be an honor to send some home."

Idly, I wondered if it would make things difficult if Carson went with this other vineyard. From what he said last night on the phone, it looked promising.

If it was meant to be, they would figure it out.

Carson stretched out beside Francesca as we continued to talk. She was a marketing major and frustrated with her father's antiquated business practices. Business was not my favorite topic. Dad had me take courses, saying it helped round out a person's education since every transaction was some sort of business deal. But still, I wanted to sit back and enjoy the beauty of the gardens while they spoke about target audiences, growth potential, and marketing strategies.

Children played. There was peace here. An old man with a cane picked up a ball and handed it to the little girl playing as he meandered across the way. It was sweet.

The afternoon progressed. Francesca drew something on one of my sketch pads. She'd minored in art. "Hold still, Carson."

He grunted and closed his eyes. "Are you going to show me?"

"Not until it's done. Be patient."

Francesca appeared to be doing some shadowing from the way she moved her pencil. I was interested to see what it looked like. We'd talked extensively about the Medici family. They fascinated me, especially because they were the reason the Botticelli survived all this time. Francesca and I both did our theses on the Medicis. We were alike in so many ways. I knew we'd get along great.

So far, she didn't seem bothered by the relationship Carson and I shared. Hopefully it stayed that way. Francesca blew some of her brown hair out of her face and glanced at me for a second. "Carson says you have a house on the beach."

"I do. I grew up there. It's home."

In a flash, Carson snatched the notebook from Francesca and took off. I couldn't stop laughing as he tried to look at it. "I think my nose is too big."

"Carson Whitmore! Give that back." Francesca jumped about trying to snatch it back.

He jogged backward and held it up above his head. It was déjà vu from our childhood; Carson used to do the same to me. He used his height to his advantage.

Francesca squealed while looking like a bobblehead. "Carson Bennett Whitmore! Give that back!"

"Make me."

I called after him, "Very mature, Carson."

Giggles erupted from a few children, and I joined in. They kept chasing each other. All of a sudden, Francesca bent over and gasped in pain. "Ouch!" she grunted.

Carson was by her side in an instant. "What happened, baby?"

Quickly, she snagged the notebook and took off. "I fooled you! I fooled you!"

Onlookers clapped. I stood and said, "Carson, you lost. Be a good sport."

He was close, so close. Francesca dodged right, left, right. "Oomph."

Carson caught Francesca with ease and hoisted her over his shoulder. "Looks like I got back what was mine after all. Are you ready, Willow?"

I shook my head as Francesca continued to yell, "Carson!" His name was barely understandable in her delight.

I picked up the remnants of the picnic and followed them to my car. They were most definitely in love.

"Signorina Russo, a delivery came for you today. I had the bellman put it in your room. Is there anything else you need before I leave for the evening?"

A yawn slipped out. I was exhausted. After the Boboli Gardens, we'd driven through Tuscany, admiring the view. We'd walked through vineyards and talked all afternoon.

I gave him a tip. "Thank you, Tomas. I don't think so. I'm so tired I'm going straight to bed. You have a great evening with your family."

This morning when breakfast was delivered, we'd chatted a few moments. He had a small daughter who was four. She was the apple of his eye and adorable in her pigtails, from the pictures I'd seen.

One day I would have a family. One day.

"Thank you, Signorina Russo. And you have a good evening, as well."

Carson had put Francesca into a car and sent her home. He planned to meet her out at her place after he reviewed a few reports. The night was only beginning in the Italian culture.

They'd asked me to join them, but I politely declined. Carson and I were heading back to the states in a couple of days, and they needed their time together. Hopefully, Francesca would decide to join him stateside over the next couple of weeks.

Tired, I trudged up the staircase. My phone vibrated in my purse as I slipped the key card into the door. It was Tack. Last night we hadn't talked. Only texted good-night to each other. I missed talking to him, but I was relieved to have some space, in a way. I'd been emotionally drained.

As soon as I was inside, I answered. "Hey, you."

He chuckled with that accent. "Evening. Did you have fun today?"

I yawned. "I did. I'm turning into an old person. It's not even eight, and I'm exhausted. I'm about to head to bed."

A large, flamboyant arrangement of flowers sat on the table. The fragrance was incredible, and I sniffed a few of the buds before locating the card.

"Did you enjoy meeting Francesca?"

I shifted the phone. "I did. I think Carson is in love. I'm happy for him."

"Me, too. Everyone deserves it."

There went that warm gooey feeling again.

I yawned again. "I think you'd like him."

As I opened the envelope, I wondered who sent the flowers. They seemed too loud to be from Tack. He seemed to be more the simply elegant type of man.

The smile faded as I read the words that chilled me to the bone.

"Willow, did you hear me?"

"I-I…" I reread the words.

The command in his voice jolted me, his accent becoming thicker. "What's going on, Willow?"

My hand began to shake as I read it aloud.

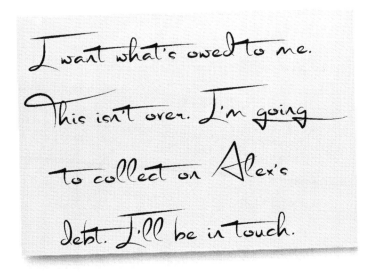

I want what's owed to me. This isn't over. I'm going to collect on Alex's debt. I'll be in touch.

"*Fuck*! Send me a picture. Call Carson. Willow, don't leave your hotel room."

This wasn't over. I had been living in a false reality, thinking I'd escaped Alex's deceit so easily. Yesterday, I'd been all over Florence by myself.

They weren't done with me.

This wasn't over.

"*Willow*!"

I took a steadying breath as my heart fought its way into my throat. "Y-y-yes."

Traffic sounded in the background. Tack was on the move. "I need you to call Carson and tell him about this. I want him to stay with you, understood? Send me a picture. Keep me on this phone. I need to know you're safe."

"Tack, why are they doing this?"

"Money. Sweetheart, I need you to do as I asked. I need someone with you." Tack remained calm, but I sensed the panic in his voice, which worried me. If he was worried, then this was more serious than I had given it all credit.

My mind was sludge. "Is this why you've been watching me in Italy?"

"Willow." The strong voice snapped me back again. "I swear we will talk about this more. But I need you to hurry. Take the picture. Call Carson."

Without any thought, I followed his command. Using the burner phone, I sent him the picture. "Okay, it's sending. Let me call Carson from my other phone."

"Good job, sweetheart."

Another honk. "Be careful, Tack. I know you're on the move. Just be careful."

"Always."

I held a phone to each ear when Carson picked up. "Hey, Willow. My conference call got canceled, so I was about to head to the vineyards."

"I need you to come to my room."

My tone of voice obviously told Carson enough. "Okay, I'm on my way. What's going on?"

I was amazed at how calm I sounded. Even though I felt anything but calm. Inside I was a frantic mess on autopilot. "I got a note. A threatening note."

"*Fuck.*"

Carson's face was intense as we talked to Trent on speakerphone. We'd switched to a secure line. The whole thing made my head hurt. When Carson had knocked on the door, I kept

Tack connected but tucked the burner phone in my back pocket.

Who knew if he was still listening. I stayed rooted in place as I thought about how this person planned to get the money from me.

I was scared to the core.

Housekeeping had delivered hot tea. I sat holding it, which brought back memories of when I first found out Alex had died.

Would I ever be free of that vile man?

I needed to be strong. Letting these people break me wasn't an option. No way.

I kept staring at the note, which was now in a plastic bag on the table. No amount. No directions. Nothing but a veiled threat.

Why play with me? Why wait all this time?

Trent's voice broke through my thoughts. "I think you need to come back to the states as soon as possible, Willow. I'll catch a flight and head back there, too."

This was news. I thought Trent was in the states. "Where are you?"

"Following some leads." Again, I studied his accent. Slightly there, but not as clear as Tack's.

I wondered what leads he had followed. We were due to meet when we came back from Italy to see his proposal. Looked like things had escalated. "Have you found anything out yet, Trent?"

Carson looked at the speaker waiting for Trent to reply. "Yes, I'd prefer to go over everything in person, just in case."

I looked at Carson and nodded. "I'll be on the next flight."

Carson added, "We'll fly back via my private jet. I'll let you know our ETA. That's the safest option I know."

"Agreed. Don't let Willow out of your sight. I'll have one security team escort you to the airport and another waiting for you when you arrive. I'll follow the Whitmore Hotel protocol to have them cleared for now unless Ms. Russo wants me to do anything additional."

Of course I had no idea what the Whitmore Hotel protocol was. I looked at Carson and shrugged.

Carson said, "That will work."

In addition, Trent had spouted off quite a few changes that needed to be made to the house security immediately. I asked, "Can we make the necessary adjustments to the house security while we're in transit?"

Some keys clicked on the computer from his end. "I'm on it, Willow. I'll have everything in place by the time you land."

I was certain whoever Alex owed money to wanted more than what he owed. Just how much… I wasn't sure. Hopefully, it was only money they wanted.

"Hey, Willow, we've landed." Carson's voice woke me. I stretched. Even with all the stress, I'd slept like the dead.

I sat up in a rush. "I'm awake. Let me get my bag."

His arm touched mine. "Take your time. Security is already in place."

Sliding off the bed, I grabbed my bag and followed Carson off the plane. Trent informed us there would be men at the house. *Men.* I expected one bodyguard, not a team. *Talk about escalating everything a few levels up.* I knew it was serious, but having someone shadow me constantly was… intimidating to say the least.

Then there was the issue of telling Nonno and Carson's parents what happened. It was all a fundamental fuckup. All because I married a lowlife, scummy, shit-eating dirtbag.

Yeah, I hated Alex. Even from the grave, he wreaked havoc on my life. *Bastard.*

Exiting in a haze, I thanked everyone for the flight. Trent had a car waiting for us. A member of my security team greeted me. "Ms. Russo, my name is Andre. I'm part of the security force. I'll be escorting you to your home this afternoon."

"It's nice to meet you, Andre. This is Carson. He'll be riding with us."

"Trent briefed me. Shall we?"

Andre was intimidating with a capital I. The broad shoulders were tense with a large frame to support his stature. Shades covered his eyes. Anyone who considered crossing him had a death wish. Apparently, he was well versed in hand-to-hand combat and had served in the military. I imagined Andre would be able to pick me up by the shirt with only his index finger and thumb. No joke.

I crawled into the back seat and then leaned my head on Carson's shoulder. "I hate that Alex is still haunting me from the grave."

"Me, too, angel. I know the whole Trent thing with your dad still bothers you, but he's the best I know. You made the right choice."

While we were on the plane, I looked at the picture I took of the note Dad wrote. I'd taken it right before I put the note in the safe—in case I wanted to read it while I was away. "I'm sure I did. It just feels like Dad had this whole other life I knew nothing about. It bothers me. And I want to know what happened."

Carson patted my hand. "Whoever this asshole is, we're going to catch him."

"I hope so." This person was brazen enough to send flowers to my hotel. The confidence exuded by such an action terrified me. A chill settled over me.

When I looked up at him, Carson was wearing a troubled expression. "What's wrong?"

"Francesca. She was short with me on the plane. I didn't tell her what happened, so she thinks I left because she mentioned wanting to have a serious talk."

My brows pinched together. "Do you know about what? She seemed pretty relaxed while we were all together."

"No fucking clue."

Sitting up, I watched Carson carefully as I asked the next question. "Do you love her?"

A million emotions flitted across Carson's face—fear being the most repeated. "I, uh. I… uh."

I placed my hand on his knee, which was jumping a million miles an hour. "It's okay, Carson. I'm not asking you to propose to her."

He visibly relaxed. "I do love her. It's just… fast. I'm just not ready for more… yet."

"Is she?"

Running his hand down his face, Carson emanated stress. "I think so. Maybe. I don't know. Hell, this just came out of the blue and we have a lot to work out. First being where we would live."

"If it's meant to be, you'll figure it out."

"Maybe." Carson wasn't going down without a fight with regard to his bachelor lifestyle. But it was apparent he loved her. He needed time. Hopefully, Francesca wasn't the type to suffocate someone, or she'd lose him for sure.

We lapsed into a comfortable silence as the car made its way closer to home. "Is Nonno meeting us at your place?" Carson asked.

"Yes. Did you want to fill your parents in on what's going on?"

"I think that's a good idea."

It was time to get the family involved since things were now escalated. I dreaded the effects increased security would have on everyone. *What would they think of me?* It was because of Alex all this happened. If only…

Carson sent a text message to his parents while I gathered my thoughts. Trent was coming later this evening.

"I can give him the wine Francesca brought me. He'll love it."

He coughed and then looked my way. "Don't mention Francesca to my parents yet. I'm not ready."

"No worries. Won't say a word." I made a motion of zipping my mouth and throwing away the key. "Maybe she could come to my art show. That might be a nice venue to introduce her to your family."

Carson's mother was extremely anxious for him to settle down and give her grandbabies. That was one of the reasons Carson was conscientious of mentioning any relationships that were a little more serious than dating.

On his leg, Carson's phone rang, and he picked it up. "Hey, Dad. Yeah, business went good. Florence hotel got the message. We should see a huge improvement. If not, I have contingencies in place. Yeah, it was good news about the new winery I found. I think so, too. Hey, I wondered if you wanted to meet me over at Willow's tonight. Yeah, we came back early. She is. I know. I will. Sounds good. See ya in a bit."

He hung up the phone. "They'll be there by the time we get there."

"I hate this, Carson."

"I know you do. We'll get this figured out."

Silently, Carson gave his support by holding my hand. I busied my mind with better thoughts as we drove.

———◆————————————◆————————————◆———

Carson and I were headed to college in a couple of weeks. We were going to be an hour's drive away from each other, which would be a first. Since grade school, we'd been in the same class. I wasn't one hundred percent sure, but I believed his dad had something to do with that.

I looked at the time. Carson was flying in from the west coast after an impromptu trip with some of his buddies before college started. Bennett and Marie sat in the family room drinking some of Dad's latest vintage he'd acquired from Italy with Nonno.

Before we headed off to school, we were having one last dinner together. With the busy semester ahead, the opportunities to do this had become limited. It was tradition for our families to get together once a month—something Mom had started.

Rounding the corner, I stopped short when I heard my name. "Do you remember that time Willow and Carson wanted to be ant farmers?"

My father laughed his boisterous Italian laugh. "They were what? Six, I think. Kendra and I came home to find ants everywhere. We had to stay in a hotel while the exterminator came."

I loved hearing stories with Mom in them and smiled at the memory. My parents had been so aggravated when they came home to what Carson and I had done. We'd spent all day gathering ants in large glass containers. The problem was we forgot to screw the lids on.

Marie piped in. "Oh, yes, I remember. Then the next week, they decided to be skunk wranglers at our house. It took forever to get the smell off them. I think we bought all the to-matoes in the state."

My nose crinkled at the memory. We stank so bad after getting sprayed.

Bennett chuckled. "That was entrepreneurialism at its finest."

Everyone laughed.

The memory had me smiling.

"It's good to see you happy. What are you thinking about, angel?"

"About the time when you came back from your weekend trip to California right before college. Our parents were sharing stories about our antics. Do you remember the ant farm and skunk incident?"

His earlier tension left as his laughter filled the car. "We had some excellent ideas."

"I think so, too."

I looked outside. As we neared the turn for the house, I saw a man in a black suit standing at the gate. No doubt he was part of the new security team. Andre rolled down the window and spoke to him with familiarity.

The gate opened, and we pulled through. Apprehension filled me as reality hit home. Whoever this was, mob or loan shark, they wanted their money and no witnesses. I swallowed hard, willing my inner bravery to come out. My palms were a little sweaty, so I nonchalantly wiped them.

The car pulled to a stop in front of the house, and I took a deep breath. Carson's parents' car and Nonno's car were out front.

What if Nonno was disappointed in me?

What if Carson's parents thought the same?

I knew I'd made a bad decision in marrying Alex.

And now someone wanted what was owed to them.

"Willow, stop whatever you're thinking." I snapped out of the moment and looked at Carson. "I know you're going through all the what ifs. Stop. Alex tricked you. Tricked all of us."

I tilted my head. "You knew something was up."

"Not at first. After you got married, yes. But he fooled us all in the beginning."

The front door opened, and my nerves increased. Three shadows appeared. *Here we go.*

"Willow, you don't have to say anything." Carson's voice sounded hurt.

I turned to him. "Yes, I do. They need to know."

As we emerged from the car, Nonno met us. "Hey, baby girl. I finally get to hug you in person. I'm so proud about the show."

He grinned, quelling some of my nervousness. "Thank you, Nonno. I missed you."

"Missed you, too. How was Italy?"

He released me, and I eased a bit more. "You know how I love Italy. I visited the Uffizi. It was wonderful. I brought you some wine from a small winery. They only sell to the locals. I think you'll like it."

"Gratzi, I can't wait to taste it. We'll have to open a bottle and toast together."

I kissed him on the cheek. "Sounds fabulous."

Bennett and Marie hugged Carson and then me. Bennett looked like Carson, only older with his hair cut short. With her hands on my shoulders, Marie looked me over. She had a smaller frame like me with dark hair and eyes.

Marie commented, "You look positively radiant. Italy did you good."

"It did. Why don't we head in to eat?"

I wanted one last dinner before I altered everyone's world.

Chapter Twenty-Two

We sat in the living room, catching up on old memories as I cocooned myself in the corner of the couch. Carson raised his eyebrows at me, silently asking when I was going to share. Mildred had retired for the evening and Chris had gone home.

I gave him the give-me-just-a-minute look. Carson gave me the I'm-going-to-do-it-myself-if-you-don't look. Then I gave him back the okay-okay-I'm-telling-them look.

Bennett stood, drawing my attention away from Carson, "Willow, your dad would have loved all of us getting together again. I know it's been a while. We need to start up the tradition again."

I agreed. "I think that sounds perfect. I'll call your office to coordinate our schedules."

"To Alfonso!" Bennett cheered.

We echoed, "To Alfonso!"

Feigning a headache, I passed on the wine. Carson set his down and waited for me.

200

It was time.

I cleared my throat. "I know we're all happy, but I need to fill you guys in on some things. Alex had been involved in some stuff I had no idea about. And now things have reached a level that I need to share the information with everyone."

Concern filled their faces.

Slightly nervous, I launched into the details of what had transpired. I felt like a general, outlining strategies that were discussed with Trent in Italy and on the plane. Tack was the only piece I left out. Bennett listened intently. Marie kept her hand over her heart as the details were unloaded on everyone. Nonno sat back with his fingers steeped underneath his chin, quietly listening.

When I finished, I looked at everyone, measuring their reactions. "So, until we know more, I think it's safest to take all necessary precautions."

Bennett asked, "And we have no idea what incident Alfonso referred to?"

Nonno sat forward. "Alfonso never mentioned anything to me. I'd have to see a picture of Trent to know if I recognized him." Carson handed Nonno his phone. He studied it with his eyebrows bunched. "He looks familiar. He might have been here a time or two when I stopped by, but nothing about it seems significant."

It was odd—no one knew what Dad referred to in his letter. Especially Nonno. It was a double-edged sword—not knowing drove me crazy… knowing meant something else had to happen. Which was the worse of the two? I wasn't sure.

Bennett stood. "I'll have my guys on it, too. These bastards won't know what hit them by the time we're done."

Before Alex had supposedly left for deployment, Nonno hadn't met him. During our brief relationship prior, Nonno had been in Italy, visiting family. Needless to say, I believed Nonno knew I'd made a mistake from the moment I announced we were married. The look of disapproval was not on his face now, but it had been replaced with something else.

I needed a break, so I excused myself to grab a quick snack in the kitchen. The conversation had moved on to precautions that were going to be taken at their offices just in case. Luckily, Mildred had been to the store recently since there were fresh-baked banana nut muffins on a tray on the white marble counter tops. The cinnamon Mildred added created the perfect concoction, and she insisted the bananas were green. I loved them.

Nonno strolled in. No doubt he wanted to dig a little deeper, which I expected, but I'd hoped it would be tomorrow after I had slept.

"Baby girl, what do you think of all this?"

Rolling my neck, I responded, "Which part?"

"Your dad."

He shot straight to the tough part. "I'm not sure. I just wish I knew why. He says it was to protect me, but what in the world did I need protecting from? It's not like Dad was involved in something illegal. It just doesn't make sense." My shoulders drooped.

Nonno hugged me. "It doesn't to me, either. But we have to remember that your dad kept his family his number one priority. Your dad had a reason, and we have to trust in that reason."

Nonno helped put it into perspective. After all that had happened, it was hard to trust, but Dad had loved me unconditionally. That was something I would never doubt.

I took a step back, knowing the questions weren't over.

"Now, let's talk about Alex."

I stared off at the opposite wall as I let all my thoughts spill out. "I keep thinking how stupid I was. How many mistakes I made. I hate Alex. I hate him with every fiber of my being for betraying me and my family like he did. And then I get mad at myself when I feel guilty for hating him. For the last year, he tried to tear us all apart and isolate me. I should be able to hate him without the guilt." I looked down at the floor. "But I don't."

Nonno put his arms around me. "Alex did all those things. I asked your dad what in the hell you saw in him. Do you know what his response was?" I shook my head. "Prior to Alex being deployed, your dad said you guys were a match made in heaven. He saw two spirits completing each other. In essence, he saw the love he'd had with your mother. Your dad believed Alex was your soulmate."

A tear slipped free. "It was all a trick. Fabricated."

His grip tightened as he consoled me. "It was. Baby girl, for some reason this is your journey. It's not finished yet. I'm not disappointed in you. I hate that your road to love has been more difficult than most, but you'll get there. And the love will be that much sweeter."

Tack popped into my head. Was the journey leading me to him? I knew I felt something pure when I was near him.

I hugged Nonno, cherishing his wisdom. "I love you."

"Love you, too. Let's go back to the living room and enjoy the evening with family who loves you unconditionally. We can take everyone some of the muffins Mildred made."

Sounded like the perfect plan.

Chapter Twenty-Three

Company had left about an hour ago, and Carson excused himself about ten minutes ago when Francesca called. I was enjoying the silence for the time being. The effects of jet lag took their toll. My phone vibrated.

Trent: I'm pulling up to the gate.
Me: Thanks for letting me know.

It was still awkward around Trent. He had a secret about my father he'd sworn to keep unless something happened. Yeah, it was messed up. I wondered what they talked about. Trent said my father spoke of me often. Had he mentioned any disappointment about me marrying Alex?

When the doorbell did its fancy chime, Andre went to the door. From the text message, I knew Trent had arrived, but Andre insisted it was protocol for him to answer. I glanced down the hall, hoping Carson had finished his call.

There was more security around the house. A man guarded the gate, and two more were stationed around the perimeter. In addition, I had a new security system—top of the line.

Trent insisted it was necessary. For the time being, I agreed.

I waited in the family room, sipping mango water. It was refreshing and hopefully gave me the energy boost I desperately needed.

"Evening, Ms. Russo. Thanks for coming back so quickly."

Rising, I greeted him. "Come in. Would you like anything to drink?"

"I'm good. Thank you." He wore jeans and a T-shirt—very casual. A sense of familiarity came over me again. I wasn't sure where I had met him before. For a second, I racked my brain if I had met him somewhere. Nothing came. "Sorry for the attire. I've been working from home all day."

It was a little weird that he knew what I'd been thinking. "No worries. I've been on a plane for what seems like forever."

"I hate jet lag, too."

Another silence fell as I listened to his accent. Tack and Trent were from Ireland, but the dialects were from different regions.

Tack.

Shit! In all the chaos, I'd forgotten to let Tack know I made it home. *Double shit.* I'd call him later.

I gestured toward the upholstered chair. "Please have a seat."

Sitting, he positioned himself on the edge of the chair. His knee bounced. "Is Carson joining us?"

"He may. He's on a phone call. You can go ahead and start." Glancing down the hall, I could see the door was still shut. You could hear the doorbell from the study, so if Carson was still on the phone with Francesca, it had to be important. I'd fill him in later. I flexed my fingers against the dark leather couch and crossed my legs at the ankle.

Trent took a steadying breath. *Why is he nervous?* "There's a reason your father's Botticelli is in the Uffizi."

That was an odd lead-in, and then it clicked. "What?" The air nearly left me.

The statement was thrown out there—I knew my eyes bugged out. I'd never known the reason for the request in his will; the letter I received with the will left no explanation. "H-how—" I cleared my throat. "How do you know?"

Trent rubbed his forehead. "While you were in Italy, I found something. And this something means I need to tell you everything."

This had to be the incident that had been kept from me. This was it. But… that meant something bad had been unearthed that led to me needing to know. By the look on Trent's face, this wasn't good. I set my drink on the table and re-crossed my legs, trying to prepare myself.

I had survived Mom's, Dad's, and Alex's deaths. I would survive this.

"Please just tell me, Trent." My voice grew stronger.

I remained silent as my mind churned with thoughts. "Nine months ago, the Botticelli was stolen while on loan for a local exhibit. You were away at college. It was a month after you met Alex. Your father and I were already good friends. He contacted me immediately. Everything was kept low key. I found it quickly. The scene was clear when we got to the warehouse to retrieve the painting."

Trent spoke in fast and short sentences making it hard to follow. I had to pause for a second before I asked, "Why didn't I know about this?"

I knew I sounded like a broken record, but I didn't understand the need to keep something such as a stolen painting from me.

Trent's crystal-clear green eyes met mine as he relayed the story. "Let me backtrack for a second. When the Botticelli was taken, there were fingerprints left all over the scene. Nothing identifiable. We found two sets. One set of prints was professionally removed, leaving only indiscernible smudges from the oil on his fingers. I almost missed it. The other set was poorly removed and left a scar pattern, almost like a finger print, which would be easily identifiable." He sighed. "Your dad didn't want you to worry. He didn't come to that decision lightly."

I'd never imagined. Not in my wildest dreams did I ever think the painting had been stolen. "Were the thieves found?"

As an answer, the set of his jaw spoke volumes. "That's why your dad put the Botticelli on loan indefinitely to the Uffizi in Florence. He thought if they tried once, they would try again, and he couldn't put you in danger like that."

So much made sense now. The security at the Uffizi was top notch. Dad knew the painting would be safe, and the change of location would take us, specifically me, out of harm's way.

It was still hard to believe Dad kept something like this from me. Trent continued when he realized I had nothing to say. "I'm sorry, Ms. Russo."

"It's fine. Continue." My head was swimming.

He pulled out his folder and handed me a piece of paper. There were two smudged fingerprints side by side. "After Martha's Vineyard, I had a thought. I went back to Cocktails and lifted one of Harley's prints to do a background check." A pause. Pauses were never good. "On a whim, I checked them against the crime scene. They matched one of the sets."

"And the other?"

Trent responded, "Is still a mystery." Another dramatic pause. I was about to strangle Trent with his dramatic pauses. "The other I think belonged to Alex."

The air left me, and I closed my eyes. "Think?"

"Yes, I wasn't able to get a set of his prints."

This was getting worse. So much worse. "When did you say the theft happened? Before or after I met Alex?"

I knew the answer but needed it confirmed. "After."

"That asshole!" I stood and paced a few steps. Trent was surprised at my outburst and stood as well. "Did Dad have any idea? Was he on to Alex at all?"

He shook his head. "Your dad asked me to look into Alex later after you got married. I found no surprises. Military background. Only child. Lived in Jersey as a kid. There wasn't anything suspicious to make him a suspect."

Sitting, I cradled my head for a second. Harley had been one of the thieves. He was in on the scam with Alex. Having Commander Taylor put a tap on my phone and follow me confirmed that. At Cocktails, Harley acted as if he hadn't known me. "Did you try to get his prints before he died?"

"No. I had no reason to."

I massaged my temples. "What's next?"

At this point, I wanted to keep Trent onboard. Carson assured me he was on the up and up.

"I think we should keep security tight. You mentioned an art show on the plane; do you have any other commitments after this art show?"

I had a feeling I was about to become a prisoner in my own home. "No, my schedule is clean."

"For what it's worth, Ms. Russo, I am sorry we kept you in the dark. I know this must be difficult."

I searched his face. There were no threatening or malicious vibes coming off him. Something still wasn't adding up. "I'm still just surprised he never mentioned anything about you."

Trent met my gaze head on. "In the beginning, we were acquaintances. Your dad helped me get into security at the major art galleries. About five or six months after we met, he saw me. It had been about two months since we last talked, and I'd been promoted to head of security. He invited me out for an espresso."

My lips turned up. "Dad loved getting to know people over espresso."

A chuckle came from Trent. "He did. I came to enjoy espressos because of your dad." Trent cleared his throat and then dragged a hand through his hair. "While we drank, he asked me what I wanted in life. I think he put it as 'what did I see my canvas looking like.'"

I sat back, lost in the story of Dad. It was similar to getting a rare unexpected prize that made him feel a little closer. After he died, I was frightened I would forget the essence of Dad—the small and special things that made him *Dad*. This refreshed it and made it seem as if he were here.

I hung on Trent's every word, and he seemed to relax. "I told him about my dreams of always wanting to own a security firm. How when I was a child, my parents had been killed in a bombing because of lack of security. It's what drives me to keep people from reliving what I had. We went our separate ways that night. A few weeks later, your Dad called me and asked me to meet him again. Alfonso told me if I showed him I was ready to run my company, he would help. I busted my ass pulling it all together. We kept talking and got to know each other better. Next, he introduced me to Carson. He called on me to help after the theft, and I dropped everything. Alfonso was my mentor. He reminded me what it was like to have a father again."

The sadness emanating from Trent touched me. "Alfonso died not long after that."

And Trent had been silenced out of loyalty to Dad.

"Ms. Russo—"

"Willow. Please call me Willow."

He smiled. "Willow, I'm going to figure this out. I promise."

"Thank you. I appreciate all that you're doing, Trent. Truly." At this point, I needed the help. "Is there anything else we need to talk about?" Exhaustion had gained the upper hand rapidly.

Trent stood. "You must be tired. One last thing—do you happen to have anything Alex touched that hasn't been cleaned? There may be fingerprints I can compare against what we found at the art gallery."

It had been nearly a month since he died. It came to me. "I have some paperwork I think Alex accidentally left. There's a bank statement, some cryptic notes, and a picture of his child."

Trent raised his eyebrows. "Can I take those for comparison purposes?"

"Sure. Let me get them."

I already had copies of everything. I took the stairs two at a time and found the satchel with the folder in it near the seating area of the room. Taking the folder out, I took a deep breath. Trent was the second man I trusted somewhat blindly. It was nerve wracking as I second-guessed myself. *Am I making the right decision?*

I stopped for a second and took a steadying breath. Dad trusted Trent. This was my decision... right or wrong.

Back downstairs, Trent lingered near the front door with Andre. I handed over the files. "Here are the files. When will you know?"

"Give me until tomorrow to confirm. I'd like for Andre to stay in the house, if that's okay with you. Is Carson staying?"

Looking at the time, it was late. "I would imagine so. There's another guest bedroom next to the one Carson stays in if Andre wants it."

In a deep timbre, Andre answered, "I'll be fine, Ms. Russo. Thank you, though."

I was too tired to argue, so I saw Trent out and showed Andre the kitchen. "I'll be up in my room. Thank you, Andre."

"Of course, Ms. Russo. Everything will be fine."

Carson came out looking frazzled from the office. "Has Trent left yet?"

"Just now. Andre is staying in the house. Want to talk about it?"

He sighed and stared at me, the dark circles prominent under his eyes. "Not really. Can we talk about it in the morning?"

Now, I was a little worried. Carson looked like I felt. We both needed sleep. "Whenever you want. I'm always here."

"Thanks, Willow. What did Trent say?"

Carson looked exhausted. I was exhausted. "Let's talk about it all in the morning after we get some sleep. Our problems will wait."

Giving me a brief hug, we exchanged good-nights. Weary, I trudged to my room. I heard my phone vibrating in my purse.

It was Tack.

"Is everything okay?"

He sounded panicked. "Yes. No. I don't know."

"What happened?"

I kicked my shoes off and sat on the chaise lounge while I moved my toes, stretching my feet. This was the scary part of the night… when the impact of the truths made themselves known. What the hell, why not tell Tack at this point? "You know the painting on loan at the Uffizi?"

Hesitantly, he responded, "Yes."

"Turns out it had been stolen."

"I know."

More irritation came to the surface. "Why did you keep this from me?"

He sighed before he said, "I found out while I was in Italy when I dug a little deeper. What else did Trent tell you?"

I took a deep breath. "Just about Dad. And the fingerprints found at the scene when the painting had been stolen."

Silence. "Does Trent know about me?"

"No. Honestly, Tack, I'm tired of playing games. Who are you? What is your end game?"

I knew I sounded short and bitchy, but I was tired and stressed.

Letting out a frustrated noise, Tack became serious. "I have no ulterior motive, Willow. My end game is you."

Oh my.

"Tack…"

"Sweetheart…"

Apparently, we were both at a loss for words. The connection between us deepened without warning. I was unprepared for it. I wanted to keep him on the phone, not ready to let him go, not ready to let the realness of the moment go.

"I don't want to hang up, Willow. Let me read to you."

"Please."

There was something so private, so intimate, and so loving about listening to Tack's words as they lulled me to a peaceful sleep.

Chapter Twenty-Four

I finished pouring the batter for the last crepe as Carson walked into the kitchen looking a hell of a lot better than he looked last night. He went straight for the cappuccino machine and made himself one without saying a word. I waited to see if he was ready to talk. I knew I was.

Last night, Tack hadn't pushed after he started reading to me… he'd simply been there, which I'd needed more than I thought. I still hadn't truly processed what all had happened with the painting being stolen. A part of me felt violated by the act. Maybe that was why Dad hadn't wanted to tell me. He'd known how it would affect me—by slightly jading my view of the world.

The thin layer of dough finished cooking, and I folded the fresh strawberries into the crepe and placed it on a plate. I added a small amount of powdered sugar. Strawberry crepes were something Mom always made after I had a rough day. She'd learned from a woman visiting Florence from Paris one summer while we were overseas. From that point on, it became a comfort food. Once, after I'd broken my arm, I got crepes with ice cream. That had been a magical day.

I handed Carson a plate and we went to the bar, where he sat beside me. The worry lines on his face were clear, which troubled me. Normally, he would have told me by now. He took a bite. "I remember your mom always made these whenever we'd had a rough day."

"I was thinking about that. I woke up this morning thinking we probably both needed these. If it gets too bad, we can always get the ice cream. I think I spied some gelato in the freezer this morning."

Some of the life was back in Carson's face. After taking a sip of his coffee, he nodded. "You first."

Finishing my bite, I turned his way. "Well, the Botticelli was stolen not long after I met Alex. That's the reason behind the indefinite loan to the Uffizi. At the crime scene, there were two sets of prints. One was professionally removed, one not so professional. Trent determined the not-so-professional prints belonged to Harley."

Carson pinched his brows together. I clarified. "The guy at Cocktails."

He nodded, obviously remembering the sleaze bag. "Trent thinks Alex was the other person. I gave him those papers I found to see if Trent could make the connection."

Carson's fork stopped halfway to his mouth. "Holy fuck. Willow... I'm sorry I wasn't there last night. I wish I'd known."

"It's okay. I promise." My throat tightened. "I was a mark from the beginning. I've known this... but it hurts. I really thought there was something there. I—" Abruptly, I stopped, knowing if I didn't, a sob fest would be eminent.

Arms came around me. "He never deserved you."

The words were sweet, but did little to take away the sting of the lies, betrayal, and deceit. I wanted to change subjects. "Your turn."

Carson sat back abandoning his crepe too the worry from earlier returning. "Francesca is pregnant. She found out the day I left, which is why she was off—she thought I bailed on the relationship. I'm going to be a dad. Her father was less than thrilled when she told him. He's old school. Last night, I arranged for her to come here while we work it out. I don't want her father stressing her out. She's on her way now."

A smile spread across my face. A baby. Carson was going to be a daddy. Children were so innocent; I knew Carson would be a wonderful dad even if the timing was less than perfect. "How do you feel about it?"

"I'm scared shitless, but this baby will be always be a miracle… never a mistake or accident." I loved his words and gave him a hug before sitting back down. Carson took hold of his fork and motioned for me. "We can't let these crepes go to waste."

I took another bite and leaned against him. "I'm the luckiest girl in the world to have you as a best friend."

"I feel the same way, angel."

We took a few more bites before Carson spoke. "Francesca and I have a lot to figure out."

I went to the freezer and pulled out the homemade vanilla gelato. "I think celebratory ice cream is in order. Congratulations, Carson. You're going to be a magnificent dad."

He chuckled. "I was wondering how long it was going to take before you got some. Give me a big scoop."

Easily, I scooped the yummy goodness on our plates. "Admit it. You were two seconds away from getting it yourself."

In response, I got a wink before the conversation turned serious again. "Thank you, Willow, for being here for me. I want you to know I'm still here for you. Whatever you need."

"I know that, Carson. And I love you for it. The same goes for you. Regardless of what's going on, I'm here for you." It was an emotional morning. I took a bite of ice cream to stave off the tears.

"Francesca is worried what you'll think. She hoped maybe she could talk to you."

Babies were so pure and innocent. They represented happiness. "Tell her not to worry at all. After she gets here, I'll plan something simple for us to do." I sighed. "I'm going to spoil that baby so much. I can't wait to be an aunt. Do you know how far along she is?"

"No, she wanted me to be there with her at the doctor to get the due date if I wanted to be."

I liked the response. "Your mom is going to be excited. She's been mentioning grandbabies since you graduated from college."

Carson shook his head. "Poor Francesca." We laughed. "So what's next?"

"See what else Trent finds. Do my show in three days. And then see where it all leads."

Three days had passed since returning early from Italy. It was hard to believe it had been a month since Alex died. So much had changed since then—I had changed as a person. To go through what I had… I believed it was impossible to not be scarred from the tragedies. But I was determined to wear those scars proudly.

At my insistence, Carson was at his house with Francesca. He'd offered to bring her here to stay with me, but they needed this time to figure things out. He checked on me regularly. However, I was more than protected with all the security measures Trent had in place.

The fingerprints from the documents I had provided took longer than expected. Trying to find oil smear patterns was a tedious job, apparently. To my knowledge, Trent's team hadn't found a match. Things were further complicated since Mildred, Carson, and I had touched them.

Tack and I talked frequently now that I was alone, though I was still surrounded by people. Last night, I'd sat in my studio watching the sunset while we spoke. We'd talked about nothing at all but everything at the same time.

I told him stories from my childhood.

Tack told me dreams of his future.

I was too scared to admit my dreams. So he avoided his childhood, and I avoided my dreams. It had worked. The past and the present collided into harmony.

Maybe it was a foreshadowing of things to come.

There was something to be said about getting to know the soul of a person before you saw them. It was hard to not feel something for him. Tack had been there in a way no one else had. But I was ready to not have any secrets and see the man behind the voice that stole my thoughts more often than not.

The next song played on my phone. "Unsteady" by the X Ambassadors. I paused while cleaning in my bedroom. The lyrics spoke to me. I wanted to be held on to and loved.

My phone paused the song when a reminder popped up.

The air left me as I sat on the bed, staring at the reminder. Having been focused on what I discovered from Trent, as well as Carson's situation, I'd forgot about my own.

My period still wasn't here.

I was never late.

Never.

Things became more real as I thought about that last night I shared with Alex. Sometimes the images came to me in my dreams, though I wanted to forget them. That last night between us had been magnificently beautiful, but then I woke up remembering the lies, which turned my reality into a nightmare.

The notification buzzed again since I hadn't hit dismiss. I'd set the reminder and forced it out of my mind, refusing to worry about something that wasn't confirmed with everything else going on.

A suspicion would either be confirmed or denied. I wasn't sure what I wanted or how I felt. To wish I wasn't pregnant felt wrong. There might be an innocent child growing inside me that had nothing to do with what happened.

Regardless of my feelings for Alex, I made a vow to love this child unconditionally. Alex was dead—not able to affect him or her if I was pregnant.

My feet were heavy as I trudged to my bathroom where I had several tests. I'd bought them on a whim while in the drug store a few days after Alex died when my head was a mess. I pulled three out of the cabinet and stared at them.

My heart beat faster.

My palms were sweaty.

I needed a minute.

Never in my life had I felt lonelier. I was scared. Terrified, actually.

Sitting on the steps to the Jacuzzi, I stared down at one of the tests I'd grabbed. In a matter of minutes, I was going to have an answer one way or another. The test was easy enough. Pee on the stick. Wait. Either the words *pregnant* or *not pregnant* appeared on the digital display.

I gripped the test lighter. *Why? Why had Alex done all this? Why had he targeted me?* If I was pregnant, my child would have a half-brother they could never know about. I knew what it felt like to have something monumental kept from you. That was the last thing I wanted to do. It also gave me a little insight as to how Dad might have felt keeping the truth away from me.

Sometimes we receive understanding in the most unexpected way.

The phone in my pocket vibrated. It was Tack. "Hey, can I call you back?" I knew I sounded off, though I tried to keep my tone even.

"You sound stressed." It was a statement. Not an answer. Like so many times before, it confirmed Tack knew me.

I heaved a sigh, happy to have someone to talk to. "I am stressed."

"Why?" Before I said anything else, he continued, "I know none of this makes sense. I know my remaining a secret is frustrating. Please don't shut me out. It will all make sense. I am here for you, Willow."

I cleared my throat. "How much longer?"

"Regardless of whether I find everything I need to or not, I'll tell you everything within a month."

A month.

That felt like an eternity, but it was an answer. Something drew me to Tack, and it was near impossible to resist.

"A month. I can live with that."

I heard him blow out a breath. "Why are you stressed?"

"I'm about to take a pregnancy test." Silence. "I'm scared to do this alone." There I put it out there. My true feelings.

He cleared his throat. "Do you want me to be on the phone with you? We can do this together. You're not alone."

"Yes." My one worded answer hung out there. "What if I'm not ready for this?"

"You're one of the strongest people I know, having endured what you have. And if you happen to be pregnant, you'll be the best mom. I know it."

This was why I had not thought about avoiding his phone call. Tack always knew the words I needed to hear to stay the course. I stood and headed to the toilet. "I'll be right back. I'm not peeing with you on the phone."

"Sounds good." The accented chuckle brought a longing to my heart... to have a man who truly loved me for me.

Quickly, I hastened to get my business done and returned the stick to the counter while the timer on my phone ticked down. "I'm back. I set the alarm on my other phone."

"Don't worry. What's meant to be will be."

Pace five steps to the left.

Turn.

Pace five steps to the right.

Turn.

Pace five steps to the left.

Turn.

"What are you doing? Are you counting?"

I huffed. "I'm pacing. It's helping."

"Willow, what scares you the most?"

I stopped pacing. "Not being enough."

"You are more than enough."

Ding.

Ding.

Ding.

Terrified, I stood frozen, my feet rooted to the ground. I'd always wanted to be a mother. To give a child something I lost far too early.

But this was real.

And the situation wasn't ideal since the child would be fatherless.

It was hard to wrap my head around it all. Still not moving I stared at the test on the counter.

"Willow?"

My voice was barely above a whisper. "Yes?"

"Go check the test, sweetheart. I'm here."

"Okay." With trepidation, I walked forward and looked at the stick.

"I'm pregnant."

"Congratulations, Willow. You will be an incredible mother."

Tears spilled down my face as I touched my stomach.

Mom.

I'm pregnant.

A nervous giggle left me. "I'm pregnant."

"Yes, sweetheart. You're pregnant. You're going to be a mom."

Staring at the test, I smiled. "Thank you for being here, Tack. I needed it more than you know."

"I will always try to be there if I can."

His words were like a vow, and I sensed they meant more than I gave them credit for. I hoped my intuition was right.

A list of to-dos spiraled through my mind. This baby was going to bring me only joy. I was determined to not let the past mar this experience.

Through all the pain, I was getting something beautiful.

A gift from heaven.

On my tippy toes, I reached for a box on the top shelf of my closet. All afternoon I'd been reading on dos and don'ts for pregnancy. My head swam with information. On Monday, I had a doctor's appointment. After I confirmed the pregnancy, I would tell Nonno.

The baby was the size of a poppy seed. So tiny.

Carson had called and asked if he and Francesca could come over. They would arrive soon. I'd already made my mind up to tell him. We were going to have children together. They were going to be the best of friends. I knew it.

Some adjustments needed to be made to my painting for a bit, which was fine. I had nearly compiled the list of what I needed to order. I was anxious to paint again as I felt a sense of new inspiration unraveling.

"Willow, are you in here?" Carson called from the hallway.

"Yes! In my closet."

The box was lighter than expected when I finally reached it and pulled it down. Francesca and Carson were at the door.

"Hey guys." After setting the box down, I hugged Francesca. "Congratulations, I'm so happy for you guys. I'm totally going to spoil this baby. Do you mind?"

I held my hands out from her stomach and she laughed. "No, not at all."

When Francesca had first arrived, she was super nervous and I had remained reserved. There was an ease about her today. Being totally obnoxious, I spoke to the baby. "This is Auntie Willow. I can't wait to meet you."

Carson shook his head at my silly antics.

"What? I need to make sure this baby knows who I am."

Francesca beamed and touched her stomach. "This baby is going to be lucky with all the love he or she has."

Picking up the box, I headed to the bedroom to give us all a little more space.

Carson motioned to the box. "What's in there?"

"My baby stuff."

His eyes grew wide—he probably remembered my confession at the beach house. Glancing at Francesca, he remained quiet, but I knew he wanted to know. I wanted her to know, too.

"We're going to be parents together. I'm pregnant."

Francesca gasped and then squealed before she took me in a hug. "This is going to be the best pregnancy. Our children will be the best of friends."

As more time passed, the initial shock gave way to elation. I was going to be a mom. "It is. I'm glad you're here, Francesca. It's going to be amazing to have children the same age. We'll be able to do so much together."

Carson busted out laughing. "And get into a lot of trouble together. Heaven help us."

I closed my eyes. "Payback is going to be a bitch, Carson. We were so naughty." Glancing at Francesca, I added, "I'm so sorry for what you're about to endure."

"Oh, dear." Francesca's eyes widened. "I'm an innocent bystander in all this."

Laying my hand on her shoulder, I concurred. "I'm so sorry. Word to the wise, we can never leave them alone. Or we'll come back to a house filled with ants and children smelling like skunks."

Francesca's only words were, "Oh, double dear."

Laughter erupted. We were in so much trouble.

Chapter Twenty-Five

Carson and Francesca left to see Marie and Bennett to tell them about the baby. They'd asked me to come along, but I wanted them to have this special time. Francesca needed to bond with his parents. It was smart waiting a couple of days to tell them until they understood a little more about what they wanted to do.

For now, Francesca had chosen to stay in the states. If and when she was ready to go back to Florence, they would work out a bicontinental arrangement. With Carson's financial situation, traveling would be easy for them.

I hated that her father refused to talk to her. It had only been Francesca and Bernardo since her mother died when she was four years old. In a way, we were kindred spirits. We knew what it was like to be without. Having each other to lean on through motherhood was a blessing.

With my mango water, I came back to my bedroom to look through the boxes. Carson helped get the other two down from the shelf before he left, giving me strict instructions to not lift anything heavy.

Sitting on the floor, I took off the lid from the box with the label *Willow's Baby Memorabilia*. The ancestral blanket was on top. This yellow knitted blanket had been in Mom's family for eight generations. It passed to the firstborn daughter when her parents were done having children. So far, there had been a girl in each generation. I ran my fingers over the soft fabric. It was tradition to have the baby's picture taken at one month of age while swaddled in the blanket and place it in the family book.

Soon, I would be adding to the picture book on the shelf in the office. Mom would be beside herself with excitement. She always wanted to have a house full of children, but she and Dad were never able to get pregnant again after me. Dad always said, *"You were the only blessing we needed."*

Next were two series of paintings, each with three paintings to complete a willow tree. I paused and looked up at the ceiling to rein in the onslaught of emotions I felt—so many good memories of these paintings. At night, Mom and Dad would read to me on my bed across from the paintings. They were the last thing I saw when I went to bed and the first thing I woke up to.

It was hard doing this alone. I always thought I'd do this with my husband and parents still here. These would be perfect in the baby's room. It was a piece of my parents for the baby to feel and see.

Thinking of the time I tried to recreate the pictures with crayon on the wall, I laughed.

Mildred walked in at that moment. "What are you doing?"

I held up the middle painting that had Dad's, Mom's, and my initials intricately painted in the tree. "Taking a walk down memory lane."

"Sometimes it's good to be connected to those we loved."

Mildred sat beside me. Picking up the painting that went to the left, Mildred held it in the proper place next to mine. "I remember these paintings. Your dad painted them as soon as he and your mom decided on a name, right?"

The acrylic felt bumpy as I ran my hands over it while I retold a story Mom always told me on my birthday. "Nonno was shocked they didn't pick something a little more… Italian. Willow was Mom's idea. Dad took her on a picnic under a willow tree for their first date. It was the memory of where they first fell in love—love at first sight."

She shook her head. "I remember. For the first two months, Nonno would randomly drop hints for other names. Like, '*Wow isn't Marcella a beautiful name.*'—Or—'*I had a dream last night I had a grandchild named Alessandra.*' Your mother thought it was funny and gave him as good as she got."

It felt good to bring the memories to life, and remembering a simpler time, I picked up where Mildred left off. "When I was born, Nonno agreed with Mom that I was most definitely a Willow. In fact, I was the prettiest baby girl he'd ever seen. The nickname *baby girl* stuck ever since then."

We stared at the paintings for a bit longer as I let the memories fill me with happiness.

Later, I sat on the beach eating a sandwich Mildred had packed in a small picnic basket for dinner. The tide had come in and a couple of dolphins played in the distance. It was peaceful.

Breathing in, I filled my lungs with the smell of the sea.

Trent approached from the side. "Is this seat taken?"

I sat up straighter. "No, go ahead. The ocean always relaxes me. There's plenty to eat if you'd like something."

"Thanks." Trent took a sandwich. His profile was handsome. "The fingerprints came back with a positive identification of at least eighty percent."

My voice became distant. "It was Alex."

"Yes."

The waves reached the bottom of my feet, giving a refreshing feel. If only my choices had been different. I'd been powerless from the moment I saw Alex. My heart had obliterated any other thought beside him. I shuddered, thinking about the fool I'd been. But if he hadn't happened, the miracle growing inside me wouldn't be there.

Looking out into the distance, I asked, "Have you ever been betrayed, Trent?"

"I have. A long time ago, by a woman I thought was the love of my life."

"It's a terrible feeling."

Trent took an introspective sip from his bottle of water. "It is. I think it was worse than losing my parents, in a way. They didn't want to leave me. She did." The hurt in his voice matched my feelings.

From what I sensed, Trent didn't have anyone in his life right now. Dad had been there for him. I wanted to be, too. "If you ever need someone to talk to, I'm here. I know we just met, but regardless, people don't understand unless it's been done to them."

More waves crashed as the ocean came a little farther up my feet. "Thanks. Only one person ever knew."

"My dad?"

"Yes."

The one-word answer hung out there. Reaching across, I touched his hand. "I'm glad we got to meet even though I would have rather the circumstances been better. Thanks for being there for Dad when the painting was stolen."

After retracting my hand, Trent worked his jaw. No doubt this was emotionally tough for him. I felt at ease with him now that I knew about the secret. Ultimately… my father trusted him, so I trusted him.

"Thanks, Willow. I sat in this very spot with your dad a lot. I miss him."

Having this connection meant a lot to me. It was like getting a piece of Dad back while sharing it with someone who loved him like a father. "I miss him, too."

Chapter Twenty-Six

C arson stopped by the house to update me on how things went with his parents. As suspected, they were over-the-moon excited and loved Francesca.

Currently, Francesca and Marie were eating before they went baby shopping.

"Are you sure you don't need me to come?" Carson was using my office for a conference call. There wasn't time for him to go back to his office, but he'd wanted to make sure to see me today. I loved him for it.

"I promise. Andre is taking me, and Trent is meeting me there. I'm only meeting with Eva at the gallery to go over all the specifics. You'll be bored out of your gourd."

He shuddered. "Yeah, I don't think I can do that much time with Eva. She's nerve-grating. I'm going to check in with Trent, too."

Ever the protective brother. "The gallery was already checked out this morning, and Eva approved of the extra security. I promise everything is fine."

That had been a chore, tiptoeing around the reason for the additional security needed with Eva. I hadn't wanted her to know about Alex or deal with all the questions that would entail. Trent made up some excuse, but when I really thought about it, he hadn't answered a thing.

"Trent knows what's he's doing, but I want to go over everything just to make sure."

I gave him a salute. "Sounds good. I'll call you on my way back."

After a quick hug, I got into the backseat of the town car. It was supposed to be armored, as per conversations I'd overhead between Trent and Andre. A bit much, I thought. But better to be safe than sorry.

I was anxious and nervous about the show. Normally, with all the other artists there, I was relaxed. Having all the attention on me and my work displayed everywhere was a little daunting.

The car was deathly quiet. "How are you today, Andre?"

"Good, Ms. Russo. Yourself?"

"Good. Thanks for taking me into the city."

"Anytime."

The staccato responses told me he wasn't in the mood to talk as he intently set forth to do his job. Yesterday, I got a briefing from Trent on who the security members of my team were. Andre, like the other members, had a military background. He had been employed with Trent since the beginning. I felt a camaraderie between the two.

I busied myself with my phone, catching upon text messages.

Marissa: The whole gang is coming to the show tomorrow. Can't wait!

Me: Thank you! Your passes will be at the check-in. Eva has ensured me that everyone is on the list. I can't believe Rosie and Mitchell are still dating!

It had been two weeks since our Martha's Vineyard trip. Dating Mitchell for that length of time had to be a record breaker. I wondered if Mitchell enjoyed the teal nightie with feathers. Thank goodness Rosie was over her Carson obsession now that Francesca was here.

Almost immediately I received a response.

Marissa: I know! They are adorable together. Got to run. Meeting with the wedding coordinator. Cake sampling today! Will be in touch about your dress fitting.

Me: Can't wait! Have fun and sounds yummy! See you tomorrow.

Marissa: See you then.

Marissa was getting married in about five and a half months. By that time, I would be over six months pregnant. I wasn't sure how to handle that. In the next couple of weeks, I would need to tell her.

I looked out the window and saw we were probably thirty minutes away from the gallery. After catching up on e-mails and finalizing my new pregnancy-safe art supplies, I sat back and watched the scenery pass us by.

Ring.

The unknown number brought my pulse to racing speed.

Ring.

Trepidation filled me as I tentatively answered. "Hello?"

The caution in my voice caught Andre's attention as the vehicle slowed and he adjusted the rearview mirror to have a full view of me.

"Ms. Russo?" My heart beat faster, recognizing the voice. Why was he calling me?

Our eyes met, and I saw Andre's body stiffen from the expression I wore.

"Yes?"

"This is Commander Taylor."

This man was not a good guy. With most of the precinct corrupt, Trent agreed we needed to leave the cops out of this.

I turned the volume up and put the phone on speaker. Yesterday, Trent had drilled this into me—if someone I wasn't comfortable with called, get security to listen in on the phone call. The car slowed a hair but kept moving.

"Ms. Russo?"

I needed to focus back on the conversation before he got suspicious. "Sorry, I'm here. It's been a crazy morning."

"Is this a good time?"

I looked to Andre, who nodded. "Yes, it is. I'm on my way to the gallery for business."

"I wanted to call and check on you after your visit last month."

The man made me sick. Regardless, the commander played both sides of the fence. "Thank you. I appreciate it. I'm doing well... moving on with my life... forgetting the past."

That seemed like a logical response, considering what he revealed to me. "Very good. Has anyone bothered you? Any suspicious activity?"

I looked to Andre for guidance, and he shook his head. My heart rate ratcheted up, and I worked on keeping my voice steady. "No. Nothing I can think of. Why?"

"I was simply checking. Call me if you need anything." The voice of the liar was smooth as silk. Who knew if he was lying or not.

Andre gave the signal to keep going. "Thank you for checking. Is there anything you need from me?"

"Not that I can think of. Congratulations on the art show. It made the front page of the entertainment section. Alex told me you paint under Willow Loren."

That was an odd change in subject. The mention of Alex's name gave me an uneasy feeling. "Thank you." I got the *wrap it up* signal from the giant in the front seat. "I appreciate the call, Commander Taylor. If there's anything you need from me, please let me know."

"I will, Ms. Russo. I wish you the best."

"And you as well."

The call disconnected, and Andre was already on his phone as he signaled for me to hand him mine. An app that recorded all phone calls I made or received had been loaded. Creepy but necessary. And now it made sense why Trent believed it was a good idea.

Andre thrust another phone back to me without a word. Social interaction was definitely not his strong suit. I saw Trent's name on the display and internally sagged with relief. "Hey, there."

"Hey, you okay?" Concern poured from the man I was getting to know better. He had a calming effect.

Leaning back against the soft leather, I answered, "Yeah. He gives me the creeps."

The city drew closer; the horn honking became louder when I looked to see where we were.

"I'll meet you at the gallery if that still works."

"Sounds good, Trent. We're pulling up. I'll see you in a bit."

A car door closed on his side. "See you in a bit."

We hung up. Andre exited the vehicle to open my door. Why was Commander Taylor contacting me? He had to have something up his sleeve. Eva burst through the doors, silencing my thoughts until later. "Willow, darling, you're here. Perfect timing."

Eva's hair stuck out to the sides in a short, spiky hairstyle. She had on a gray fitted suit with metal-studded black heels. Very artistic looking with the metal rings placed on her jacket. We entered the gallery with Andre shadowing me, which was oddly comforting. It smelled of paints, and I loved it.

The gallery had been swept and surveillance added. I couldn't see any changes, which eased my apprehension.

Eva and I went through the lighting and how to display the series. No doubt, Eva was brilliant at her job. Seeing how they glowed in their places along the wall, I had to remind myself that I painted them.

This is my work.

A sense of accomplishment overcame me as I took it all in. Only one change needed to happen—the order of two paintings had been switched.

Eva received a phone call and excused herself. I took a step back and looked at all the paintings again.

The pain.

The betrayal.

The lies.

In the middle of the series was the painting I'd done after my last night with Alex when I'd become pregnant. It was a stark contrast to the before and after.

There was hope.

There was peace.

There was love.

I touched my stomach. At least my baby was created when I felt light in my life. That had to count for something. For some reason this baby was meant to be, and I would always treasure the gift.

"Andre, I'm going to use the facilities."

He radioed something. "I'll wait out here, Ms. Russo. The restroom has been checked."

I gave him a slight nod and made my way to the restroom. Andre stopped following me about ten steps from the door.

The restroom was plush with a round stool in the middle of the sitting area. Two roses sat on it. A smile spread across my face.

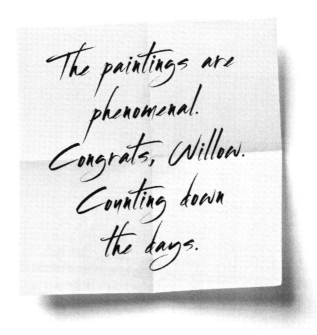

I whipped out the burner phone, my heart beating with excitement.

Me: Are you here?
Tack: Yes.
Me: I need to see you.
Tack: Not yet, Willow.

Walking into the restroom, I put my hand to my forehead. This was all so fucked up.

Tack: Will you promise to keep your eyes closed? I need your word.
Me: Yes. I promise.
Tack: Walk to the door in front of you. Close your eyes. I'm trusting you, Willow. Don't open them.
Me: I've been trusting you for a while now.
Tack: Same here, sweetheart.

For the first time, I noticed the door at the end of the room. Right before it, I stopped and closed my eyes.

He was close.

Tack was here.

I was about to be with him again.

It was hard to contain the delight.

Creak.

I felt the charge in the air change. A hand touched mine, sending tingles through me. His touch was always electric. I thought my imagination had made it more. But it hadn't. The feeling was better, so much better.

Willingly, I took a few steps, and he pulled me into the closet. "Tack."

"I feel it, too, Willow."

He was right there with me. "Isn't this crazy?"

"No. Not to me." I felt the heat of his body move closer. I licked my lips. "How did you get in?"

"I have my ways. Your security is top notch. I swear no one else is getting to you."

Only one explanation remained if my security was that good. "You have a friend who works for Trent."

His forehead came to mine. His breath intoxicated me. "How are you feeling?"

Previously, Tack had said he would never lie to me. His not answering kept that promise. I leaned in infinitesimally. "No morning sickness yet."

"Good. I'm glad."

I felt his breath get closer, and I leaned in further. His lips brushed against mine. "I'm doing everything I can to make sure there are no more secrets between us, Willow."

"Good."

His lips tenderly touched mine. "I want to kiss you until you think of nothing else." I went to move my hands, but he kept them at my side. I leaned in a little further and his lips pressed against mine again. The warmth spread through me.

Then... he was gone.

"We've done too much already. When I really kiss you, I want you to know what my face looks like—know who I am."

Disappointment radiated through me. Then his forehead was against mine again. "Soon, Willow. I swear it."

"Soon." I echoed his words.

"You need to head back out there before someone gets suspicious." Again, his lips pressed against mine so quickly I thought I imagined it. "Call me when you can."

"I will."

A gentle tug on my arm led me outside the door.

Click.

The door shut, and I turned around. My eyes opened. I wasn't able to tear my gaze away—Tack was behind that door. Through the slits, he could see me.

I stood there transfixed in place.

My phone chimed.

Tack: It's time to go, sweetheart. Soon, I promise.
Me: Soon.

Knowing he was in there, I refused to use the restroom. My business could wait until I got home or I'd ask Trent to stop somewhere. After checking the mirror to make sure I looked put together, I left the bathroom, and Andre fell in slightly behind me. He stood there stoically, not moving except for his eyes, which were constantly scanning.

Eva greeted me. "Willow, darling, is there anything else we need to change?"

My eyes drifted for a mere second to the bathroom door before I focused back on Eva. "No other changes. Is there anything else you need from me?"

Her hands fluttered through the air. "Another series so I can book a show. Willow, you have no idea the interest this series has garnered. I must have more."

Dad would have been so proud to see me build my name like this. Most people had no idea I was his daughter. "Thank you, Eva, for everything. When I have something else ready, I'll let you know. You'll have first dibs."

"Perfect." She kissed her fingers again. The front door swung open and Trent entered wearing slacks and a polo shirt.

With a bright smile, he greeted us. "Hello, ladies. Thank you, Eva for being so accommodating through the security changes."

A quick lick across her lips indicated Eva was practically melting in a puddle in front of Trent. "Yes, it's going to be fantastic. She approved the layout."

"Can't wait." He turned his attention to me. "Willow, whenever you're ready, let me know and we'll head out. I'm going to discuss a few details with Andre. I'll be right around the corner."

Eva kissed her fingers again. "It'll all be marvelous. If you could get here about twenty minutes prior to the show, we'll be all set."

"Perfect."

We'd walked to the door when she remembered. "Oh, I have something for you. It was delivered earlier. Let me get it."

Eva disappeared behind a wall while I waited by myself. Trent was beyond the partition toward the front door speaking with Andre. Moments later, she reappeared. In her hand was a turquoise box with a white ribbon. I took the box and tucked in into my purse. I had forgotten about the gifts that accompanied a show.

"Bye, darling." Eva gave me air kisses while we exchanged good-byes.

The hot sun was brutal on the streets of New York City. The air conditioner in the SUV was a welcome relief. Trent sat in the back with me while Andre drove with Dwayne, another security guard, in the passenger seat.

Trent pulled out his phone. "I need to make a quick phone call."

"Sounds good."

Ensconced safely inside, we took off through the busy streets. I always loved how the city never slept. While Trent was on the phone, I decided to open up the gift from one of the guests. It wasn't uncommon to get gifts leading up to an event like this. Honestly, it was my least favorite part.

From the color of the box, I assumed it was some sort of jewelry. I pulled the ribbon off and then removed the lid.

Everything stopped moving. I couldn't tear my eyes away from the box. This wasn't happening. I put the lid back on the box.

Not enough air in the car.

"Air." My voice came out hoarse, barely audible. "I need air." I wasn't moving. No one heard me. A sickness came over me. "I'm going to be sick." My voice came out shallow but with a little more voice. "Trent!" Finally, I got his attention. "Pull the car over. I'm going to be sick."

He looked semi-relieved, probably because he thought I was dealing with a bout of morning sickness and not some sicko. "Andre, pull over for Ms. Russo."

I had told him about the pregnancy yesterday since I had a doctor's appointment on Monday.

With the lid back on the box, Trent had no idea. Before we'd come to a complete stop, I jumped out of the car, hearing a string of curses from everyone. This was against protocol, but I didn't care. Technically, opening an unknown box was, too, but I hadn't thought about that since it was normal to receive gifts. I leaned against the brick and lost everything in the alley of the busy city. The smell of the garbage bin intensified my sickness.

This was terrible.

Dry heaves wracked my body as the image replayed over in my head. Trent was beside me in an instant. "What's wrong, Willow?"

I managed to say, "Look in the box."

More dry heaves.

"Get me the box," Trent demanded.

People moved around me as I vomited more. I took deep breaths—in through the nose and out through the mouth. The box appeared, and I glanced at Trent. Alarm rang in his eyes, and he said, "Oh *fuck*!"

Chapter Twenty-Seven

"**A**ndre, take this."

"Yes, sir."

Everyone was on high alert as I leaned my forehead against my arms on the brick. A soft touch patted my back. Trent's soothing voice was tinged with worry. "Willow, we need to get back in the car and get out of here."

Without a word, I walked over to the SUV with Trent guiding me. Trent gave further instructions. "Andre, take us back to the house."

This was so bad—worse than I imagined.

"Yes, sir."

I looked up at the vehicle's ceiling, trying to keep the bile down. The decaying finger smell still lingered in my nose. "That was Alex's ring, Trent. And the note…"

The picture of the note flashed through my mind.

"We're supposed to check every delivery. I'm seeing what happened, Willow."

Not much remained of the finger. I gagged thinking about it. The missing finger hadn't been a trophy, but a gift... to me. I gagged again. Trent grabbed my hand. "We're going to figure out what the hell is going on."

Ring.

Ring.

Ring.

Trent shuffled to get to his phone. "Yes. Find him. I understand."

Find him? That doesn't sound good.

This terrible day kept getting worse by the minute. The hate within me for Alex continued to grow. What had he been thinking? With this threat, the situation escalated to a whole other level compared to simply wanting money. All I wanted was to go back to a simpler life. If only I had never crossed that street where we first met.

I was pregnant.

What if someone got to me?

The baby was the most important thing in my life. How in the world had Alex done these things having a child of his own? The games he played were dangerous… in fact, they seemed deadly. I touched my stomach. *I will protect you, little one.*

Trent mentioned the finger, and I forced the thought away. The last thing I wanted was to be sick again.

After hanging up, Trent informed me of his conversation. "That was Paul. He's working on locating Commander Taylor. Within fifteen minutes of the call he made to you, we identified that he was not at the precinct or his house."

An involuntary shudder went through my body, remembering the decaying encrusted finger. The thought of being taken terrified me. I swallowed again, refusing to vomit anymore.

"We'll get to the bottom of this. I swear it. I have good men on my team. Dedicated men."

Never again was I opening unknown boxes. Never. Again.

I wasn't able to form any coherent sentences that added anything. All I kept thinking about was someone figuring out a way to get through the protocol. Tack had and now this person. How had they? The knowledge concerned me.

There was a minibar off to one side in the back of the SUV. Trent handed me a ginger ale. "Drink some of this for your stomach. It'll help."

Tentatively, I took a sip. The ginger ale burned a little but helped soothe the turmoil.

Whoever'd had the package delivered knew my schedule. I pulled up my phone and scanned the article about the show. It mentioned nothing about me going there today to review the paintings.

Besides security, Carson, Tack, and Eva… who else knew where I would be? "What are you thinking about?"

Finally, words returned to me. "Who else knew I was going to be at the gallery today. It's been the only place halfway accessible since the house is like Fort Knox. Every delivery is monitored. There are cameras and motion sensors everywhere. You have people patrolling the perimeter. It doesn't make sense."

Trent took out his phone. He pushed a few buttons and then my voice played over the phone. It was from my conversation with Commander Taylor.

"Ms. Russo?"

"Sorry, I'm here. It's been a crazy morning."

"Is this a good time?"

"Yes, it is. I'm on my way to the gallery for business."

The recording paused. "That motherfucker knew where you were going to be."

Trent made another phone call. "Send me all the details of where Commander Taylor has been since we started tailing him. Call Eva at the art gallery and ask her why the fuck protocol wasn't followed on that gift."

Time passed as my mind contemplated all the different possibilities of what had happened. The gates to the estate opened, and I felt safer. Another SUV was parked in the circle part of the drive. The mood was tense as we all walked into the house.

I wanted this over with.

Another security guard emerged from nowhere as though they multiplied on demand.

The box came into sight, and I turned the other way, afraid the ginger ale would not stay down. I never wanted to see the contents again.

"Andre, please take this and wait for me outside."

Thank goodness, the finger left. Just the thought. I focused on the patterned curtains while getting my thoughts under control.

"Let's sit, Willow. You look a little pale."

I felt pale. I sat on the couch, and Trent joined me in the chair next to me. Carson walked out of the study with his hair pulled pack. "I wasn't expecting you back so soon. Everything go well?"

I shook my head. "I got another message."

Carson's eyes went wide. "What type of message?"

I motioned for Trent to tell him. The putrid smell still lingered. "Willow received a box with a finger and a note stating they were coming for her."

"Oh fuck." Yeah, that was putting it mildly. "How in the fuck did that happen, Trent?"

Trent ran his fingers through his hair. "We're checking into that. I'm going to take the finger to a trusted lab. Run some tests. See if there's anything."

Andre came to the door, and Trent excused himself. The burner phone dinged in my purse. *Shit. I forgot to turn down the volume.* Quickly, I found the phone and silenced it without bringing any attention to myself.

"Francesca and I are staying here tonight. I don't want you alone."

I looked over at Carson, the tears finding their way to the surface as the shock wore off. "Thank you. I appreciate it."

Carson brought me into a hug. "You're not alone, angel. I'm here for you. We're all here."

The silent tears came fast. Trent cleared his throat, and I hastily wiped them away. "The box was delivered to the business upstairs of the gallery while Eva was visiting a friend. She tucked it in her purse and didn't think about it."

These people were good. Really good. My eyes widened, and Carson was in front of my face. "Don't let your thoughts go there, Willow. No one is taking you."

The words weren't reassuring at this point, but I put on my game face.

Trent walked further into the room. "We also found out why Alex sent money to Apple Blossom using the money he wired from your account."

"Why?" I asked.

Trent sat in the chair across from me. "It's a special needs school. His son goes there under the alias Toby McIntosh."

Carson jumped in. "Why does his son go there?"

Trent answered, "Gabriel Alexander Thompson the Second has autism."

This little boy was an innocent bystander in all of this, too. Alex, the king of bastards, had potentially put his child in harm's way. If whoever sent the note was willing to take his wife, a child would be icing on the cake. In college, I had taught art to autistic children. It had been part of my curriculum.

Children weren't able to pick their parents. "What's the status of his tuition?"

"The account is in arrears since the drafts stopped a little over two weeks ago. If his mother doesn't become current on the account within two weeks, it looks like he'll be released from school."

I cradled my head in my hands. This was terrible. I thought about my baby. I was fortunate to not have financial stress added to the situation. The image of the little boy came to mind—he was a little Alex through and through. We were both victims of the same circumstances. I wanted to help this little boy any way I was able to without becoming directly involved in his life.

After clearing my throat, I asked. "Can we set something up to pay the tuition? I don't want them to be able to take cash out, but I don't want this little boy to pay for the sins of his parents if this school is legit and he truly does have autism."

Running his fingers over his forehead, Trent thought for a second. "Let me do some additional checks. If everything looks legit, I'll get it figured out how to funnel the funds through without you being involved. I'll bring it to you to sign off on."

"I can look, too, Willow, if you want." Carson offered.

"Yes. Please." I put my attention on Trent. "Run it by Carson. He'll send it to my accountant."

Trent stood. "I'll make it happen. Let me check in with my team. Reorganize. I'll keep you posted."

We stood. "Thanks, Trent."

He left with the phone to his ear.

This was all too much. *Where in the world do I start to think about it all?*

I was tired. "I'm going to go lie down."

"I'll be here. I've informed Francesca of the change in plans."

Francesca had to be wondering what in the world had happened. Touching Carson's shoulder, I made a decision. "Tell her everything if you want. I don't want there to be any secrets between you."

"Thanks, angel. Let me make some arrangements. I'll be down the hall if you need anything."

"Okay."

Safely inside my room, I took out the phone and checked my messages. There were numerous ones from Tack that all read about the same.

Tack: What happened?
Tack: Are you okay?
Tack: Willow, I need you to answer me.

I checked the time. The last one came ten minutes ago.

Me: I'm okay. I got another threat. I was with Trent and Carson.

My phone rang.

"Hello."

He sighed. "Thank fuck you're okay. I saw you pulled over. I thought you were sick. What happened?"

I got under the covers. "Commander Taylor called me today to check in. It was creepy. I disclosed where I was headed, not thinking about security. While Eva visited her friend upstairs, a package was delivered to her for me. She brought it back and put it in her purse without thinking. I opened it without telling Trent. It was a clusterfuck, really. In it was a finger with Alex's wedding ring. And a note that said '*We're coming for you.*'"

"Where's the note?" A shiver ran down my spine at the steel in Tack's voice.

"Trent and his team have it. They're analyzing it. They're also trying to find Commander Taylor."

We grew quiet for a minute. "I'm going to be coming to you soon, Willow. Sooner than a month. I'm missing a big fucking piece of the puzzle, and I can't figure it out yet. But I'm not jeopardizing you or the baby's safety. Are you staying in tomorrow?"

"Yes. I want this all to end." My voice cracked.

"Me, too, sweetheart. Me, too. Keep your ringer on when you're alone in your room."

"I will."

He paused. "And Willow?"

"Yes."

"I'm counting down the seconds until there's nothing else between us."

My heart jumped in anticipation. "Me, too."

Chapter Twenty-Eight

"Hey, Nonno, sorry I missed your call earlier. The Whitmores were over for lunch. We roasted marshmallows for old time's sake."

Having everyone over had proven to be a great distraction from yesterday's events. It had been Francesca's idea.

A chuckle came from the other end of the call. "Did Carson still burn the shit out of his?"

"Yes, he gave up and had me make them. I'm afraid Francesca is as bad as he is." Nonno had witnessed many a roasting disaster throughout the years.

Another laugh. "Sounds like a match made in heaven. Is everything set for the show tomorrow?"

The show. I had so many mixed emotions. Apprehension was winning at the moment. "It is. Your ticket will be at the check-in. If you need anything, let someone know. Marie and Bennett are going to pick you up."

"I'm so proud of you, baby girl. You did this on your own. If your dad was alive, he'd tell you the same thing."

Pride was evident in his voice. I hoped Dad and Mom were able to see me from heaven.

"Thank you, Nonno. Thank you for sharing."

"Anytime, baby girl. Never doubt his love or how proud he was."

"I won't."

Ring.

Ring.

Ring.

I fumbled with the phone on the nightstand. Who the hell was calling this late? Or maybe it was early? Whichever it was, I wanted the annoying noise to go away.

"Hello?"

It was Tack, and he was wide awake. "Willow, has Trent called you?" An urgency similar to the situation in Italy filled Tack's voice.

"No. What's going on?"

"Commander Taylor was found dead."

I gasped. "What?"

"Yes, burned like Alex." Dread filled me. "Whoever's doing this is—"

I cut him off. "Is tying up loose ends."

"It appears that way."

I hated Alex. He met me. Found out about the painting. Then he tried to steal it for his payday. When that didn't work, he played me. And now my life was inside out and upside down. And my innocent baby was being dragged into this mess, as well.

Tack's voice came back. "No one is getting near you except me. I need to get to the crime scene to see if there's anything that will help. Will you let me know if Trent knows anything? I'm sorry to call and wake you, but I wanted you to know."

"Yes, I'll tell you what I find out. Be careful, Tack."

"Always."

Chapter Twenty-Nine

W e were on our way to my art show. I felt like I radiated nerves. Surprisingly, I had forced the events in my personal life aside for the day after Trent told me about Commander Taylor. There were no additional leads. I'd let Tack know he was empty-handed, also.

Tomorrow, the problems would still be there; today, I enjoyed my accomplishment and the events after the show—Carson planned to propose to Francesca at my house. This filled me with delight. She had no idea and wasn't pushing for the proposal. Mildred had made Carson's favorite ravioli to celebrate.

Afterward, he planned to take her to the beach house he'd ended up buying through all this madness. That home would be the perfect place for them.

After checking my phone for the tenth time, Trent's hand came on top of mine. He was dressed in a tux, looking quite dashing. "There's nothing to be nervous about, Willow. I, or another member of security, will be with you the entire time.

Don't take anything from anyone. I'll intercede in a professional manner if need be."

"I got it."

He released me. It was a brotherly feeling. Comforting. Flexing my fingers, I resisted the urge to check my phone… again.

I adjusted my lavender chiffon dress, careful not to snag any of the teardrop beads dangling from it. It was sophisticated elegance. I found it earlier this year, and I'd been dying to wear it. The dress had been love at first sight. I never dreamed I would be wearing it to my own art show.

My fingers went to turn over my phone, but I resisted. Trent smiled and shook his head, trying to suppress a laugh. "I know. I know. I feel like a neurotic mess."

"I don't think I said this before, but congratulations, Willow, on your show. It's an incredible achievement. Having worked security for many, I know how significant this is."

"Thank you. It's pretty surreal."

The gallery's brick building came into view. A few press members hung out front. Generally at any event like this, there were a few paparazzi hovering in hopes of catching someone rich and famous dropping by.

The box with the finger flashed through my mind. Whoever was after me knew I would be here tonight.

Put it aside. Enjoy tonight. I will be safe.

Trent reassured me. "I promise everything will be fine."

And I was beginning to truly trust him—and not simply because my father had. We veered off the main road to the alley that led to the back door to enter without anyone in the way.

A beep signaled a text message on Trent's phone. He quickly read it. "Everyone is set up. Some security will filter in as guests. There will also be normal security around so the increase in personnel doesn't raise suspicions. If anything is bothering you, look at me and blink three times. We'll get you out of there. No questions asked."

Andre radioed someone from the front seat and the alley door opened. We were quickly ushered inside. I looked over my shoulder, wondering if the person causing all this was watching and waiting for the perfect moment to take me. The kidnapping threat had everyone on high alert. Commander Taylor's murder only added to the stress.

Eva greeted us wearing a pink ombré silk gown. Her hair had been elegantly smoothed down. In her element, Eva exuded enthusiasm. "Hello, darling. Everything is set. We've already had someone buy one of the paintings. It's above asking price, so I went against protocol and sold it. I hope that was okay. I have a feeling tonight is going to be stupendous."

"Really, which—"

"Eva, there's a member of press outside who would like a comment." One of the female staff dressed in a cream colored suit interrupted our conversation.

"Perfect." She turned to me. "If you need anything, let anyone know and we'll make it happen. I'll be back."

In a flutter she was gone. Andre took a step to the side and nodded to me. Trent used his earpiece to check in with various people.

I wondered if the person was here... watching me. *Stop it, Willow.* I focused on the here and now. It was the only way my nerves would make it through the evening.

Eva pranced back into the room. "People are filtering in and asking about you. Another painting has already sold."

I was stunned. Normally I sold the majority of the paintings chosen for a particular showcase, but that was *after* the show had started. "Wow, that's amazing. I can't believe it."

Eva looked pleased as she beamed. "I know. It's fabulous. Are you ready to greet your guests, darling?"

"Yes."

Italian opera played low to give the perfect ambience. Growing up, this is what Dad played at all of his shows. Truly it felt like old times. People lined up to enter the gallery. With Trent by my side as my "date" and Eva directing, she led me to the first group to meet.

A permanent smile was affixed to my face as I talked about the paintings and the emotional mood. Overall, I avoided the reason behind the paintings regarding Alex's betrayal. As an artist, you bared yourself on canvas. However, like my father, I left it to the observer to take away what the meaning meant to them.

People projected their own personal lives into art. If they were hurting, they saw the pain. If they were happy, they saw the love. If they were sad, they saw the heartache. There was no right or wrong answer… it was just true emotion connecting to the image in front of you.

I took a quick sip of water and looked up to see Nonno with Carson, Francesca, and his family come inside. Last night, Carson had told Francesca everything about what was going on. Afterward, Francesca had come to my room to check on me and let me know if I ever wanted to talk, she was there for me. I'd always hoped I would be great friends with Carson's wife.

Briefly, I'd hugged each of them. Before I said anything else, Eva pulled me away again to meet more guests.

Appetizers circulated and filled the air with a tasty aroma. As a tray passed, I snagged a puff pastry. "I'm starving."

Trent chuckled before shoving a pastry in his mouth. "Me, too. You're doing great."

"Thank you." I beamed at the praise.

Someone tapped me on the shoulder. "Willow, I love these darker-toned pictures you've done. What inspired you?"

Launching into the pre-rehearsed spiel, I explained it was a period of finding myself. Eva approached, and the balding man signaled to Eva he wanted to purchase.

Whew, I was exhausted.

How many paintings had sold? I checked the time. Only two hours into the show, and things had progressed faster than anticipated. It was hard to believe. I remembered seeing Dad's art sell quickly and hoping one day I would reach the same success. It seemed like I had realized one of my dreams.

I loved it.

So far, no one had mentioned Dad, which was good and showed I stood on my own two feet when it came to my art. There were some who knew he was my father, though I never advertised it.

I finished my water. Within seconds, Andre had another glass for me.

A tap on my shoulder caused me to turn. "Marissa! Rosie! You guys made it!"

Marissa spoke first. "Wouldn't have missed this for the world. Clay and Mitchell are at the bar. The rest of the gang is stopping by a little later."

We all exchanged hugs. "Thank you guys for coming. It means the world to me."

"Clay and I took a quick tour while you were talking to someone. Amazing. It's some of your best work yet."

"I agree," echoed Rosie.

The response to this night overwhelmed me at times. I felt like a recorder on repeat, unable to verbalize the appropriate words for what I felt. "Wow, thank you."

The rest of our friends joined us after handing the girls their glasses of wine. Carson arrived with his arm around Francesca. Earlier, she'd been introduced to our friends shortly after they walked through the door. Marissa, of course, treated her like they had been friends for years.

It was still odd seeing Rosie with someone in this new dynamic. Mitchell hooked his arm around her waist. She looked radiant. I was happy she'd finally found someone who put up with her kind of crazy. With Francesca by his side, Carson was the most relaxed he'd ever been around Rosie. A giggle I'd suppressed tried to escape as I thought about him running from her in Martha's Vineyard. I made a mental note to share it with Francesca.

Clay spoke to Carson, showing him something on his phone, after Marissa excused herself to the facilities. Small talk ensued before Eva pulled me away. I took it all in as I sipped my water, thankful I had my friends back in my life. Alex hadn't taken everything from me. In some ways, he helped me see how precious some things really were. Sometimes even the faintest of silver linings helped you get through a difficult situation.

Eva approached. "I have some news for you, Willow."

"What's that?"

The hairs on the back of my neck prickled with a familiarity I wasn't able to place. Quickly, I scanned the room. It wasn't apprehension but something else.

Clumps of people stood in front of the paintings. Nothing stood out. I kept scanning. An old man with a cane walked my way. Our eyes caught, and I wasn't sure why I kept staring. I couldn't place him.

"Willow, did you hear me?"

I turned my attention back to Eva. "I'm sorry. What did you say?"

"The show is completely sold out."

My mouth dropped open as her words registered, taking my focus away from the man. "Every painting?"

"Yes, darling, every painting."

This was beyond words. I wanted to jump in excitement, but I refrained and took a deep breath while smoothing out my chiffon dress. "I'm speechless. Wow, thank you, Eva." There I went—like a broken record again.

She raised her eyebrow in complete seriousness. "Thank me by getting me more paintings."

Giving a small laugh, I replied, "I'll see what I can do." Honestly, the woman wore me out with her insistence.

A tap on Eva's shoulder from one of her associates took her attention. She gave an excited clap. "More business to attend to. I'll be back."

The water felt good as I took a small sip. I was more tired than normal, which was understandable with the pregnancy. Only Carson, Francesca, Trent, and Tack knew at this point.

Carson leaned into my ear. "Fuck, she drives me nuts. She's like a squeaky, energetic mouse."

Coughing ensued as the water threatened to come out my nose. Finally, I managed to speak. "You dated her for a bit, if I remember correctly."

"Worst decision of my life. It only lasted as long as it did because I was gone ninety percent of our relationship."

I had no idea she drove him nuts. They always seemed friendly with each other. In a playful mood, I raised my eyebrow. "Did she keep going and going and going?"

Carson shuddered. "You know, Eva tried for a while to reconcile. Hell, she even showed up at places to run into me. Then, she stopped. I figured she'd sunk her claws into someone else."

Tapping my chin, I thought out loud for only Carson to hear. "You seem to make the girls go a little crazy. I think it's the cologne. Should I warn Francesca?"

"Payback, Willow. Don't forget about payback."

We laughed as Francesca approached, trying to hide a yawn. The doctor confirmed she was ten weeks pregnant yesterday. They had been dating for a little over three months. Carson wrapped his hand around her hips.

A shoulder bumped into me. Marissa waved her arms as she spoke. "You will not believe who is here. Oh my gosh! I can't believe it. There's some actor here. Oh my gosh! They were talking in the restroom. I must find him to take a picture to Tweet." In all her excitement, Marissa grabbed Francesca's champagne glass and downed it.

Knowing Marissa, she would get her picture before the evening ended. Clay just rolled his eyes.

Marissa's face scrunched in an expression of horror. "What the hell are you drinking? Was that sparkling cider?"

Carson and Francesca broke out in huge grins. With so much pride, Carson announced, "Francesca and I are pregnant."

Cheers erupted as Marissa put her hands on Carson's shoulders. "Well, hell. Someone finally tamed you, Carson. This is amazing. Congratulations!"

Carson's hand touched Francesca's stomach. I restrained from touching mine as he said, "I can't wait to meet this little person. I'm the luckiest man alive to have Francesca be the mother of my child."

The word *mother* still brought a thrill of excitement to me. I was going to be a mom, too. I added, "Carson, I hope it's a little girl to drive you wild."

"Me, too." He gave me a wink, no doubt elated the news was out.

Marissa engulfed them in a giant hug. "Congrats you two. I'm so excited."

"Thank you."

"O' Sole Mio" by Luciano Pavarotti played throughout the room. It was low, but the memories of Dad and Mom filtered through my head. In that moment, it felt like Dad and Mom were here smiling down on Carson and me. Things were going to be okay once we got through the storm. I knew the sun would be on the other side.

Chapter Thirty

The night wound down as the crowd left, leaving only a few people behind. All through the night, I'd barely spoken to Bennett, Marie, or Nonno. I hated that I hadn't been able to spend more time with them. I was about to search them out when I saw they were approaching. I leaned against the wall, exhausted. There was still about a half hour left of the show.

Trent was nearby but had moved back some with Nonno approaching. All night long he had been intercepting business cards, gifts and drinks handed to me. It was done in such a manner no one suspected a thing from what I was able to tell.

Nonno enveloped me in a hug. "So proud of you. Amazing show, baby girl." Pulling back, I saw he was tired. It had been a long show.

"Thank you. It completely sold out." I noticed Carson speaking to his dad. Both had huge grins on their faces. This was an exciting time for them with the proposal coming later under the disguise of celebrating my show. The plan was to leave a little early with Francesca. They were going to stop by Carson's to pick up something Bennett had supposedly left before bringing Francesca back to my place, where Carson would be waiting.

He gave me a kiss on the cheek. "Eva told me. That is fantastic news. Your dad would be on cloud nine."

"He always said, '*When we follow our true destiny, the mind and soul will lead us to success.*'" We reflected as we thought about his words. They were spot-on, as always. The only thing I wished for tonight was to have Dad here by my side.

Yawning, Nonno gave me one last hug. "I'm going to head out with them." He gave me a wink. "Maybe rest in the car before the next surprise."

"Bye, Nonno."

Marie and Bennett were next. "I'm sorry I was so busy tonight. It was crazy. Thank you for coming. It meant the world to me."

In a simply elegant black dress, Marie waved my worries away. "We were so proud watching you in your element."

Francesca joined us. "I'm going to leave with them, too. Carson's going to stay. This first trimester has me nearly worn out all the time. But it was all amazing."

"Thank you for coming and making Carson so happy."

"I love being part of this family."

Hugging me one last time, everyone made their way to the waiting limo. I socialized with the last few stragglers of the show, and then we were alone. I was ready to leave. Carson stood talking to Trent a few feet away. The doors were locked, and I kicked off my heels. It was over.

Francesca was right. The first trimester was exhausting.

Eva presented me with an initial spreadsheet with all the purchases. I was shocked at what the paintings went for this time. Signing my name, I felt such a sense of accomplishment. After exchanging thanks and good-byes, Eva went to the back to wrap up a few details the way she normally did.

Trent walked up to me. "Andre is going to drive you home. Paul will be with him in the passenger seat and I'll be close behind once I wrap up a few details here. I'll catch up to you guys before you get to the house."

A tired sigh left my lips. "Sounds good. See you at the house."

The refreshing unseasonal crispness of the night hit me as we left the gallery. Carson was at the curb talking with Paul. He was in full business mode.

A limo pulled up, and Carson opened the door. "I have never been prouder of my best friend."

I ducked inside the dimly lit limo, and Carson slid in and tossed his jacket on the opposite seat. "Thank you. It was amazing. In about an hour, I'm going to be saying the same thing to you when you propose to Francesca."

"I just don't want Francesca to think I'm proposing because of *him*."

Earlier, Carson had told me Francesca's father officially excommunicated her from the family because of the shame she'd brought on them being pregnant out of wedlock. *Who does that?* I hated that for her. If Dad had willingly tossed me aside, I knew the pain would be excruciating.

I grabbed a water from the mini bar. "Hopefully her father will come around. If not, we will be the only family she needs."

Carson nodded. "He's stubborn, so we'll see." His knees began bouncing. "I hope Francesca loves the beach house. I thought it would be a good place for us to make our home."

Gently, I placed my hand on his knee. "Don't stress. She's going to be overjoyed. I loved growing up by the ocean. We'll have to have beach playdates."

Maybe changing the subject to the baby would help.

"I can already see the trouble we're in store for."

"Me, too."

A comfortable silence lapsed as Carson texted who I assumed was his dad to get updates. The part of the road we were coming up on was my favorite. The bend overlooked a steep ravine. In the daylight, the waves always crashed about, fighting to make their way in. The colors of the sea were beautiful. I closed my eyes to imagine it since it was dark outside.

A voice came over the intercom. "I need you guys to get buckled. We have headlights quickly approaching from the hill to the right. Trent is a minute from catching us."

Car approaching? There was no road on the hill to the right. Why was there a car coming? *Oh God.* They were coming for me. They were here.

My breaths came fast as I fumbled with the buckle. Carson hands grabbed my seatbelt. "Here. Let me help."

"Carson, get buckled."

"I will."

The intercom came on. It was Paul this time. "We're going to have impact. Brace yourselves."

My seatbelt clicked. Carson reached for his.

Crash.

The car swerved, and I gripped the armrest on the door. Andre worked to get the car back under control as my body jolted. "Carson! Get buckled!" I screamed.

They were here. If they pushed us too much, we would go over the cliff. The car straightened.

Carson's buckle was almost locked.

Crash.

We lurched forward. The seatbelt stopped me, but Carson went to his knees and quickly scrambled back to his seat. This wasn't happening. I clutched my stomach with one arm while I braced myself with the other, readying for another impact.

Paul came on the intercom. "Trent has us in sight."

Trent. He made it. I frantically looked at Carson. With his belt in hand, he slid it into the buckle and relief washed over me as we reached for each other's hand. Our fingers gripped like a lifeline.

"Everything is going to be okay, Willow."

Carson's words were like a balm. "I know." I wasn't for sure, but I hoped.

Crash.

The car spun.

For a moment, I felt weightless.

My scream pierced the night.

Thud.

Boom.

Crash.

Everything was black.

I wasn't able to tell which way was up.

The sound of metal crunching filled my ears.

My heart galloped in my chest.

Carson.

The baby.

This was it. This was the end. I wasn't ready to die.

Then...

Chapter Thirty-One

P ain.
    There was a lot of pain.
    Throbbing.
My head was killing me.

I tried to open my eyes, but I was only greeted with darkness. My body throbbed. There was something warm next to me. With a scratchy voice, I said, "Carson?"

Nothing.

Only silence.

Wait, was that something?

There were shallow breaths.

Close.

Were we on our sides?

I couldn't get my bearings straight. A hand grabbed mine, and I nearly wanted to weep at the familiar touch. It was my best friend. He was here.

Louder, I said, "Carson?"

There was a cough. "I'm here."

Relief.

Carson was okay. The baby. I ran my hand over my stomach. There wasn't any pain. That was a good sign. It had to be a good sign. I prayed for it to be a good sign.

We had to be in the ravine from the tumble we took.

Shouting from outside the vehicle caught my attention as I tried to move my head. Everything was stiff. It was hard to move. The shouting came again from somewhere outside the limo. The voices were above us and drawing near.

We were saved.

Carson coughed again. I realized he was close to me but on the wrong side of the limo. Why was he not buckled?

"I wanted—" Carson coughed again, unable to finish his sentence.

At least we were both awake.

Everything was okay.

There was more shouting. They were yelling Andre's name.

I coughed, too, as dust filled my throat. "We're going to be okay, Carson."

"Tell Francesca I love her."

Those weren't words of hope. Those were words of despair. No, no, no. I refused to believe the tone I was hearing from Carson. My voice grew stronger. "You're going to tell her yourself, Carson."

The darkness came again as I fought to keep my eyelids open. It was hard to stave off the tiredness that threatened to consume me. "I love you, too, Willow."

I knew the impending exhaustion was about to win, but we needed to remain conscious. "Carson, fight. I love you, too. You're my best friend."

"I know, Willow."

Our voices were growing more tired. I knew it. He knew it. We needed to save our energy. I wanted to sleep.

"I love my baby, Willow. I want to be a father." Now he sounded scared.

I was scared. I wanted to respond, but nothing came out.

The darkness had come to claim me.

Blackness.

People surrounded me. There were so many flashing lights, and they hurt my head. "Get her IV hooked up. What are her vitals?"

The plastic oxygen mask covered my mouth. I slapped at it. A hand stopped me. "Careful, Ms. Russo. We're loading you into the ambulance."

"Pregnant." It took everything I had in me to say the one word. The mask kept it from being understood.

Someone moved closer to me. The mask lifted. "What, Ms. Russo?"

With the last of my energy, I managed to say louder, "Pregnant."

The darkness claimed me again.

My body refused to respond. More people were talking.

Nonno. Why was Nonno here?

Where was I?

Carson. Where was Carson?

My baby. Was my baby okay?

The blackness tried to pull at me again. I fought it as I strained to listen to the voices. It sounded like Bennett was here, too.

"Did you know?"

"No, I didn't."

"Thank goodness they're okay."

"I know, Bennett."

There was a sadness to their voices.

Why were they sad?

The blackness moved in more aggressively.

No, no, no! I needed to hear more.

It was useless. I succumbed.

Lips pressed against my forehead. "Thank God you and the baby are okay."

Tack was here. *Tack.* He came for me.

The sludge kept me from responding. He was here, within reach. I wanted to be near him. See him.

"I need to leave, sweetheart. I won't be far away ever again. I'm never going to let anyone come near you again."

Tack. I needed him to stay.

Another kiss. "Fight, Willow. Fight for the baby. Fight for us. Don't give up."

And then I was pulled back under.

More voices.

Bleach filled my nostrils.

There was beeping.

"When will she wake up?" Nonno was here again. Worried.

There was a clearing of a voice. One I wasn't familiar with. "Her body is healing. Hopefully within the next twenty-four hours."

Another day.

How long had I been sleeping?

I wanted to scream I was here, but nothing worked.

Carson. Where was Carson?

My baby. How was the baby?

The blackness approached again. I wanted to run away from it, but nothing worked. I was vulnerable. Fighting the impending slumber, I strained my ears.

Nothing.

Chapter Thirty-Two

B *eep.*
Beep.
Beep.

My eyes fluttered open but then squinted shut at the brightness. It hurt like of son of a bitch as pain radiated through my head.

Beep.
Beep.
Beep.

What was that noise? This time, I barely opened my eyes to keep some of the light out. Nonno sat in a chair beside me, sleeping. His hand was on top of mine. Odd. I hadn't noticed it until now.

"Nonno?" The voice coming from me sounded like a stranger's. Rough, like sandpaper.

He stirred and his eyes grew wide. Quickly, he pressed a button near the side of my head. "Thank God. I'm here, baby girl."

More pain shot through me, and I closed my eyes. Barely, I managed, "The light."

Mercifully, the light in the room dimmed.

"Where... am... I?" The dryness in my throat became more apparent. I needed water.

Nonno spoke again. "You're in the hospital. There was a wreck."

Wreck? I tried to remember something... anything.

We were at the art gallery. Then the limo. I think we talked about the future. Andre came over the intercom.

Bits and pieces came to me, but it was all a jumbled mess.

We were hit. Near the ravine. The car tumbled. I spoke with Carson. Then I remembered nothing.

The baby.

The monitor beeped a little faster. *I can't lose my baby.* "What about the baby?"

A sniffle came from my left. On instinct, I moved my head to look.

It hurt. Everything hurt.

Marie was by my side with a tear-streaked face. She reached down and touched my hand. "The baby is fine. You were in distress, but you've both pulled through."

I nodded. The baby was fine.

"Carson?"

Nonno grabbed my hand. "He's in the hospital, too."

Carson was fine. We were fine. Everything was going to be okay. "What... happened?"

Bennett stepped to the side. How many people were here? I closed my eyes again. "A Hummer approached from the hill and pushed your car off the road into the ravine. Andre carried you to the road before the ambulance got there, saving precious time we didn't have. He got Carson out of the car, too.

He saved your life. That's all we know. Trent has a team here and hasn't stopped investigating."

There were so many words to focus on that I'd have to ask again later. The door opened, and I cracked my eyes. A doctor and two nurses came in. He was an older gentleman. "Good afternoon, Ms. Russo. We've been waiting for you to wake up."

"Hello." Again my voice sounded like sandpaper, and I started coughing from the dryness. With a nod, the black-haired nurse put some ice chips in front of my lips. Gently I managed to get them in. "The baby?"

I knew Marie had told me, but I needed the doctor's confirmation.

He looked at a sheet the nurse gave him. "You sustained a head injury from the car accident. A few bruises and minor cuts. With the trauma, we were afraid the baby would abort itself, but you have a fighter on your hands. We're going to monitor you and limit the amount of tests we do to make sure the baby stays unaffected. It's important you follow our directions."

"I will. When can I see Carson? What about Andre and Paul?" All the information wore me out. My eyes fought to close.

Nonno stepped in. "Tomorrow, baby girl. Francesca is with Carson right now. Andre had a few bumps and bruises. Paul is here, too."

I had no remaining energy to demand to see Carson now. At least there was comfort in knowing we were okay. "Tell Paul and Andre thank you from me. Will you tell Carson I'm awake?"

Marie took my hand. "Of course we will. We're going to head to his room shortly. We've been keeping him updated."

Our last conversation flitted through my mind.

I coughed, too, as the dust filled my throat. "We're going to be okay, Carson."

"Tell Francesca I love her."

Those won't words of hope. Those were words of despair. No, no, no. I refused to believe the tone I was hearing from Carson. My voice grew stronger. "You're going to tell her yourself, Carson."

The darkness came again as I fought to keep my eyelids open. It was hard to stave off the tiredness that threatened to consume me. "I love you, too, Willow."

I knew the impending exhaustion was about to win, but we needed to remain conscious. "Carson, fight. I love you, too. You're my best friend."

"I know, Willow."

Our voices grew more tired. I knew it. He knew it. We needed to save our energy. I wanted to sleep.

"I love my baby, Willow. I want to be a father." Now he sounded scared.

A half smile appeared since my energy had waned. "Tell him thank you for fighting and I love him."

Tears filled Marie's eyes. "I will, sweetheart."

My eyes fluttered closed.

I stirred as the nurse adjusted the blood pressure cuff on my bicep. It was dark outside, like it had been the last few times I had awoken. After clearing my throat, I asked, "How long was I out?"

"Just a bit. I'm going to call the doctor. He wanted to run a few tests the next time you woke up. The Whitmores took your grandfather to the cafeteria to eat. I've been in here with you since they left about ten minutes ago."

I readjusted myself slightly. "Good. Nonno needs to eat."

She gave me a reassuring look. "He's a sweet man."

I shifted my legs. Everything was still so damn sore, like I'd been run over by a car. "How's Carson?"

"We'll get an update when they come back. I just came on shift." Her hand lay on top of mine.

"Thank you."

Another doctor came in the room. He was younger than the one earlier. Everything was still slightly hazy. A light was shined in my eyes and my reflexes were checked. "Things are looking better, Ms. Russo. It seems both you and your baby are fighters."

I nodded and winced slightly. The doctor hadn't missed it. "I'm going to give you something for the pain. It's safe for the baby."

"Thank you."

Moments later, the nurse stuck a syringe into the IV, and fuzziness clouded my mind. Before I knew it, sleep claimed me once again. The more I slept, the faster tomorrow would be here for me to see Carson.

I awoke feeling more refreshed than I had the last few times. This was the longest day of my life. Each time I came to,

Nonno and Bennett told me tomorrow hadn't come yet when I asked to see Carson.

Apparently, I had only taken a nap.

Doctors checked me often. With the light bothering me, the shades were drawn. My diet was limited to liquid only.

Time wasn't making much sense at this point. The ache in my body still hurt like a son of a bitch, but it had ebbed slightly.

The doctor came in, checked me, and then nodded to Nonno. Things were progressing and the baby was fine. "Nonno, when do I get to see Carson?"

"Today, baby girl."

Excitement bubbled through me. I needed to see that my best friend was okay. The nurse came in with a breakfast tray. There were two roses on the tray next to the protein shake. "Those are beautiful."

She pointed to the flowers. "I guess someone fancies you in the kitchen. Special treatment."

Tack.

Had he been here?

I knew those were from him. They had to be. My arms were steadier as I reached for the petals and caressed them. He was watching me; I knew it. It was his way of saying he knew the baby and I were okay—the reason for two roses.

The Whitmores walked in, having changed from the clothes they'd been wearing.

Taking my shake, the nurse commented, "By dinner tonight you should be on solids."

"Sounds good." A weariness settled over the room. The mood instantly shifting

"What's going on?" I cautiously asked.

Marie sat beside me and took one hand. Nonno took the other. Bennett's head tipped downward before meeting my eyes.

This was bad.

Dread filled me. What happened?

Whatever came next was going to change my life forever. I felt it to my core. My eyes scanned everyone as the telltale monitor with my heart rate beeped faster. No one spoke. "Please tell me what's going on... now."

Nonno cleared his throat. "Carson sustained much worse injuries than you did. His seatbelt came undone and he was thrown around. He's on life support."

"No, no, no, no!" This wasn't happening. No way was this real. I shook my head, ignoring the dull throb that reared its ugly head. My chin trembled. "You said... you made it seem." I was close to hyperventilating when Bennett stepped in front of Marie. He gently took my face in his hands.

"Willow, I need you to breathe. In through your nose and out through your mouth." He exaggerated the motions, and I followed. "Do it again." I followed his instructions. "Listen, I get that we misled you, but we had to get you through the critical stages. The stress isn't good for you or the baby."

I followed his breathing again before I asked, "How much time has passed since I woke up?"

"Three days."

"Th-three days? Three *days*?" They'd been playing this game with me for three fucking days! I was furious. I was tired of the games—all of them. Alex had manipulated me, and now they had, too. It hurt my family would distort the truth for three days. I stared at them, trying to comprehend.

Beep. Beep. Beep. My heart rate escalated.

"Willow, I need you to breathe with me," Bennett said. I followed his motions. "The doctors aren't going to let you see Carson if your vitals are all over the place. Carson needs you to be strong. He needs to hear your voice."

He was right. I kept doing the deep breathing exercises. The beeping on the monitor slowed. "What's wrong with him?"

Bennett ran a hand through his hair. "He had some internal bleeding. During the operation, he went into cardiac arrest three times. They had to put him on life support to stabilize him. His body couldn't handle much more."

Tears formed and cascaded down my face. There was no stopping them. "Were they able to get the bleeding to stop?"

"They think so. The brain swelling hasn't gone down yet. We're waiting for that, and then hopefully we'll be able to tell more."

My heart broke thinking of my best friend in the hospital... broken. I felt lost. *Francesca.*

"Where's Francesca?"

"She's up in ICU with Carson. Each person is allowed two hours a day for the time being."

He was going to be a dad.

He was going to be a husband.

We were going to have our kids together.

Chapter Thirty-Three

The wheelchair squeaked against the linoleum as a nurse took me to ICU. For now, my movement was to be limited. Plus, I still had an IV attached to me. At this point, it was easier to be in the wheelchair than walk.

Seeing myself in the mirror, I'd been shocked at the face looking back at me. I had cuts and bruises from head to toe. My hand rested on my stomach. Thank goodness this baby was a fighter.

Thank you for not taking my baby.

The wheelchair stopped at the doors that led to ICU as the nurse signed me in. I overheard them say as soon as the young lady left we would be buzzed back.

Francesca came through the doors with a tear-streaked face. She stopped, apparently not expecting to see me. "Willow!" She rushed to my side and knelt beside me. "Thank goodness you're okay. I've been so worried."

Dark circles under her eyes confirmed how much this affected her, too. "How is he?"

She shook her head and grabbed my hand, unable to speak.

I reassured her. "Carson is a fighter. His last words were of how much he loved you and the baby."

"I need him to fight, Willow. I can't do this without him."

She burst into sobs, and Marie was instantly by her side. I felt helpless in my wheelchair. "Let's get back to the hotel, dear. You need rest."

Francesca nodded, and she was led away by the Whitmores without another word. She looked utterly broken. The wheelchair started to move again, and I held up my hands as my bottom lip quivered, fully realizing what I was about to see.

This was real.

Carson was hurt.

His life hung in the balance.

The nurse checked on me. "Ms. Russo. Are you okay?"

I shook my head. "I need a moment."

A tear raced down my cheek, followed by another. My heart was broken—for all of us.

The nurse crouched down in front of me. "If this is too much, we can try again later."

The doctor's words about too much stress flitted through my head. I had to be strong, or they were going to take me back to my room.

I *had* to see Carson. I *needed* to see my best friend.

Forcing the tears away, I repeated the breathing exercise Bennett had done with me earlier. "I'm ready."

The door buzzed open to the secure ICU area. I knew I had to remain outwardly calm though I was terrified on the inside. The wheels squeaked again.

This was hard.

Harder than I imagined now that I was here, in the moment, rolling down the hallway to his room. I bit my lip to stave off the tears. *Carson needs me.* Monitors beeped while patients lay motionless in their rooms.

This was my reality, yet it felt like a dream.

We stopped at the door to what I assumed was Carson's room, and the nurse opened it.

I gasped and the tears fell against my will.

My sweet best friend lay broken in a bed, battered far worse than I was, a white gauze bandage wrapped around his head.

I must stay strong. I must stay strong. They cannot take me away yet. I need to see him.

The nurse touched my shoulder. "I know this is hard, but I truly believe it helps to talk to them."

I nodded, unable to speak yet.

She rolled me closer to the bed. His only movement was the rhythmic rise and fall of his chest. The noise from the machines filled the silence. I wanted to see his blue eyes looking at me with love and him to tell me everything was going to be okay.

"Buzz me if you need anything, Ms. Russo." The nurse gently laid Carson's buzzer in my lap. "I'll be back in an hour to check on you unless you need me sooner. At that time, we'll see how you're feeling to stay for the second hour."

"Thank you." My voice was hoarse. I cleared it after the door closed and I was alone with Carson. I would force myself to remain calm if it meant more time with him.

I must stay strong.

It was hard seeing him lifeless. In my mind I could hear him say, *"Everything is going to be okay, angel."*

Quickly, I glanced away and took a deep breath. *Please wake up, Carson. Please. We need you.* I cleared my throat again. "Hey, it's me, Willow."

With shaky fingers I touched his scraped-up hand. "We had an accident. The doctors say the baby and I are going to be okay. The seatbelt saved my life. You saved my life. I—"

The words caught and I swallowed. Needing a moment, I touched his hands.

"You're always there for me when I need you. Now I'm going to be here for you. I'm sorry I wasn't here sooner. They had to get me a little stronger before I could come up to ICU."

Memories of what was said in the dark flashed through my mind. The warmth of his hand soothed me. "I saw Francesca. She misses you. Marie is taking her back to the hotel to rest. We still have a big proposal to witness."

With no response from my best friend, I felt the desperation clawing its way out. But I took a deep breath and pushed it down. The nurse was going to check my vitals when she came back. I had to be strong enough to stay the entire time. I cleared my throat again. "When I was out, I heard some of the conversations around me. If you can hear me, know I'm here for you. I'm going to be fighting right alongside you."

My thumb stroked his hand, and I closed my eyes at the familiar touch. "Nonno asked me to say hi. You're like a grandson to him."

Silence.

This was beyond hard not hearing Carson's words. I wanted to scream for him to wake up. Never in my life had I felt so helpless.

"I love you so much, Carson."

I looked over and saw no change or response. I leaned in and winced. Repositioning myself, the pain left.

287

Carson's body was too still. "Carson, I need you to fight. I need you to find your way back. For Francesca. For your baby. For me. For your parents. We need you. Fight, Carson. Don't give up." I took a breath, feeling my strength return. I was going to be here for Carson and fight for him if I had to. "Do you remember the time you busted your leg during the triathlon? You refused to quit and finished that race. I waited for you at the finish line. We're here waiting, Carson. Come find us. Please."

The tears trickled down, but I forced myself to sound strong. I talked about everything... mainly memories of our life together.

Nearly five days had passed since I saw Carson for the first time after the accident. The swelling had gone down in his brain, but no changes occurred in his situation on life support. They'd tried to take him off of it once, but his vitals quickly declined.

Knowing a few machines kept him alive was enough to nearly send me into a mental meltdown as I considered every negative outcome. But I kept it all inside, bottling it up for the time being.

Francesca was a wreck. Yesterday, she'd fainted and was now being observed for stress. If all went well, she'd be released with me today.

Andre had been released three days ago. His injuries had been less serious than mine since his airbags deployed. Paul was still in the hospital but hoped to be released by the end of the week. He had a broken arm that ended up requiring surgery four days ago.

But I was determined. We were going to weather this storm to find the rainbows on the other side—all of us.

The two hours a day never seemed enough time for any of us.

In the bathroom, fresh out of the shower, I caught my appearance in the mirror. I brushed my finger against my cheek where the bruise had turned to a more purplish yellow. Still tender, I carefully dressed in yoga pants and a T-shirt. The soreness had lessened, but I still felt the effects from the wreck.

A door opened and shut in my room. I assumed it was Trent coming to take me to the Whitmore Hotel where we were staying for now. He'd been checking on me regularly. When I insisted Nonno be taken to rest, Trent stayed with me to keep me company. I had learned he grew up in an impoverished part of Ireland. After his parents died, he was adopted here in the states within a year. Shortly after, his new mother died from cancer and his new father killed himself. Trent had no one. I felt for him. Until Dad had come into his life, Trent had isolated himself almost completely, except for work.

I knew Trent was working around the clock to figure out who was behind the wheel of the Hummer. Unfortunately, no leads had developed thus far.

Stepping into the room, my suspicions were confirmed. Trent was seated in a chair speaking with Bennett. Everyone looked tired from the weary days and the sleepless nights. *Carson* hung out there, unspoken, on the lips of everyone.

Trent stood. "I hear we're busting you out of here today."

"Yes, I'm so glad to be leaving." Being in the hospital kept me on edge with all the monitoring and beeping. I looked forward to uninterrupted sleep.

Marie walked in with Francesca, who looked more rested. Yesterday, I'd gone to her room for a few hours to keep her company and talk. For Francesca, it had been love at first sight with Carson. She'd known he wasn't ready to settle down and had respected that. On top of everything, Francesca had been terrified Carson would initially think she'd trapped him.

Francesca had an honest soul. I sensed it.

"Did they release you?"

Obviously relieved, she responded, "Yes. I got to visit with Carson this morning. He's looking better."

So much hope resided in her voice. It was good to see her more rested, especially for the baby.

"I saw him, too. I agree, some of that ashen color is gone."

It was still hard seeing him so beat up and broken, though I knew I looked fairly bad myself. From time to time, I saw Nonno looking at me the way I knew I did with Carson.

"Come in and sit."

Marie stayed at the door. "I'm going to see Carson. Francesca wanted to leave with you if that's okay, Willow. Or Bennett can take her."

"I'd love the company. Francesca can show me the ropes of the hotel." I gave her a wink which earned me a genuine relaxed smile. Though we were getting close, I knew Francesca was lonely and felt like she was intruding. Nothing could be further from the truth. I think the baby helped us hang onto hope. We had a piece of Carson.

At my insistence, Nonno went to the hotel to sleep for a bit. Being here most nights with me had worn him out. The last thing I wanted was for him to get sick. Francesca still hadn't heard from her father even though she had left a message to tell him what happened.

He sounded like a genuine asshole.

The door cracked open and one of the security guards leaned in. "A Mrs. Rene Adams is here. She said Mr. Whitmore is expecting her."

Bennett stood. "Send her in. I know about this."

I knew what this was about as Bennett had told me this morning she would be stopping by. Hopefully, it helped Francesca. Everyone clung to anything to do with Carson. It kept him here in the present and not in ICU, hooked up to life support.

Mrs. Adams was an older lady in jeans and a yellow summer cardigan. I'd met her a few times when I was with Carson. "I'm sorry to intrude. Hello, Willow. It's good to see you again, even under these unpleasant circumstances."

I gave her a hug. "It's good to see you, too."

She looked at Francesca. "You must be Francesca."

Shocked, Francesca glanced at me as Rene handed her a key.

"I'm Rene, Carson's realtor. These are for you. I know Carson is in ICU, but I think he'd want you to have them."

A gasp left Francesca's lips as she looked at the key and then cradled it to her heart. Tears flowed. I walked up to her and hugged her. "He's still here, Francesca. He loves you so."

More tears as she gripped me harder. "Did you see it yet?"

"No, but he told me about it."

She showed me the brass key. I took it and read it. It had a simple silver heart key ring attached. An inscription in elegant script appeared down the key.

My fingers traced over the wording. *I will not cry. I will not cry.* He hadn't told me about the engraving. Carson always paid attention to the details.

In a low, voice she asked, "What is it to?"

I looked to Bennett, and he nodded. "It's to a beach house where you and Carson can live in and become a family. It's a little more kid friendly than his loft."

Another tear slipped from her eye, causing some to form in mine. Rene approached her. "I know you don't know me, Francesca, but I hope my words give you some sort of comfort. I've helped Carson broker deals for many hotels. He's an impeccable young man. About a week ago, he called me to finalize the deal on the beach house. He said it was for the most special person in his life. The one who would always own his heart."

I sniffled as the emotions broke free. *Damn it. I want to be strong, but I'm an emotional wreck. Carson, you are one sweet man. Please wake up.*

Tracing the heart key chain, Francesca said, "My surprise," as more tears sprang free. They rolled down her cheeks uncontrollably.

Yesterday, Francesca mentioned Carson had told her about a surprise he had. I was glad Bennett reached out to

Rene to get the keys. I thought it would help her through this difficult time to realize how much Carson truly loved her.

"Yes, your surprise. He was so excited to give it to you."

Shaking her head, she replied, "Thank you. You have no idea how much I needed this. Not the house, but something to keep Carson close to me."

Bennett gave me a nod, silently thanking me for asking him to do this. I was already able to see more hope in Francesca's eyes. This was good for the baby. I knew it.

Francesca clutched the key to her chest again.

Please pull through this, Carson. I'm begging you.

Coming to me, Francesca asked, "Can we go out to see it? I need to have him closer to me. Will you come?"

I wanted to be there for Francesca. "I'd like that."

Trent touched my shoulder. "Let me make a few arrangements while you finish getting discharged. We'll go to the beach house from here and return before it gets dark."

"Thank you, Trent. That will work."

Bennett added, "I'll come, too. There's something else Carson wanted Francesca to have."

Her eyes danced with excitement. Over breakfast, Bennett had asked if he should give her the engagement ring. I knew Carson would have wanted Francesca to have it to know how he felt until he was able to tell her himself.

The security guard let Marissa and Rosie in as Trent left. This was a busy place today. They'd frequently stopped by along with my other friends. Each time so far, I'd either been with Carson or asleep.

"How are you?" Marissa asked with concern.

Each one gave me a gentle hug. None of my friends knew about the baby yet. "I'm hanging in there. There's no change in Carson, but I'm hoping for the best."

I had to stop before I cried. Between the emotional stress and the hormones, I was a basket case.

Marissa gave me an understanding look, and Rosie grabbed my hand. "I know, sweetie. We're here for you."

"Thank goodness Francesca wasn't in the car, too. Have they found any leads?" Rosie gave me a gentle squeeze along with a sympathetic look while waiting for a response.

Francesca took a seat beside Bennett, looking at the key chain. She had reached her limit for talking. I understood.

I shook my head. "Nothing yet. It appears to be a hit and run." That was the answer I had been instructed to give anyone who asked for now. Trent wanted to keep everything on a need-to-know basis. However, this was planned.

"I hope they catch that motherfucker." Marissa's sternness startled me for a second.

I echoed the sentiment. "Me, too."

The nurse walked in. "Ms. Russo, I have your discharge papers."

Finally, I was leaving.

Chapter Thirty-Four

In the back of the SUV, we rode in silence with Trent at the wheel. There was one car in front and another at our back. Bennett rode in the car behind us with Francesca. I was grateful to have some time to myself, not needing the silence filled.

I hadn't heard from Tack. My stuff had been taken to my house after the accident. The offer to stay at the Whitmore Hotel had come afterward. Tomorrow I would ask to get some things, including my phone. From the rose delivery on my tray every morning, I knew Tack kept tabs on my wellbeing. It was the only way we had to communicate since people stayed close to me almost every second of the day.

Not too long ago, Carson and I made this same drive. It was to give me comfort. Now, we made the same drive to give Francesca comfort. The world certainly came full circle sometimes.

I focused on good memories of our childhood as scenes from the car wreck tried to overwhelm me. He *had* buckled.

Why hadn't the buckle held? I thought back to our conversation after seeing Carson for the first time in the hospital.

Trent walked into the room. "It's good to see you awake. We've all been worried about you."

"Thanks. It's good to be seen."

He came further into the room. "Is now a good time? I assume the police will be here shortly. I want to prepare you for their questions."

After my visit with Carson, I was emotionally raw. "Umm... yes."

He sat next to Nonno in jeans and a blue T-shirt. There were dark circles under his eyes. "We've been going over every detail. At this point, I believe the best story to give the cops is that it was a hit and run."

Nonno agreed. "I can do that." My voice was barely audible as I remembered Carson talking about how much he loved his baby.

After a few minutes, I looked at Trent. "What have you found so far?"

Regret shone in his eyes. I hated it. "We can't find any traces of the vehicle except for the description Andre gave us. Whoever it was came from over the hill and left the same way until they got to the dirt road on the other side. From there, we can't find a trail. We're looking at all rentals, traffic cams, anything we can think of."

"So, we have nothing." I needed to talk to Tack to see what he knew. Hopefully, he would reach out to me.

"I won't stop until we figure this out, Willow. I swear it."

Trent had that determined look in his eyes that told me he was a man of his word.

Pulling up to the beach house brought a smile to my face. I remembered the night Carson brought me here to get away after Alex died. He'd burned so many marshmallows it was a miracle he hadn't burned the house down.

When he woke up, I was going to roast him all the damn marshmallows he wanted.

"All is clear, Willow." I looked at Trent, and he continued, "We've done an internal and perimeter sweep. I have a man stationed in the study on the main floor and two upstairs. I'll be outside on the front porch. Francesca has asked for a few minutes by herself."

"Of course. I'll wait here."

Bennett walked Francesca to the front door. She sobbed as she took it all in for the first time. I totally got it. The beauty had overwhelmed me.

Carson was going to wake up. He had to. I glanced out at the ocean to give Francesca a little privacy as she walked around. I imagined beach playdates here. Kids buried in the sand. We had a beautiful life ahead of us as soon as Carson came back.

Francesca walked in while Bennett stayed on the front porch. I wasn't sure when she wanted me to come or what she wanted me to do, but I was here. However she needed me.

Life was cruel, making us suffer as we had. How much loss was one person supposed to withstand?

My mother.

My father.

Alex.

And now, potentially, Carson.

Please come back to us, Carson. Please.

I knew the importance of remaining optimistic, but a piece of me was gone until he came back. For my entire life, he'd always been there.

Bennett gave me the ten-minute signal and walked in. Trent stayed nearby in full-force observation mode. There were a few security guards around. Hopefully later, Trent and I would be able to talk more in depth. With the constant interruptions, we'd kept our conversations more surface level.

Looking up at the second level, I remembered Tack coming to my room. I needed my phone. Once I heard his voice, my nerves would calm.

When ten minutes had elapsed, I walked to the door with Trent not far behind.

The house was just as I remembered it as I walked through and saw the fireplace we had sat in front of for hours, talking.

I paused. We were going to have more of those moments.

Beyond the living room, I walked to the open patio doors.

Bennett was on the back porch with Francesca. I gasped at the sight. Carson had recreated their night from Italy. It was painfully beautiful to see Francesca clutching a velvet box to her chest. I touched the gauze curtains that swayed in the wind at the door.

It would have been perfect for them.

A night to start the rest of their life.

"Carson was going to propose to you that night," Bennett said to Francesca. "I'm certain he would have wanted you to know how much he loved you by me giving you this. He was so excited about the baby and finding his true love. That morning he called me and said this was the first day of the rest of his life."

I bit the inside of my cheek. Bennett kept going. "I told him how proud I was of him."

Francesca opened the box. "He has to pull through, Bennett. He has to."

Everyone's future hung in limbo. Francesca needed Carson's strength. The baby needed a daddy. I needed my brother... my best friend. Life was not the same without Carson here. In fact, a hole—a Carson-sized hole—grew inside me while he lay immobile on life support.

As I stepped out, she stared down at her ring. I gave words of encouragement, taking a few steps forward. "Carson is strong. He's a fighter. I know he's trying to get back to us. I know it."

They turned toward me as Bennett wiped a tear away. "Yes, he is."

Francesca, unable to speak, showed me the box. The antique square diamond set sparkled in the afternoon sun.

"It's beautiful, Francesca. Carson had it specially designed for you."

Francesca took a deep breath as she slipped the ring onto the third finger of her right hand. "When Carson wakes up, I'm going to have him put it on my left hand."

I gave her a hug. "I think that sounds like the perfect plan."

Chapter Thirty-Five

I walked into Carson's room and kissed his forehead. I paused for a moment, expecting him to say something. "Good morning." I then brushed aside some of his blond hair I'd misplaced.

Touching his cheeks, I noticed the cuts were getting better. That had to be a good sign he was healing.

"We took Francesca to the house last night. It was beautiful, Carson. She's going to be here in a little bit. The doctor is checking on her and the baby. Your mom is with her. She's still on cloud nine about finally becoming a grandmother."

Happiness floated through my voice. I checked the monitor, hoping I reached him today. There was something different about today. I could feel it. Something big was going to happen.

Taking his hand, I squeezed it. "Your dad gave Francesca her engagement ring. She loves you so much. I know your love is strong enough to get through this."

Time passed far too quickly before I had to leave and Bennett came into the room. "He's looking good. I think he has more color."

Bennett gave me a hug and looked at Carson. "I think so, too. Marie is switching times with me today since she's with Francesca and the baby."

"Good. Francesca needs someone with her."

Each day was easier and harder at the same time. Easier because Carson was healing, and I became stronger. Harder because he wasn't waking up. I overheard the doctors saying the longer he stayed on life support, the more worrisome it became.

Shaking my head, I refused to let my thoughts go there.

Trent was across the room on the phone. "How was Carson today?"

"He's looking better, but there's still no response. Are we ready to head to downstairs?"

The doctor here at the hospital wanted to check my vitals within twenty-four hours of being released. It had been six days since the accident. In the elevator. I noticed the circles underneath Trent's eyes were more pronounced.

"Do you ever sleep?" I asked

He shook his head, and his steely eyes grew fierce. "Not lately. This motherfucker has pissed me off."

Taking Trent's hand, I held it with gratitude. "Thank you. It means a lot that you're here."

He held on to me while meeting my gaze. "I've cleared all the cases I can. My top guys are on this, Willow. I won't let your dad down."

"You're a good man, Trent."

Trent gave me a smile as we got out of the elevator. Once in the waiting room, I checked in with the nurse, who quickly got me back in. Now that I was pregnant, I noticed pregnant women more. Knowing my flat stomach would become round brought a grin to my face.

The doctor came in with my chart after the nurse took my vitals. "Everything looks good, Ms. Russo. Next week, at six weeks, we'll do another trans-vaginal ultrasound, and we'll hopefully be able to hear the heartbeat."

"Really?"

The doctor confirmed. "Really. Bring whoever you feel comfortable with if you want anyone else to be here for that."

"I will." Tomorrow I would tell Carson about the appointment. That would be positive news to share with him. "Hopefully Carson will be able to make the next appointment for Francesca."

The doctor looked at his charts. "I hope so, Ms. Russo."

Faith and hope was what I would cling to.

It was midafternoon, and we were headed to the Whitmore Hotel near the hospital. Bennett and Marie had offered it while I'd been unconscious. With each of our homes nearly forty-five minutes away, the commute each day wasn't sensible. Plus, we were close if anything happened. Trent's men had also taken over a room for security headquarters. Last night, I had briefly seen their operation. The main room had a dozen computers. There was gear for the men everywhere.

The car turned sharply, and I grabbed the door handle and closed my eyes. Cars still made me a little on edge; every little thing made me remember the crash.

Mercifully, the ride was over before I knew it.

The hotel was pristine as expected with grand chandeliers and ginormous flower arrangements. Cherry wood ceilings gave an extra amount of opulence.

We used the private elevator—it was the only elevator that had access to the top floor. There were only two ways to get to our floor; the private elevator or the stairs. Both had constant security and surveillance from Trent's men and the hotel.

The top floor was cleared of all guests. Nonno and I were in one of the suites, each with our own bedroom. He had an appointment this afternoon with his accountant. Of course he'd offered to cancel, but sometimes it was good to be alone to organize and process my thoughts. Having time to get my emotions in order helped me stay mentally strong. Lately, someone remained at my side at all times.

Last night, it had been wonderful to sleep in peace, alone.

We excited the elevator. "Tomorrow I'll have someone go to your house to get your purse, if that works. I know last night we'd discussed doing it today, but I had to keep that man on surveillance on your place. One of my men had to leave for a family emergency."

"Yes, of course. Family first." I understood, but inside I was disappointed. Another day before I was able to reach out to Tack.

Where is he?

He had been able to reach me at the gallery, and I was sure he visited while at the hospital. Why hadn't he made contact? It bothered me. More and more my thoughts drifted there, wondering what was going on.

We passed Bennett and Marie's suite. Francesca had been offered the option of having her own or staying with them.

She'd chosen to stay with them, which was a good decision, in my opinion.

Trent walked me to the door. He slid the key card into the lock. It beeped and unlocked the door. Turning to me, he asked. "Can I speak with you a minute?"

"Sure. Would you like some water?"

"Water would be great."

I walked into the large suite. The living room connected to the dining room, which led to the kitchen. Nonno had given Trent's team the larger suite since it had more bedrooms. I liked the small coziness of ours.

The cream colored distressed table seemed like a good place to have our discussion. So we sat. "I wanted to wait until we were alone to share some new findings with you."

Shit.

There was more on Alex. And from his tone, I wasn't going to like the news.

I hated this. Was it ever going to end? I was ready for it to be over with, especially after the stress of the last few days. Taking the bottle cap in my hands, I gave myself a mental pep talk. *I am strong. I can handle this. It will get better.*

Looking Trent straight in the eye, I felt an inner strength return. "What did you find?"

Trent took a drink and cracked his neck to relieve some of his stress. "If this is too much, tell me. I don't want to stress you and the baby out."

I placed a hand on my stomach. "I'll be fine. What did you find?"

A file I hadn't seen landed on the table. "I've tracked down an additional loan shark Alex was connected with. He's the worst of his kind. He goes by Jack De Luca."

The name sounded familiar. Had Alex mentioned him from one of his fake undercover stings? The answer was on the tip of my tongue. I knew there was something familiar about him. "Why does that name sound familiar?"

The folder flipped open, revealing a man with dark hair and dead brown eyes. Deadly was an understatement with regard to this man's vibe.

"Jack De Luca was under arrest for murder. The case was dropped because all the witnesses wound up dead. Burned, actually."

The news. That was why the name seemed familiar. Alex and I had been in the living room when news of Jack De Luca came on. He'd been obsessed with the case. "Alex made a comment about Jack De Luca. His arrest was on television. Alex said that's what happens when good guys win. Jack was going to get what was finally due to him."

Trent scribbled a few notes. "Did he say anything else?"

"No, that was one of the only times he made reference to his job. Or what I thought was his job." I asked the obvious. "Do you think Jack had something to do with Alex and Commander Taylor's deaths? Since they were both burned?"

A hand scrubbed down his face. "I think so; it's too coincidental. Alex may have betrayed him. I think that's a motive to come after you. Mob guys don't get satisfaction from the person themselves. They go after the family, too."

The baby. Me. We were Alex's family in Jack De Luca's eyes. They were coming after me. They wanted me. I massaged my temples. "Will this ever stop?"

All I wanted was to live an Alex-free life with my baby.

Trent's hands were fisted on the table when I opened my eyes. "If I have anything to do with it, it will. I won't stop until you're free to live, Willow."

"Dad would be proud of you. I wish I'd known you when he was alive."

The tension eased as he sat back. Trent was a little scary when he was worked up. A sad smile came over his face. "Me, too." He took a deep breath and brought us back to task. "We're going to keep an eye on Jack De Luca. He's the strongest suspect we've got." After making a couple of notes, he added, "I've wired the money for Alex's son at Apple Blossom. The account is still current. We have a tap on Alex's first wife to see if anything is said. We're working on getting one on Harley."

I tried to fight it, but a little tired yawn came out of me.

Trent stood. "One last thing; I had this ring designed with a panic button installed. You press in these two places—where the diamonds are—simultaneously for three seconds." Trent showed me to two spots on the ring.

He handed me the ring, and I slipped it on.

"Try it."

With minimum effort, I pushed in the stones. His phone beeped with an alert. My hand shook as I looked down at it. *I had a ring with a panic button.* My life was not my own. Trent's hand landed on top of mine. "It's only precautionary, Willow. There's a tracking device in it, too. All of these precautions only make it safer for you and the baby."

I took a steadying breath. "I won't take it off."

"Good. I'm going to share your frequency with the men." Gathering his stuff, Trent walked to the door. I followed. "Get some rest, Willow. We'll be right outside the door if you need anything. The room has been swept multiple times."

"Thanks. Goodnight, Trent. Try to get some sleep."

"Once I catch this motherfucker, I'll sleep."

And like that, he was gone.

I yawned and plodded over to the couch with my phone. I was going to close my eyes for only a second.

Chapter Thirty-Six

I n a haze, I awoke and looked at the time. Nearly four hours had passed since I'd fallen asleep. It was early evening. A text from Trent flashed on the screen of my phone as a reminder that I hadn't read it.

Trent: Mr. Russo came back and retired early. He wanted me to let you know if you needed anything to knock on his door.

Me: Thanks. I just woke up. I didn't hear him come in.

Trent: That's what he said. He also confirmed he refuses to learn how to text. His whole life he's gone without it. No reason to start now.

Me: Sounds like Nonno. I'm going to bed shortly, too.

Trent: Sounds good. I'm briefing Andre outside.

I got up and opened the suite door to see Andre there. I hadn't seen him since the accident. The doctor had released him from the hospital but hadn't signed his release to return to work. He gave me a grin, and I threw my arms around him. "Thank you for getting us out of the car like you did. You saved our lives."

He patted my back. "I'm glad I could help, Ms. Russo. Wish I could have done more."

"You saved us. You saved my baby by getting us out so fast and meeting the medics. You gave us enough warning to buckle up."

"Just doing my job."

I gave him another hug. "I'm glad you're okay." Pulling back, I saw him blush as he nodded. "Let me know if any of you guys need anything. I saw Paul today after I visited Carson. He's healing well, too."

"Yes, he is. Sleep well, Ms. Russo."

"Thank you, Andre. When it's time for you to sleep, I hope you rest well, too."

I headed back into the suite, changed into my pajamas, and washed my face. Andre was back. Paul was healing. Now, all we needed was Carson to wake up.

Mildred had sent several changes of clothes and my toiletries to the hospital when they initially set up camp here. It felt good to have my things. Heading back out to the main area, I folded the blanket and put up the empty waters from earlier.

My stomach growled. *I should probably eat something.* Bennett and Marie had stocked our fridge with food as well as given us cart-blanche access to room service.

A quick sandwich would be perfect. I set about making it, wondering when I would be able to fill Tack in. He still hadn't made any contact, which worried me. What if he was hurt? Or in trouble? I pushed away those thoughts.

The sandwich tasted heavenly.

Ring.

Ring.

Ring.

An unknown number showed up on my display. I pushed Talk.

"Hello?"

"Willow, its Tack."

Tack. He called me. Finally. The lilt of his voice was something I'd needed to hear more than I knew. "Are you okay?"

"Yes, I'm sorry it took me a bit. It's been a clusterfuck. I visited you in the hospital."

It hadn't been a dream. I felt warmth spread through me. "I kind of remember. I was pretty out of it. But the baby and I are okay." Without thinking my hand went to my stomach.

"I know. I kept close tabs on you. I was scared shitless."

"Me, too." The hairs on my neck stood, and I looked around at the familiarity I felt. The area was empty. No one was here.

"Willow?"

My voice became a whisper. "Yes."

"I need you to keep an open mind. We don't have much time with the delayed recording on your phone."

"O-o-okay."

My heart sped up. What in the world did Tack need me to keep an open mind about?

There was a long sigh. Then his accent morphed into something familiar. "Promise me you'll keep an open mind, sweetheart."

"What happened to your Irish accent?"

My heart hammered in my chest again, and I knew my life was about to be turned upside down.

A few seconds passed before Tack said, "Remember... keep an open mind, sweetheart. Look toward the bedroom door."

Goose bumps raced along my skin. My eyes darted to the bedroom door. A body appeared in the darkened doorway.

My body pulsed.

Adrenaline raced through my blood.

The body moved into the light.

Everything in me froze.

Nothing made sense.

How was this happening?

There was no way.

This is not happening.

Shocked, I whispered, "Alex?"

Continue reading the conclusion of Willow's story in

black truth.

Sometimes the *black truth* is scarier than the *white lie*.

Below is a list of songs that remind me of
White Lies and Black Truth

Unsteady – X Ambassadors

Yours – Ella Henderson

Close – Nick Jonas

Jar of Hearts – Christina Perri

Every Time We Touch – Cascada (Yanou's Candlelight Mix)

Jet Black Heart – 5 Seconds of Summer

Listen to Your Heart – D.H.T., Edmee

For You – Demi Lovato

Stone Cold – Demi Lovato

Black Magic – Little Mix

Stay – Rihanna

Should've Been Us – Tori Kelly

Far Away – Nickelback

You Ruin Me – The Veronicas

Heart of Stone – Iko

4 In The Morning – Gwen Stefani

PILLOWTALK – ZAYN

Let It Go – James Bay

Say Something – A Great Big World

Hurt – Christina Aguilera

Take A Bow – Rihanna

Beneath Your Beauty – Labrinth

Never Say Never – The Fray

Cry – Rihanna

Heaven – DJ Sammy

Can't Help Falling in Love – Haley Reinhart

Say You Love Me – Jessie Ware

Please Don't Say You Love Me – Gabrielle Aplin

Wild Horse – Natasha Bedingfield

Poison & Wine – The Civil Wars

Salvation – Gabrielle Aplin

Concrete Angel – Christin

Thank you from the bottom of my heart
for making this journey possible.
It's because of you I get to submerse
myself in the magical word of writing.
Thank you infinity factorial
Xoxo Kristin

Other Books by Kristin Mayer

Available Now

The Trust Series

Trust Me
Love Me
Promise Me
Full-length novels in the TRUST series are also available in audio from Tantor Media.

The Effect Series

Ripple Effect
Domino Effect

The Twisted Fate Series

White Lies
Black Truth

Stand Alone Novels

Innocence

Bane

Finding Forever (co-written with Kelly Elliott)

Coming Soon

Whispered Promises – January 2016

Untouched Perfection

Flawless Perfection